THE MILDEW GANG

THE MILDEW GANG

BEING THE FIRST VOLUME
IN THE MILDEW GANG TRILOGY

An Inspector Cauldron Classic Crime Novel

by

S. FOWLER WRIGHT

WRITING AS "SYDNEY FOWLER"

THE BORGO PRESS

An Imprint of Wildside Press LLC

MMIX

CONTENTS

CHAPTER I

Concerning Murder at the Old Jersey

The reception-clerk of the Old Jersey did not like detectives. He thought that anything beyond the most distant contacts with the police derogated from the dignity of a first-class hotel where wealthy citizens of the United States were accustomed to stay. The pavement, not the lounge, was the place for them.

He recognized that when guests murder one another (as those of sufficiently good social standing to put up at the Old Jersey should not be expected to do) the intrusion of the police becomes an unavoidable evil, but it is still not one to be freely encouraged, nor to be allowed to continue indefinitely. Mrs. Houghton had now been dead for three days. Her husband, after shooting her, had had sufficient good breeding to leave the hotel immediately. The body of the dead woman had been removed. The police had been allowed to poke about the room as it was their nature to do. After that, it had been put into order, and was now eligible to be let to less violent guests. It had become time to let the past die.

When he saw Inspector Cauldron enter the revolving door, and give a word of friendly greeting to the head-porter, though he had not seen him before he recognized him for what he was, with the acumen which reception clerks are expected to have, but he did not look pleased. His "good-evening," as the inspector approached the counter, was cold, and his voice had no more than a minimum of civility as he stated that Miss Bingham was not in.

"Then I must wait she returns."

"I don't think I should do that, if I were you. I don't know when she'll be back."

Inspector Cauldron was conscious of the hostility with which he was met. It was an attitude to which officers of the C.I.D. become accustomed as their years pass. It is not one to rouse their suspicions beyond the normal temperature of those who are in constant contact with violent or cunning crime. An uneasy conscience may be more anxious to please.

Had he said frankly: "I am a young officer, only recently promoted, to whom this first chance of handling an important case has unexpectedly come, and I am concealing a good deal of nervous anxiety lest I make some blunder of inexperience, such as might damn my prospects for many years," he might have met a more friendly reception. But official dignity and his own character were double barriers against such a confession as that. He said only: "You don't mean that she's left the hotel?"

The clerk glanced at the key-board. "She's taken her key with her, if she has."

Inspector Cauldron knew it to be one of the first lessons of his profession to maintain such conversational exchanges so long as there be possibility, however remote, of learning something which might prove useful at last, and his mission was to reap in a field from which an experienced senior officer had already gathered all the harvest he could. "I suppose," he said, "they sometimes do that."

"Sometimes isn't the word! But that's mostly when we know they're leaving, and they overlook handing them in. As a matter of fact, the lady said she rather hoped you'd call—the other officer, I suppose, she meant. I don't think I've seen you before."

"Chief Inspector Barnes has been taken suddenly ill. I'm handling the case now."

"Well, Miss Bingham said I could tell him, if he came any more, that she wasn't going to spend the rest of her life answering the same questions put backwards and sideways and upside down."

"You mean she went out to avoid being questioned further?"

"I daresay she'd had enough. But I believe there was something about arranging for Mrs. Houghton's funeral. I understand she'd had permission from you."

"From the superintendent? Yes, that's right. She's got an order to take the body. Only she mustn't cremate.... Was she sober when she said that about being questioned sideways and upside down?"

By the look the clerk gave in response to this question it seemed that his resentment had been freshly aroused—possibly by the suggestion that the amount of liquor consumed by any guest of the Old Jersey should be the occasion of comment by the police. But he only answered: "Yes. Quite," and Inspector Cauldron, rightly judging that, for the moment at least, there would be nothing more to be got from him, said: "There's a maid, Janet, I should like to see, if I may. I suppose she's on duty now."

"You can see her down here if you like."

"I'd rather see her upstairs, if I may. I should like to see the room where it occurred."

"You're not going to start it all over again?"

"No. I hope to be less trouble than that; but there are one or two points I've got to be a bit clearer about an I am now."

The reception-clerk turned to the telephone. A moment later he said: "Janet's at dinner, but she can with you in about three minutes. I'll tell the liftman to show you up."

Janet was the head chambermaid on the floor on which the murder had occurred. She had been in personal attendance both upon Miss Bingham and the murdered woman, and she had been the first of the hotel staff to reach the scene of the tragedy. Her statement was already filed among the *dossier* of the crime.

Inspector Cauldron said that he would go up; and as he waited in the softly carpeted corridor of the third floor, his mind went back to reconstruct the event as he had studied it that morning in Chief Inspector Barnes' concise and lucid report, upon which it may be convenient to turn a backward glance more comprehensively than he had yet been able to do.

The two Bingham sisters, prominent members of the social aristocracy of New York, had inherited so large a fortune from a millionaire father that their money had, for them, no practical limit. Its manipulation was in the hands of legal gentlemen of equal caution and integrity, and they had never found it to be inadequate to the demands which they had made upon it, which had not been light, for they belonged to that much-advertised but numerically inconsiderable proportion of the aristocracy of the United States who live wildly upon their wealth.

James Cadell Houghton, an Englishman, born in Preston, had begun his business career as a patent broker in the depressing atmosphere of that northern town. A single fortunate transaction, such as is the dream of all who enter his precarious profession, had made him a comparatively affluent man, and transferred the centre of his business interests to New York, where he had opened offices in 43rd Street, and rented a Fifth Avenue apartment, on a scale which showed that he did not intend to rebuff the smile which Fortune had turned towards him.

Money which had come easily was allowed to go with equal readiness, as will most frequently be. Whether he made further successful business deals during the short hours that he spent in his comfortable offices was a matter best known to himself at the time when he met the Bingham sisters, and proposed to, was accepted by,

9

and married the younger, with a celerity more characteristic of their own country than the slower-moving methods of his native land.

Isabel Bingham had no reason to ask or care what his financial status might be, having ample dollars for both. It was enough that he attracted, and professed to be attracted by her, and that he had fallen into their affluent, indolent, wasteful, pleasure-seeking ways. If she had had a further and subtler motive in at she did, it was something that Chief Inspector Barnes had had no means of guessing.

All he knew was that they had come to England—the elder sister, who had remained with the married pair, still making the third of a trio such as might be congenial or the reverse, according to the relations and temperaments of the three. But he had no evidence whatever to suggest that there was any connection between this triangular position and its supervening tragedy. He had only met one of the three alive, and she had professed a natural wish that there should be retribution for her sister's death.

Of the tragedy itself, the known facts were simple and few, and might not have been beyond the ability of a clever advocate to mitigate, if not to explain away, with some ingenious theory of misunderstanding or self-defence, if James Houghton had not condemned himself by his instant flight.

Four shots, almost as one, had sounded—not loudly, for the walls and doors of the Old Jersey are solid, and I carpets are soft and thick—in the suite opposite the staircase on the third floor; and a few moments after Mr. Houghton had stopped, and entered, a descending lift, hurried to the outer hall, said in a voice of agitation to a lady-clerk who was in temporary charge of the counter: "Send someone up to my rooms at once. There's been an accident," and disappeared through the revolving door into the street so rapidly that the porter had scarcely had time to rotate it for him, as it was his duty to do.

Naturally, he had not been stayed. It is not customary in good-class hotels to detain visitors by force if they mention that there has been an accident in their rooms, on the assumption that their meaning is that they have just murdered their wives.

He went through the revolving door, and had not been seen or heard of again. He had been fully dressed at the time, which was not surprising, it being 10:30 A.M., but the dead woman had been unclothed, except for a bathrobe which she could merely have been holding round her with one hand, for it had spread open when she fell, shot twice through the body, as she had apparently been coming out through the bathroom door.

But she had not died, it seemed, without attempting her own defence. A small silver-plated revolver lay by her dying hand, and it had two chambers empty.

Mr. Houghton's heavier weapon, with his name engraved upon it, had been thrown down on the other side of the room, after its deadly work was done. It also had two empty chambers, and there was no doubt where their bullets had gone. One had splintered a lower rib on the right side of Isabel Houghton's body, and then followed its course in an inner curve, stopping when almost touching the spinal cord. The second had pierced the aorta with a resulting haemorrhage which must have proved almost immediately fatal.

Of the two bullets that she had fired, one had been found imbedded in the opposite wall, but the other had not been discovered, even by the most diligent and intensive search of the whole apartment.

There were features about the affair which were not easy to understand, and which might be variously interpreted, but when a man takes to instant flight, having shot his wife two minutes before, it is not the first duty of the police to propound ingenious theories reduce the seriousness of the crime. The task of explanation may be left to him and his legal advisers, when he has been placed in the dock, where he must surely expect to be.

Yet, in view of the superintendent's words, when he had instructed him to take over the case, Inspector Cauldron thought that it might not be unprofitable to consider these facts with a freshly open mind. "I don't know what Barnes had in mind, but I got an idea that he wasn't quite satisfied that everything had been just as it appeared. But you'll remember that the murdered lady and her sister are—or were—both American citizens, of some importance in their own country. We don't want them to think on the other side that we can't handle a case like this neatly, or get justice done when we catch the man—as we're sure to do unless he does for himself, and I don't say it mightn't save a bit of trouble all round, if he has that much sense...."

There was nothing unusual in the fact that Mrs. Houghton had not been dressed at that period of the morning. Indeed, the telephone call for breakfast to be served had not been made, as was quite frequently the case at that hour. But it did seem strange that a lady clothed in nothing but a bathrobe should have a revolver so near her hand that she could return her husband's fire, even though she had not used her weapon with equal coolness, nor to such deadly effect.

It seemed strange also that—but at this point Inspector Cauldron's reflections were interrupted by the appearance of Janet, with the keys of the room he sought.

CHAPTER II

What Janet Said

The citizen of God's own country lives in centrally-heated buildings, the atmospheres of which are both hot and dry, so that he is in constant need of moisture. He takes this inwardly in the form of iced water, of which he has copious supplies beside him at every meal. Outwardly, he comforts his dry skin with continual baths.

The hotel proprietors of his own land are so conscious of these vital necessities that they supply the iced water free of charge; and, so that there may be no delay, even to cross a passage, when the desire for bodily immersion becomes urgent, they provide a bath for every bedroom. There are simple-minded Americans who take pride in the existence of these numerous baths, as indicating a superior standard of cleanliness, which is an error of diagnosis. The bath which is a pleasant luxury to the Englishman is a continual and urgent necessity to his Transatlantic cousin. Habits, however acquired, are not easily modified, and the American visitor to the older world, being introduced to an hotel bedroom, looks round with plaintive, bewildered eyes for the bathroom which may be anything from five to fifteen yards away.

Mr. Monro, the present proprietor, having purchased the lease of the Old Jersey, and knowing that American citizens (in 1922) were London's most affluent visitors, had determined to adapt the hotel to their requirements, without troubling his mind concerning pathological explanations of their condition. He had therefore added about fifty baths to the fourteen which had been previously installed, and their introduction involved some structural alterations, and many minor adjustments of the accommodation of the hotel.

The suite which the Houghtons had rented consisted of a lounge, a dining-room, a double bedroom (Isabel Houghton objected to the idea of married people having separate rooms), and a bathroom which was so placed that while it could be entered from the bedroom, it had another door, normally kept locked, which led to the dining-room, that being the central room of the suite. Both the dining-room and the lounge had doors which opened on to the corridor, but the bedroom could be entered from the dining-room only.

Miss Bingham's separate suite, consisting of bedroom, bathroom, and a small boudoir, was on the opposite side of the corridor, and a short distance away from the Houghton suite, which faced the lift and a broad flight of stairs; but they had been in the habit of taking their meals together, the dining-room and lounge being used equally by the three.

It was at the bathroom door which opened into the dining-room, and which was normally locked, that Isabel Houghton had fallen. The key had been, and still was, on the inside of the door, so that it appeared probable that, unless it had been unlocked previously, she must have opened it herself. She had been coming to her husband, rather than he seeking her, and he, when the shots were exchanged, by the evidence of the weapon that he had dropped and the bullet in the wall, had been almost opposite to her on the further side of the dining-room, and therefore close to the door of the corridor through which it appeared that he might have retreated, had he wanted to do so.

Janet had already made a statement of how she had heard the dull sound of the shots in the linen-room at the end of the corridor, but not loudly enough for her to be alarmed, or to guess what they were—she was a practical woman, indisposed to curiosity in regard to what was not her direct concern—and almost immediately after there had been a shrill scream from Charlotte Bingham, on hearing which, but still not expecting serious tragedy, she had put down the washing-book, told the girl who was with her to go on checking it till her return, and gone to see what was happening.

She had come upon Miss Bingham standing near the top of the stairs in a distracted condition, and her words, which Janet professed to remember with exactness, had been: "Oh, get a doctor! Do something! He's shot Isabel. Oh, the blood!"

Miss Bingham's own statement had been that she had heard the shots as she was completing her toilet, and—being much nearer than Janet—she had recognized what they were. She had run at once, scantily dressed as she was, to the dining-room, at the door of which she had met James coming out. He had said to her—so she said—"Well, it's done now"; and she had pushed past him, and seen next moment how her sister lay. It was then that she had screamed and run out of the room.

Before Janet, with more leisurely movements, had arrived on the scene, James Houghton had disappeared.

Such were the facts as the first enquiry had disclosed them, and Miss Bingham's further evidence had been that the couple were on normally affectionate terms, and that she could offer no explanation of what had occurred. She said that James had obtained a licence to carry a pistol from the New York police, on the ground that he was liable, in his business dealings, to have large sums of money or valuable documents upon him, and that he had once been the subject of an attempted hold-up while on his way to the bank. Her sister had had such a permit for a much longer time, having represented herself as a lonely woman, afraid of burglars, and having many valuables in her flat; and she had practised with her tiny weapon until she had become of moderate proficiency. She herself (she said) disliked firearms, which she never handled.

She could not account in any way for the fact that Isabel appeared to be coming out of the bathroom with the loaded revolver in her hand, as though anticipating attack, nor why that locked door should have been open at all. She had never known it to be opened previously, nor even that it had a key on the inner side.

In fact, she had represented the tragedy as being an inexplicable mystery to her, both in its circumstances and itself. It was an attitude difficult to disprove, particularly as James Houghton had disappeared and his wife was dead. If it were a false pose, it was far less vulnerable than would have been any invented explanations, such as could have been tested with the patient skill that the C.I.D. know so well how to apply.

Only if James Houghton should be arrested, and give a different account of his relations with his wife, or of how the tragedy had occurred, would it become necessary—or perhaps possible—to examine how far Miss Bingham's evidence might be coloured either by a natural desire to protect the dead woman's reputation, or—perhaps equally naturally—to bring to justice the man who had taken her sister's life....

Janet, a sandy-haired, pleasant-mannered, efficient Scotswoman, may have shown no more than the native caution of her race when she had previously declined to express opinions upon the three guests, or to enlarge her statement beyond the actual facts of the tragedy, as they had come under her own eyes. But Chief Inspector Barnes had recorded the opinion that she was too shrewd not to have observed more than she had allowed herself to say, and that she had restrained herself from abstract caution, sympathy with one or more of those concerned, or a feeling that loyalty to the hotel guests was an obligation that took precedence over the "duty of every citizen" as it is interpreted by the police.

Inspector Cauldron risked how she might respond to a direct appeal. "Janet," he said, "I want to ask you seriously to give us any help that you can. We're hunting for James Houghton now, and before long he may be on trial for the murder of his wife—well, you see how we stand! We want to get a conviction if he did murder her, but not otherwise. We just want the truth, and we shall need everyone's help if we're to get that now."

"What is it you want to know? I didn't see it happen, if you mean that."

"I never thought that you did. I think you've told us all you can about that. What we want to know is more about the people themselves, what their relations were with each other, and anything which could supply a motive for them to be letting off at one another in the way that two of them certainly must have done."

"You want guesses or facts?"

"I shouldn't be ungrateful for a good guess."

The woman's answer came with a downright energy for which there had been nothing to prepare him in the tone of her previous question. "And that, Inspector, is where I should say you go wrong! Years ago I saw a poor boy sentenced for something that I knew that he hadn't done; and that was brought off by some of the cleverest guessing you ever heard. But there's such a thing as being too clever, and forgetting what's said in a better book than the English law. *At the mouths of two or three witnesses shall every word be established.* You can't have better justice than that.

"It doesn't tell the jury to make a good guess, such as they might think well enough in their own business affairs—that's a judge's phrase we often read in the papers today—and I'll give you any fact that I know, but you'll get no guesses from me."

Inspector Barnes saw that her mind was biased by the sharpness of some past experience of an unforgettable kind.

He avoided argument, and held to his own course with diplomatic adroitness. "Well, Janet, we won't differ about that. I'm not sure that there isn't a good deal of reason in what you say. Only, when we make a good guess, it mayn't do no more than let someone in. It may let someone out. But I won't ask you to guess anything. If you'll give me facts, I won't ask for anything more."

"I don't know that I've got any facts to give you. Not about the poor woman's death."

"Well, you won't mind me asking a few questions. And if the answers aren't any use, I shall be no worse off than I am now.... Did they get on well together, or did they quarrel among themselves?"

"Mrs. Houghton did. I mean she sometimes quarrelled with her sister, and sometimes with Mr. Houghton. Mr. Houghton and Miss Bingham didn't. Not that we ever heard."

Inspector Cauldron observed, without appearing to do so, the plural pronoun. He concluded that, if Janet had not discussed the murder freely with other members of the staff, there had been reports taken to her.

"You don't know," he went on, "what they quarrelled about?"

"No...I wouldn't like to say that."

"Was it generally when Houghton had had rather too much...? I'm not guessing about that. We've seen the hotel bills."

"You mustn't put all that to him. The ladies drank as much, if not more."

"Well, if we divide by three, they didn't suffer from lack of moisture. Did you ever see any of them the worse for drink?"

"That depends upon what you mean. Mrs. Houghton was excited at times."

"So it wouldn't be far wrong to say that it was Mrs. Houghton who sometimes drank rather too freely, and at those times she got quarrelsome, either with her husband or sister?"

"No. Not far wrong. James, the waiter, might tell you more about that."

"Did you ever hear any of them threaten one another?"

"No. I didn't see as much of them as you may think."

"Very well. I'll ask James.... Do you know whether the bathroom door leading into the dining-room was usually locked?"

"It was locked when they took the suite. I can't say for sure beyond that. I used to do the Houghton suite myself, and when I cleaned the bathroom I never used that door. I reckoned that it was kept locked. It might have saved time sometimes to come out that way, but I couldn't have locked it again—not on the inside—when I'd come through."

"I see. And do you know where Mrs. Houghton kept her pistol?"

"No. I didn't know that she had such a thing at all."

"And there's nothing more you can tell me that might be helpful?"

"No. I don't think there is."

The denial was definite, but Inspector Cauldron waited patiently, with an instinctive perception that she was hesitating over some further statement. The reward of his patience came when she said doubtfully: "You might have a few words with Doris. It may be nothing to do with it; but it may be right you should know."

17

Doris was a younger girl, normally brisk and pert, who worked under Janet, and whose duty it had been to attend to Miss Bingham's apartment.

"When Doris was questioned before, she said she had been in the linen-room all the time, and knew nothing about it whatever."

"So she was. But I wasn't thinking about that. I'd better have a few words with her first."

Janet went off to find the girl, leaving Inspector Cauldron in some hope that he had not been wasting his time. She came back in a few minutes, leading a sulky, obviously reluctant girl.

"You'd better tell the inspector just what you saw," she said, with uncompromising severity, "or else say that it's made-up lies. You've told enough other people whom it doesn't concern."

"I'm not going to be dragged into any court," the girl said sullenly. "I didn't see nothing wrong."

"The question of giving evidence may not arise, the inspector answered. "But if you've seen things that you won't tell us, you may get called and treated as a hostile witness, and you wouldn't like that, would you?"

This vague assurance, and still vaguer threat, appeared to have some effect on the girl. She answered, in a more subdued tone: "I didn't want to tell tales to do any harm."

"We don't want you to do any harm. We just want the truth, so that no one will get misjudged."

There was a moment of sullen silence, and then the girl said:

"It was about half-past eight. I saw Mr. Houghton go into Miss Bingham's room."

"You mean at night, or on the morning that Mrs. Houghton was shot?"

"In the morning?"

"Did he know that you saw him?"

"No. I'm sure he didn't."

"Which room do you mean? The bedroom?"

"No. The boudoir."

"Was he fully dressed?"

"Yes."

"At half-past eight! There doesn't seem to be overmuch in that. Did you see him come out?"

"He hadn't come out at nine; and after that, when I went in to change the flowers, I heard someone speak, and then the key turned in the bedroom door.

"Did you recognize the voice, or hear what was said?"

"No. It was too low. It was only a word. And then someone turned the key very quick."

"Would Miss Bingham expect you to be going in at that time?"

"No. The orders were that she wasn't ever to be disturbed till she rang."

"But you usually changed her flowers in the morning?"

No. Not till I did the room. I hadn't done it at that time before."

"I suppose it was really an invented reason for going in to see or hear what you could?"

"I didn't see what business he had staying there."

"And you didn't see him come out?"

"No. I went off duty at nine-fifteen."

"Shouldn't you naturally expect Miss Bingham to be up at half-past eight?"

"Not when she never was. Besides that, it was after two when they came in the night before."

"How do you know that?"

"I was on duty during the night."

"Were they all sober when they came in?"

"Nothing to notice. Mrs. Houghton was talking a bit loud."

"Had you known Mr. Houghton go into Miss Bingham's bedroom before?"

"We thought he'd been there once or twice."

"Why did you think that?"

"Oh, there are things you can see."

"What things?"

"Oh, things."

Thank you, Doris. I think that will be all now."

Having finished with her, Inspector Cauldron descended to interview James, the waiter, who had served breakfast regularly, and sometimes other meals, in the Houghtons' dining-room. He added little of definite fact to that which had become evident already, but, unlike Janet, he had no objection to guessing. He expressed a confident opinion that Charlotte Bingham had killed her sister. He said that the two women hated one another, and were jealous concerning James Houghton. It was a case, to his mind, of a woman trying to seduce her sister's husband, and the two women having a shooting-match in consequence. Inspector Cauldron pointed out that it was James Houghton who had bolted the moment that the tragedy had occurred, that it was his weapon from which the fatal bullets had come, and one or two other facts somewhat difficult to reconcile with this theory, but James remained unshaken in his belief. The inspector formed a correct opinion that Miss Bingham had not made herself popular with the dining-room staff.

CHAPTER III

Miss Bingham Desires Revenge

Inspector Cauldron felt that he had not done badly. He expected that the widespread net which had been cast for the snaring of James Cadell Houghton would be drawn in before many days were over, having the desired fish in its meshes. When that should happen he must be ready with a plausible construction of the crime, and such information concerning the characters and relations of the murderer and sisters as would be potent in cross-examination to break down any lying tale that he might put up in his own defence. How many criminals, he thought, have fallen to rope or jail because they lacked the kind of courage which will risk the implications of stubborn silence, and so have been led on a path of lies which has supplied the evidence against themselves, which could have been obtained, in legal form, in no other way!

He knew what he had to do, and he felt that he had already made substantial advance toward understanding of the tragedy—perhaps more than Chief Inspector Barnes, so inopportunely afflicted with that acute attack of appendicitis (or should "opportune" be the word?) had succeeded in doing.

But, he told himself, he must not indulge too early in such self-gratulations. There was still much to be done. When he had interviewed Charlotte Bingham, complacency might have more solid grounds.

Next morning he was at the Old Jersey at too early an hour for it to be likely that she would have left the hotel He would rather wait till she should be up than miss her again. Wait he did—for nearly three hours.

It appeared that the lady had come in late the night before (there was nothing unusual in that), and her orders were that she should not be disturbed until she should ring for breakfast.

She did this at nine-thirty, and said she would have it in bed. After that she took long to dress.

21

Inspector Cauldron, sustaining this long delay with difficult patience, not unaffected by the atmosphere of latent hostility by which he was surrounded, and the grudging permission he had received to remain in the hall, concluded that if she could telephone down from her room he could telephone up to her, which, overcoming some expostulations from the reception clerk, he succeeded in doing.

"I am Inspector Cauldron of Scotland Yard," he said, when the connection was made. "I am anxious to have a few words with you in reference to Mrs. Houghton's death."

There was a rather long pause before a woman's voice with a strong American accent answered him: "You can't today. I've got things more important to do."

"I'm afraid I can't agree that anything can be more important than this."

"Then we've just got to differ. My sister's funeral's at two-thirty this afternoon."

"I beg your pardon. I wasn't thinking of that. But I shan't keep you long."

"I don't see what use it would be. I've told Chief Inspector Barnes all I know, and he's got it signed. You'd better talk it over with him."

"Chief Inspector Barnes is in hospital with appendicitis."

"That's just too bad! But I don't see why I should begin all over again because of that. I've made a written statement of all I know. I suppose you haven't got James?"

"No. Not yet. Though we soon shall. But there's one point that your statement doesn't cover, that I'm bound to clear up. I needn't keep you many minutes for that."

He saw that the time might be inopportune. He might have left his call till the next day, had he given more thought to a thing he knew; but the ladies apparent reluctance to see him—natural as its explanation might be—had stirred him to an obstinacy which would not yield. Now he must listen to an impatient and unexpected reply:

"Then why don't you say what you want to know?"

He was not instantly prepared for that. He had no intention of being cut off with a curt reply to a telephone question. He wished to see the lady; and his one question might well lead to a dozen more. He replied, with some truth: "I'd rather not speak from here. It's not quite as private as I should like it to be."

"Then you'd better come up now."

Satisfied with this abrupt surrender, Inspector Cauldron took the lift to the third floor, knocked at Miss Bingham's bedroom door, and heard her reply: "If that's the policeman, come right in, and come through."

He entered an empty room, and, seeing an open door on its farther side, supposed correctly that he was invited to the bedroom beyond.

Miss Charlotte Bingham lay in bed, with her empty breakfast tray on a table at the farther side. Inspector Cauldron, an observant man, as detective-inspectors are likely to be, saw evidences in the empty dishes that her appetite had not been impaired either by the fact that her brother-in-law was in flight from a capital charge, or that she was to attend her murdered sister's funeral that afternoon.

He saw a woman still in the early thirties, with auburn hair, rather fine eyes, cheek-bones of some prominence in a face too highly coloured for the beauty to which she could otherwise lay some claim in a florid style. She concealed an opulent figure in a dressing gown of crimson silk, which he observed, as the interview progressed, that she was excessively careful to keep not only tightly closed at her throat, but with the sleeves drawn down her wrists. It seemed incongruous to her manner in other ways. Was it habit or pose? He had a moment of puzzled wonder, and passed it by for more obvious questions.

The hands that drew the sleeves so carefully down were not only well groomed, they were well shaped. On the left one he saw two over-large, very splendid rings.

He summed her up rapidly. Rich. Vulgar. Pleasure-loving. Selfish. Good-humoured, if all went well. Not to be disturbed from her habits of physical indulgence by any calamity that left herself and her fortune free.

That she had no colour sense was obvious from the crimson silk she wore, which had no mercy on the high colouring with which she paid for the pleasures the table gave. But wealth, if not culture, was evident in the litter of the untidy room.

He did not think her a fool. He thought there should be things she could tell him—if she would—which might be helpful to hear. But he must seek first to learn what her feelings were toward the dead woman and fugitive man, for their value might hang on that.

He saw signs that she had been dressing when he rang, and had got back into bed to receive him. Well, that would be the natural thing for her to do. These speculations would not take him far! He must see what she had to say.

He had promised to be brief. He went to his point at once. "I believe," he said, "that you told Chief Inspector Barnes that you had not seen either your sister or her husband on the morning of her death, until you heard the shots and rushed across the passage to find out what had happened."

"You don't *believe*," she answered bluntly though with a voice and manner pleasanter than the words. "You *know* I said that. It isn't what I *told* anyone. You've got it on the statement in black and white."

"And you are sure, on further consideration, that that was true?"

"You bet it was! We'd been out rather too late the night before, and I don't say we hadn't done ourselves well. There's no sense in getting up too soon on the morning after. And Isabel wouldn't have been in the best of tempers to meet. No, I wasn't in any hurry for that."

"You mean they'd been quarrelling?"

"No, I don't. I mean what I said, as I mostly do. After what they'd taken the night before, they'd both wake up with a bad head."

"I see…. And if anyone says that Mr. Houghton had been in here with you an hour before the shooting occurred, he'd be saying something that wasn't true. "Oh, that! You said *he*? You've been talking to that little slut Doris. But yes, James did come here for a moment, I didn't think it was worth mentioning. It couldn't have had anything to do with what followed. He only came for a book."

"I was told he was here some time. I haven't suggested that it had anything to do with what followed, but I wish you'd be as accurate as you can."

"You might pass me that book. Yes, the red one on the table there."

Curious as to what the coming explanation could be, and with some admiration for the frank coolness with which Miss Bingham met the evidence of her previous inaccuracy, Inspector Cauldron passed the book. As he did so he observed the title: *Three Murders at Blackmire Grange*. He knew it's hero to be one of those detectives of fiction who turn in their murderers as regularly as the milkman delivers the morning milk. And that in spite of complications a thousand times greater than he was likely to meet in this simple case! We'll, if the occasion should come, must hope he would do as much.

Miss Bingham turned the pages with a deliberate scrutiny. "There," she said, "you'd better judge for yourself. Page 260 to the end—that's page 282. That's twenty-two pages. How long would it take to read those while someone stood fussing at the foot of the bed?"

Inspector Cauldron saw it to be a question to which there would be no certain reply. The care with which the pages were read—the interruptions which might be made. "You mean," he said, "that Mr. Houghton came in for that book and waited for you to finish it before he took it away?"

"Yes. I mean just that. He wanted this book, and I said he'd have to wait, as I hadn't got much to read."

"I suppose he'd expect that you'd have been up at that hour?"

"No, he wouldn't. He'd expect just the other way. If I'd been dressing, I should have put the bolt on the door. After we'd come in late, James used to get up a lot earlier than Isabel or I, and he'd mooch about like a lost dog. Isabel wouldn't let him have breakfast. He had to have it with her when she was dressed. So did I, if I wanted the day to have a good start."

"Could you tell me about what time it was that Houghton came for the book?"

"No. You'd better ask Doris that. I wasn't watching the clock."

There was temper in the tone as well as the wording of this reply, and the inspector was too discreet to press further a question the answer to which he already knew. He said: "Wanting to borrow a book to read isn't quite what you'd expect from a man on the point of shooting his wife. Wasn't anything said at all that gives you any clue to what happened afterwards?"

"Not a word he just wanted a book he was half through, and hung about till I let it go. He might have been a bit on the sulky side. But not more than he often was at that time of day."

"And you thought this wasn't worth mentioning?"

"I don't see that it is now. I don't see that it helps you at all."

"But when you were asked directly whether you had seen anything of him that morning, wouldn't it have been more natural—?"

"I thought Inspector Barnes meant whether I'd been up and with them before it happened. I told him what I thought wanted to know."

"But it's surely better to give a true answer, even if you don't think it important. I gather that Mrs. Houghton was rather difficult to get on with?

"What makes you think that?"

"For one thing, what you said about breakfast."

"She certainly liked having her own way. Most people do."

"But some are more considerate than others."

"She liked James to toe the line, if you mean that."

"So that they were not very happy together?"

"I wish you wouldn't put words into my mouth! It was just the opposite way. You might say she was never happy apart."

"Do you mean she was jealous?"

"I daresay she was. You might say all women are."

"Not equally. Do you think she had given him any cause to be jealous of her?"

"I know she hadn't. It was about the last thing she'd be likely to do."

"And you can't suggest any motive for what happened?"

"I've said that already. I've no more idea than you."

"And you would naturally wish that the man who killed your sister should be brought to justice?"

"I'd say I should! But that's your business, not mine. And I don't suppose you'd take any advice from me."

"On the contrary, I should he very grateful for any hint you can give."

"Inspector Barnes asked a lot of questions about where he'd lived in Lancashire, before he came to New York. He seemed to think he'd make for there, more likely than not."

"It does seem probable."

"Well, you ought to know! But I should have said that James wasn't quite such a fool as that."

"Perhaps not. But we find that most criminals are.... Was there any other direction in which he could obtain money?"

"That's a bit more than I'd say. I don't even know he could get it there."

"And you don't think he had any on him when he left?"

"He might have had a few pounds, more or less. I shouldn't say he stopped to pick anything up."

Miss Bingham paused, and the inspector waited in patient silence, thinking that there was something further to come. Her eyes had fallen. Her hands moved restlessly, pulling down the sleeves of her dressing-gown in the manner which he had noticed before. Then she asked: "If I told you something, you wouldn't let anyone know that it came from me?"

"I can't promise that till I know what it is."

"It isn't the kind of thing you'd want to use in evidence. It's what might help you to know where to look."

"If it's no more than that, it would be confidential with me."

"It's only that he once said, when there was some-thing in the papers about a murderer being caught, that he deserved it for bolting the way he did. He said that if the man had taken lodgings in the next street he'd have been a lot harder to find."

"Thank you, Miss Bingham. That may be very useful indeed. I won't hinder you longer now. If there's any point I haven't got thoroughly clear I'll come and see you again."

Inspector Cauldron rose and went, with the feeling that he had not wasted his time. He was sure that he had not been told all the truth, and dubious of that which had been said with much appearance of frankness. But even that *might* be true. Servants' gossip and inventions might have put a too-evil construction upon what had been no worse than loosely unconventional ways.

It had been clear before that the dead woman had been violent and uncertain in temper and of frequent insobriety. By implication Miss Bingham had admitted this, though it was natural that she should desire to shield her sister's reputation.

But he was convinced that she could say more, if she would. Those two people would not have started shooting at each other without some prefacing quarrel. And with guns in the hands of both!

If Mrs. Houghton had come out of the bathroom, threatening her husband with a revolver, which seemed, in some respects, the most probable construction of the event, what had led to that sudden out-break?

How had his own weapon been so ready to his hand? The woman must almost certainly have fired first, though it might be by no more than an instant of time. For she must have been incapable after those better-aimed bullets which were directed against her had found their mark. She must have collapsed at the first, and the second struck before she had sunk to the ground.

There was something—if not much—in the man's favour there. But if he had been in fear of his wife's violence, why had he not retreated through the door at his side, instead of reaching—where? for his own gun.

And whatever her condition might have been, he had been sober and cool. That was, if Miss Bingham's evidence were not entirely untrue. Sober enough to be looking for a book with which to pass the hours till his wife should rise, and they could order the morning meal.

Well, when they had him, and heard the account of the event which he would be certain to offer, it would be strange if there were no material for questioning Miss Bingham further to be abstracted therefrom. He knew how often truth will emerge from two sets of discordant lies.

And the hint which Miss Bingham had given him, apart from any value it might prove to have (of which he had a sanguine hope) was important as indicating her real feeling toward the missing man. To bring him to justice while keeping her sister's reputation unslurred, appeared to be her not unnatural aim.

CHAPTER IV

Mr. Houghton May Not Be Far

Inspector Cauldron started the next day in a less confident mood. He had discussed the case with his senior officers, and they had endorsed the wisdom of the course which James Houghton was said to have approved. If all those who commit murder in London should simply move to a new lodging anywhere within a ten or fifteen mile radius, taking a new name, they would be much harder to catch than they now are. If they should take such a lodging, and establish a separate identity *before* committing the crime, so that there would be nothing to arouse the suspicions of those immediately around them, their immunity would be further increased. Fortunately for the community, few murderers calculate so coolly, or plan in anticipation of what they do. In the case of James Houghton, it approximated to certainty that he would not have anticipated the crime. When he hurried out into the street through the rotating door of the New Jersey Hotel he would have been acting on the elementary instinct of flight, but with no settled refuge to which to flee. But if, as Miss Bingham said, he had been already of a settled opinion as to the course of safety, under such an emergency as had suddenly become his, it was extremely likely that he would have acted upon it.

It was, at least, a theory well worth an intensive test. As it was, Inspector Cauldron knew that, while there might be no corner of the British Isles where both the detective and uniformed officers of the law were not watchful for the appearance of anyone similar to the photograph or description of James Houghton which had been circulated to them, there might be nowhere in the whole of that wide area where the search would be more perfunctory than in the immediate vicinity of the old Jersey Hotel. It was a lesson of experience, if not a verdict of common sense, that their quarry would not be there.

But now the inspector proceeded to alter that. He saw a possibility, in addition to his general charge of the case, that he might become the actual discoverer of the fugitive, which he had not thought that opportunity would allow.

He not only roused every officer in the Metropolitan area to a new alertness by circulating an instruction that the man was believed not to have left London, he devoted his own time to a systematic search, particularly of the smaller hotels and boarding-houses to which a man in such extremity would be likely to go.

He considered, with some acumen, that an intelligent man so placed would be likely to consult the advertisement columns of the daily papers. It would be some introduction, if not much, to say: "I noticed your advertisement in the *Daily Telegraph* this morning." Better, at least, than ringing at a bell with no better reason for having selected it than a window-notice that there was accommodation to let.

Pursuing the idea, he procured a comprehensive file of the London daily papers of the date on which the murder had occurred, and made systematic enquiry during the next three days at many hundred addresses—a proceeding rendered less onerous than it may sound by a previous tabulation which enabled him particularly in the Blooms-bury and Bayswater districts, to go almost from door to door. In a very great majority of cases a brief question would obtain a conclusively negative answer, and he would leave a closing door to proceed on his monotonous quest.

It was one of those patient, persistent efforts characteristic of the methods of the C.I.D. which may be said to have deserved success, but, as so often happens, the first hopeful news—leaving aside various false reports which collapsed on closer enquiry—came in a more casual way.

P.C. Wrexter, a young and inexperienced member of the uniformed branch of the service, telephoned that the cashier of the South Street branch of Atlas Restaurants, Ltd., had called him in from his beat and reported that a man whom she felt sure to be James Houghton had been coming in regularly about 3:30 P.M. every day from about that on which the murder had occurred.

By a fortunate chance, Inspector Cauldron was in when this message came through, and it was no more than fifteen minutes later that he entered the restaurant, and presented his card to a middle-aged lady, of plain features but pleasant manners, whose tale, reasonably and intelligently told, gave him solid ground for hope that this most important part of his work was done.

"I daresay," she said, "you'll think that I ought to have communicated with you before, when I tell you that I've had some suspicions for the last three or four days, but I didn't want to put you to

29

trouble for nothing—I've heard that you get hundreds of dud clues every day of the week—and I hesitated till I felt sure.

"I noticed the man first because he comes in regularly at about half-past three, and always sits in that far corner over on the right. It's a time when we're nearly empty, and that's the darkest corner of the shop, as you can see for yourself. He always has a pretty good meal, without taking too long about it, and when he pays me as he goes out he scarcely looks at me. I don't mean he avoids it exactly; it wouldn't be fair to say that. But it's as though he's got something on his mind that he can't forget, so that he's hardly conscious of what he does.

"I tried yesterday giving him his change a shilling short. I'd thought before that he never looked to see what it was. Well, he took it without noticing, and of course I called him back, and said I'd made a mistake."

"You say he started coming here the day of the murder?"

"I couldn't say to a day or so either way. Not for sure. Of course, I wasn't noticing particularly. But it was just about then."

"And you say he looks like Houghton?"

"Well, that's for you to judge. He's so like that he reminded me of the picture I'd seen in the *Record*. That was what put the first suspicion into my mind. And I didn't trust to memory. I turned up the paper and brought it with me yesterday. I had it under the shelf here while he was having his meal, and when he paid me I felt sure enough to call in the policeman, and tell him what I suspected."

Inspector Cauldron considered this, and saw some probability that he wasn't wasting his time. Even murderers must eat. What more likely than that the hiding man should go to a class of restaurant which his acquaintances would not probably enter, and at an hour when it would be comparatively empty? What more natural than that he should select a retired corner, and that his thoughts should be on other things than the amount of his change when he paid his check?

All the same, there was nothing tangible in this beyond the resemblance to the wanted man which the cashier professed to have noticed. If he should be accosted and simply deny that he was Houghton, giving another name—which, whether Houghton or not, he would be likely to do—the grounds for detaining him would not be strong.

Such risks have to be taken, and some mistakes are unavoidably made, but they are not liked at the Yard and a young inspector will not improve his reputation by perpetrating them. Inspector Cauldron preferred to be sure.

From the restaurant he went straight to the Old Jersey, with the intention of securing a witness who would make identification positive.

But here he met difficulty. The manager was out. The reception-clerk, who professed authority in his absence, did not refuse to allow any eligible witness to be released, but he suggested that it was improbable that much assistance would be rendered. He pointed out that Mr. Houghton had only been there for a short time, and that the Old Jersey had many guests.

He said this in the hearing of the hotel porters, who may have passed the words to others. Anyway, that was the position taken generally by the hotel staff on the ground floor. It only varied from a definite assertion that they would not be able to identify Houghton, to a non-committal attitude, which neither promised nor denied. Inspector Cauldron wanted something better than that.

He tried the liftman, and was rebuffed again, this time by what he felt to be an honest reply: "Not to swear to, I couldn't. There's too many as comes and goes."

"Very well," he said, "then I'll go up to the third floor." He felt that either Janet or Doris would be quite capable of the identification he required. They had been in close contact with the Houghton party, and they had sharp feminine eyes. Janet might be difficult to persuade, but he thought there might be more than one way in which any reluctance on the part of Doris could be overcome.

But when he reached the third floor, it was neither of these, but Miss Bingham whom he first saw.

She was leaving her room, dressed to go out, as Inspector Cauldron stepped from the lift, and she hurried forward to check its descent. But the inspector stood his ground, blocking her way. It had occurred to him that, if she could be persuaded to make the identification, her evidence would be more conclusive even than that of one of the maids.

She looked younger and more attractive than when he had seen her in the bedroom before, being more completely groomed; and a skilful tailor had cut her costume to give the impression of a symmetry of form which was not hers. Inspector Cauldron did not think that she was grieving overmuch for her sister's death, but such hardness was quite consistent with willingness or even desire that the man who had killed her should pay the legal penalty of his crime.

However that might be, it was clear that she did not welcome further conversations with the police. Her cheekbones reddened beyond their normal floridity, as she observed who it was who now blocked her way to the lift.

31

"May I speak to you a moment, Miss Bingham?"

"Yes, if you must. I suppose here will do?"

"I wondered whether you would be free to spare me an hour tomorrow afternoon?"

"What do you want me to do?"

"We want you to identify a man whom we believe to be Mr. Houghton."

"You mean that you've arrested James?" There was no doubt that the lady's interest was now fully aroused. She had ceased to look toward the descending lift.

"No. Not exactly. We are watching a man whom we believe to be he. It is your identification on which the arrest will depend."

"You mean he's in London?"

"Yes. The hint you gave us appears to have been well-founded."

"I think I'd rather you got someone else to do that."

"I thought you might prefer to do it yourself, rather than have others mixed up in your—family affairs."

"They're scarcely that now."

Inspector Cauldron was conscious that he had not struck the right note. "Of course," he went on, "we want to be sure that we're not arresting the wrong man. I thought I might get Janet or Doris to have a look at him; and then I thought you might prefer to make the identification yourself."

"Does he say that he isn't James?"

"He hasn't been asked anything yet. We wanted you to have a look at him first."

Miss Bingham remained silent for a moment. Inspector Cauldron could have no knowledge of what she thought, but he had a feeling that the atmosphere changed. With a view to drawing her finally over the bridge of hesitation, he added: "Of course, if it should be Houghton, we're bound to find out; even if he shouldn't admit it, as he most likely may, your identification wouldn't make any real difference. But if it isn't, you'll be doing a good turn to an innocent man, and save him from even knowing how near he's been to an unpleasant experience."

With an expression that still left the inspector slightly puzzled, feeling that there was something he could not read, she asked abruptly: "Just what is it you want me to do?"

"I want you to come with me tomorrow afternoon to a restaurant not more than half a mile away, and take a look at the man, if he should be there, as there is reason to think he will. I can put you where you'll get a good look at him without much chance of being seen. He needn't even know that you've been there, if you'd rather not."

"And, if I refuse, you'd get Janet or Doris to go?"

"I shall do my best to get one of them."

Miss Bingham still showed indecision, but Inspector Cauldron was right in thinking that the game was won.

"I don't see," she said at last, "why I shouldn't do that. But of course it may not be he. What time do you want me to go?"

"I'll have a car here for you at two-thirty."

"Very well. I'll be ready."

With more affability than she had shown previously, Miss Bingham wished the inspector good-afternoon.

Inspector Cauldron reported what he had done when he got back to the Yard, and received only qualified praise."

"You'd have done better," Superintendent Backwash said, "to have got one of the maids. If Miss Bingham's got any reason for not wanting the case to come into court—and, if the chambermaid's suspicions had any truth in them (which they quite likely didn't, you needn't trouble to tell me that) she's probably got one very good one, if not more—she'll be quite likely to stare at her brother-in-law and say she never saw him before, and where will you be then?"

"I haven't overlooked that possibility," the inspector replied with the patience due to the criticism of a superior officer, however unreasonable it may be, "even if she should refuse to identify him, I meant to have him followed, and kept under observation, till we've made quite sure who he is. But after the trouble I'd had, I didn't mean to lose a chance by letting the lady walk past me. And I think Janet would have refused, though I'd got a good hope of the younger girl."

Superintendent Backwash made no comment on this, which was as near to approving the actions of his subordinate officers as he was accustomed to go; and the reasonable doubt which had entered both their minds proved to be groundless, for, next afternoon, the suspected man took his usual seat, and ordered his meal in ignorance of the fact that Miss Bingham (who had been introduced to the kitchen quarters through the West Street entrance) had him in clear, view for twenty or thirty seconds through the service hatch, and identified him with an ease and decision consistent with the close acquaintance of previous days.

CHAPTER V

The Arrest

Inspector Cauldron put Miss Bingham hack in the car, for her part was done. He walked round to the front entrance of the restaurant. His previous experiences had not included the arrest o£ a man who was accused of a capital crime, and he was not entirely free from anxiety as to how he should acquit himself if any position of difficulty or delicacy should arise.

But he was outwardly cool and self-possessed as he walked in.

So far James Cadell Houghton had been little more to him than a name, without objective reality, except as one who had killed his wife, and then taken to abortive though troublesome flight. Now he saw a man who was young, and well-enough though rather carelessly dressed. His face was thin, and might have been described as of an intellectual type, though without imputing lack of courage or of capacity for prompt decision.

He appeared worried and preoccupied, but showed no sign of alarm or interest as Inspector Cauldron came to his table. He gave him one unseeing glance, and turned his eyes indifferently elsewhere.

Inspector Cauldron knew that it is the etiquette of the Yard that such arrests shall be quietly and politely made. The man who murders his wife through some unendurable matrimonial difference is not usually a habitual criminal. Beyond that, there is most often a tale which he is anxious to tell in his own defence. It is seldom, indeed, that such a man will make violent resistance if he be circumspectly approached. But, for all that, each case has its individual differences. There is no certain rule.

Now Inspector Cauldron leaned slightly forward. "Excuse me," he said, in a low and toneless voice, his glance fixed watchfully upon the one who seemed so indifferent to him, "you are Mr. J. C. Houghton?"

As it was said it sounded less a query than a statement of fact, but the man who was thus addressed looked up with a surprise which, if it were not genuine, was remarkably simulated. "Am I?" he asked. And then: "May I ask how my name concerns you?"

"I'm afraid I have an unpleasant duty to perform, Mr. Houghton. I am Inspector Cauldron, of the Criminal Investigation Department. I have a warrant for your arrest for the murder of Isabel Houghton. It is my duty to warn you—"

The other man interrupted him. "Never mind that patter," he said. "You are making a mistake. That is not my name."

The inspector smiled slightly. "I'm afraid that won't do," he replied. "You admitted it a moment ago.

"Oh, no, I didn't. I asked you what business it was of yours." The voice was curt now, and slightly irritated.

But the inspector was unimpressed. "Well," he said, "you know now. I suppose you'll come quietly…. I've got a taxi outside."

Mr. Houghton (if such he really were) appeared to repress an angry answer. He became silent, as though considering an unprecedented position. "I'm not going to knock you down, if you mean that. And I am not going to resist arrest, if you assure me that you have proper authority for what you do…. I suppose it's no use telling you again that my name's not Houghton?"

The detective smiled. "Not the least. We know quite well who you are. You were positively identified less than five minutes ago."

"Perhaps you have my fingerprints?"

"I daresay they could be found."

"I wonder…. Well, I suppose that would settle it, one way or other…. I must hope you haven't."

"We've no need to depend on them in a case like this."

"No? I suppose not. And anything I say will be put in as evidence? Do you mind if I write it down?"

"There's no need to do that now. If you want to make a statement there'll be lots of time after you've been properly charged."

But the accused man had already drawn out a pocket diary, and was writing rapidly on an empty page. Inspector Cauldron thought that there could be no harm in letting this performance proceed. His aim was to secure his prisoner as quietly as possible. There was no reason for haste. But he remained alert for any sudden movement, either of aggression or flight. If the man were foolish enough to make a statement, it could scarcely fail to simplify the work of the police, as such documents always do.

The present one was unusual in at least one particular. It was brief. The accused man had not had occasion to turn the page, which he tore out, and passed across the table.

Inspector Cauldron looked at it with a wary eye. Was it intended to divert his attention while his prisoner would bolt suddenly for the door? But he made no movement, and the words could be quickly read:

I say three things:

(1) I am extremely surprised.
(2) I have not murdered anyone.
(3) My name is not Houghton.

The inspector read these assertions with an expressionless face, though he smiled inwardly. His thought was that Houghton had helped himself a long way on the road to the hangman's shed. Innocent men, when they are arrested, do not deny their identity. But he said only: "This will be put in evidence, of course. We'd better be going now."

The man who denied being Houghton made no motion to rise. Actually, he was playing for time while he endeavoured to remember everything that his pockets held. He said: "I'm very inexperienced in these matters. What is the procedure?"

"You can't have bail, if you mean that. Not in a case like this."

"I wasn't thinking about bail. I only wondered whether you propose to take any further steps to identify me with your friend Houghton, and whether it would be etiquette to enquire for any details about the murder which I am expected to prove that I didn't do."

"I don't think we shall worry much about the identity," was the cheerful answer. "The charge will be read over to you at the station. You don't really think it's worth while to go on saying you're not Houghton, do you?"

But behind the confident, almost derisive tone Inspector Cauldron was aware of a puzzled doubt, which he would not show. He had the best of reasons for confidence that he had not made any mistake. But that did not prevent him observing the unusual behaviour of the man he was arresting. It was not quite the attitude—not quite *any* of the attitude with which he was familiar on the part of those whom it became his duty to accost in this manner. But still less was it one likely to be adopted by an innocent man.

His opponent appeared to be faintly amused by the repeated question. "I told you," he replied, as though wearied of repeating that which was of no great moment to him, "that my name is not Houghton. I see no occasion to go on saying the same thing."

"If you were not the man I want, you would say whom you are, and you would have every opportunity of proving it."

"Can you tell me any reason why I should do your business for you?"

"Most people would think it to be very much their business. If you seriously want to prove to me that you are not the man I am after, you will give your name and address, and no doubt you could get others to identify you. If you won't do that, you can blame no one but yourself that your assertion is not taken seriously."

"Really? It sounds illogical. Shall we go?" He added as he rose: "I suppose I may pay my bill? Or do you undertake such little responsibilities for me?"

The inspector had no objection to his paying his own bill. He had put it in his waistcoat pocket when the waitress had given it to him a few minutes earlier. He drew it out now, and walked to the pay-desk, the inspector keeping closely to his right hand. There was an open fireplace on his left. A fire burned brightly, with a centre of glowing heat. As he passed he threw a small folded paper into the red heart of the coals.

It was quickly done, but Inspector Cauldron's eyes were quick, too. With an exclamation of annoyance he sprang at the grate. He looked for fire-irons. There was only a short poker. He seized this, and jabbed the paper clear of the coals. But it was already tinder.

Meanwhile his prisoner, neither slackening nor hastening his pace, was walking toward the door. He had no choice but to follow. He said hurriedly to the two young women—the cashier and waitress—who had watched the performance with wide-open eyes: "Save that ash for me. I'll give a pound for it if it isn't crushed."

"Houghton," he said angrily, as he regained his side, "you'll find that sort of thing does you no good."

The arrested man smiled almost genially. He answered with his usual query. "Really? You didn't mention that you had a warrant for my correspondents' envelopes."

The inspector did not reply. He took his prisoner's arm in a grip which was too firm to be comfortable. But the victim showed no resentment. They passed the swing-doors together and entered the waiting taxi.

At the police station there was a more detailed interrogation, and, a diminished politeness. The prisoner was formally charged. He was generally warned once again. He was unceremoniously searched and relieved of some loose money, a pocket-knife, a set of keys, a wallet containing seventeen pounds in notes, a pocket diary in which little was entered, and some figures on loose sheets of paper of no apparent significance.

He was invited to state the nature of the paper that he had burned, but his assurance that it had borne nothing but his own name and address was received coldly.

Having declined to have his finger-prints taken, he was told that he was free to summon legal aid, if he wished to do so, and locked up for the night.

CHAPTER VI

The Evidence of Charlotte Bingham

The stipendiary magistrate looked at the memorandum which, at the prisoner's request, Inspector Cauldron had produced in the witness-box. He raised puzzled eyes to the man in the dock as he asked: "Do you persist in this?"

"Will you believe me if I assure you that I wrote no more than the truth?"

"It would, of course, be necessary for you to bring evidence— very strong evidence—in its support."

"Then it seems useless to say it again."

"Do you mean that you withdraw a useless denial?"

"On the contrary, it was because I did not intend that there should be any possible ambiguity on that point that I did not rely upon a verbal statement, but wrote it down"

"Very well. It will be recorded that you have denied that you are James Cadell Houghton. Who do you claim to be?"

"Is not that more than you have a right to ask me to say?

The magistrate paused. He knew it to be highly unlikely that the police would have arrested the wrong man in connection with such a crime. The man whom they arrested might, of course, he able to show that he was innocent of the charge. But when they set out to arrest the husband of the murdered woman it was very improbable that they would put a stranger into the dock.

But if James Cadell Houghton, having lost his head on being arrested, had uselessly denied his own identity, and were now persisting in that futility, he was acting with extreme folly, and gravely prejudicing whatever defence might be his of a better kind He had understood that nothing, would be done to day beyond a formal remand, and it had been a reasonable presumption that the accused man would obtain legal aid before the case should come into court again. Now he said: "I think it to be very desirable that you should he legally advised."

"If I feel that I require legal aid I will make any application that may be necessary."

"Very well. The answer to your question is that we have a right to ask, and you may be within your own rights if you decline to reply; but there will be a natural inference from your silence that you have made an assertion which you know that it would be hopeless to attempt to prove."

"I should have supposed it to be the duty of the police to prove I am whom they say."

Mr. Otbury, the prosecuting solicitor, rose. "My instructions are that there is no shadow of doubt on this point, and that Houghton is merely wasting the time of the court. I submit that his refusal to state whom else he professes to be substantially disposes of that defence. But, with your permission, I will call evidence at once to refute it."

"I think, Mr. Otbury, it might be a wise course to adopt."

"I call Charlotte Bingham."

Inspector Cauldron stepped down, and a moment later Miss Bingham entered the court and mounted the witness-box. Having been sworn, her examination proceeded: "You are the sister—the only sister, I believe—of Isabel Houghton, who was fatally wounded at the Old Jersey Hotel in Cranbrook Road on Tuesday last?"

"Yes."

"She was living with you, was she not, up to the time of her marriage to James Cadell Houghton in New York about six months ago?"

"Yes."

"And you became well acquainted with her husband, both before and after the marriage?"

"Yes."

"You actually came to England with Mr. and Mrs. Houghton on the *Britannic* about three weeks ago?"

"Yes."

"And stayed together at the Old Jersey Hotel?"

"Yes."

"Now, Miss Bingham, I want you to look carefully at the man who is in the dock."

The solicitor paused for a moment, as though to give her leisure for a careful inspection and a considered reply, before putting the vital question. The silent, almost breathless spectators saw her gaze straightly at the prisoner, who stood not more than five yards from her in the dock of the little court, and he looked back at her, not as being afraid of her identification, but with a mocking, challenging, even derisive expression, almost inexplicable considering the position in which he stood, unless he were confident that she was about to speak the words that would set him free.

"And now, Miss Houghton, will you tell the court whether you know him, and, if so, who he is?"

"He is James Houghton, of course."

"The man who married your sister?"

"Yes."

"You are absolutely certain of that?"

"Yes, of course I've known him for years."

The magistrate interposed: "Miss Bingham, I think you should know that the prisoner denies absolutely that he is your brother-in-law, or that his name is Houghton at all. Bearing that in mind, are you able to identify him absolutely, or is there any possibility that you may be misled by a resemblance perhaps an exceptionally strong resemblance to the man you think him to be?"

Being thus admonished, the lady gazed at the prisoner for a further instant, but rather as one who obeyed the order of the court than as feeling any necessity to do so.

He's wearing different clothes, of course," she said, "but I know James too well to make a mistake." She added: "It's just the sort of thing he would say, more likely than not."

The magistrate turned his eyes to the prisoner, who was now looking openly amused. "Do you wish to ask the witness any questions?" he enquired, with a cold severity in his voice which told what his own opinion was.

"I might if I thought she would answer truthfully. I should want to know what the game is."

"You are doing yourself no good by this attitude. That will be all, Miss Bingham. The remand will be till 10:30 A.M. on Wednesday next. You will be prepared to go on then, Mr. Otbury? Very well." The magistrate's glance turned again to the occupant of the dock. "You will be wise to obtain legal assistance," he said, "as promptly as possible; for which you will receive every facility, and any necessary assistance, from the police."

The reporters, leaving the court with better copy than they had expected to get, would have been additionally gratified had they been able to overhear a conversation between Mr. Otbury and Inspector Cauldron which followed immediately.

"I suppose," the solicitor asked, "there's no danger of coming a cropper over this question of identity?"

"It doesn't seem likely, after what you heard Charlotte Bingham say."

"No, it doesn't, especially as the man can't or won't say who he's pretending to be. But it was just that woman's evidence, and the way the man took it, that put a doubt into my mind. It seemed to me that he was more surprised at the first that she swore he was Houghton than she was when she was told that he denied it. And that was the wrong way round.

"Well, I can't say I noticed that. And it isn't sense that when we're after the man who killed her sister she should go out of her way to point out someone else. It isn't as though, even if she had a motive for such a thing; she could hope that it could be sustained. But as you feel that way, I don't mind saying that I haven't been quite as easy about it as I should like. I heard just before I came into court that they've succeeded in deciphering the writing on that envelope he burnt. I suppose he wouldn't think that we could do that! It doesn't prove anything. There were some notes that seem to have been of no importance on the back, and it was addressed in a woman's hand to J. Limbrook, Esq., 17 Charmian Crescent, W.1. It looks as though it really were the address that he wished to destroy; and when we've had time to find out who Limbrook is, and whether he's still about, we should know a lot more than we do now."

Mr. Otbury agreed that everything possible was being done. He said that the Limbrook clue alone ought to clear the matter up, one way or other. And with Miss Bingham's positive identification, and the man refusing to say who he claimed to be—well, if he were not Houghton, he must be finding a prison cell more attractive than most men would!

CHAPTER VII

A Queer Bargain with Mr. Limbrook

It was on Tuesday afternoon that Inspector Cauldron entered a cell which might be hygienic, but could not be considered cosy by the most vivid imagination, and found it solitary occupant appropriately studying the Book of Job. The inspector had a photograph in his hand. He said sourly: "Mr. Limbrook, before you leave here perhaps you'll be good enough to tell me why you have put us to all this trouble."

"Do I understand that you now want me to go?"

"We shall withdraw the charge against you tomorrow morning. You needn't have been here at all if you had been franker at first."

"I am not aware that I have made any complaint."

"I don't see that you've any cause. I think it's we who should do that."

"Really? You know, as a matter of abstract argument—but I could hardly expect you to admit that!"

Inspector Cauldron ignored the tone of restrained and yet almost bantering levity with which he was met. He had something more to say from which he would not be turned. "Naturally, we have had some curiosity to discover who Mr. Limbrook is, and what his occupation has been during the last few months."

"I hope you haven't been persuaded to arrest him in mistake for me?"

"I suppose you think that's a joke! I must tell you that we've found out some rather serious things."

"It may occur to you that, so far as they may be true, I am not likely to be very interested, as I must be familiar with them already; and so far as they may be mistaken (a possibility we are bound to recognize after the events of the past week), they are still less likely to rouse any excitement."

"They are sufficiently serious to render it necessary to ask you for explanations."

"Am I to take that as a threat? It should, if I may venture to offer you some good advice, be a mistake, especially after what has occurred already."

"I haven't threatened anything yet. I've only said that there are some things we should like to know."

"Well, that's a bit better! There is a condition on which I might even gratify your curiosity."

"I don't know that I could make any bargain before I heard."

"Oh yes, you could. Why don't you wait to hear that the deal is? If you'll undertake not to withdraw the charge tomorrow, I'll talk for as long as you care to remain in this homelike atmosphere, and I may tell you some rather surprising things."

Inspector Cauldron stared. He felt that he had heard one already. He exclaimed: "Not withdraw the charge! We can't go on prosecuting you when we know you're not the right man."

"You can ask for another remand."

"But we've got to get the right man into the dock."

"Well, you can go on looking for him. And I suppose you'll be asking the lady who knew me so intimately a few questions. Your next conversation with her ought to be quite interesting."

Inspector Cauldron said that he thought it would. He added: "If you're really serious about not having the charge withdrawn at once—"

"I'm quite serious about that. The lodging here is remarkably cheap, and so long as I put my coat on the bed— Can you tell me, Inspector, why, if a man be suspected of murder, he requires so few bed-clothes at night?"

The inspector said that he was sure that an extra blanket could be arranged.

CHAPTER VIII

Inspector Cauldron Reports

Inspector Cauldron was an anxious man. He was on the biggest case which had yet been entrusted to his hands, and he knew that it had developed so that he might be praised or blamed, and it was difficult to decide which it was the more likely to be.

He might not be blamed for putting the wrong man into the dock, in view of the fact that he had been obliged to rely upon Charlotte Bingham for identification, and that she, with whatever object, must have deliberately misled him. Rather, it might be said that he had shown some ability in checking upon and exposing the error so promptly; and the information which he had obtained from Mr. Limbrook was of a nature to condone much.

But he knew that his superiors required that a high standard should be maintained, not only of effort and judgement, but of success. They did not like the idea of putting innocent men into the dock, however good the excuse might be—and still less did they appreciate the unavoidable sequel of publicly fetching them out.

Now he had been instructed to report to Superintendent Backwash, who would then discuss with his superiors what would be done, and to whom the further conduct of the case should be given.

That was what he had most to fear. That the case—there were really two cases now—when he had reported all that he knew, would be considered to have become too big for him, and that one, if not both would be taken out of his hands.

But there was one certainty with which he could encourage himself. Superintendent Backwash would listen to all that he had to say. In his silent, non-committal way, he would listen well. He would he fair, though there might be no margin of generosity in what he might say or do. It would be Inspector Cauldron's own fault if his case were not fully and fairly put to those with whom the final decision lay.

The superintendent received him better than he had expected. "I hear," he said, "that Houghton's photo's conclusive. Sir Henry's relieved that we've got it over in time to prevent us going farther down the wrong road. But there must be some funny business going on.... I just want to hear what you've been able to do with Limbrook, and then you'd better get hold of the Bingham woman.

"You can threaten her with the Public Prosecutor, and a perjury charge, if she doesn't come clean, as the Yankees call it; but don't promise her much if she does. She may have killed Houghton herself for all we could swear to yet."

"There's the fact that Houghton bolted."

"Yes. There's that. But there must be some other facts that we haven't got, and facts have a funny way of knocking each other out. You never know what any one of them means till you've got the lot."

"I'll go after Charlotte Bingham, of course. Six months' hard wouldn't be too much for her. But I suppose I've got to try to get her to talk before we even think of running her in."

"You can use your discretion about that. If she can't put up a decent-looking excuse—and it's not easy to see what it can be— you'd be justified in bringing her here. You can't arrest for perjury, but we could put the charge in another form."

"It's quite true that I don't want to lose any time before I hear a bit more of that woman's tongue, but there's something I've got to report first that you may think even more important, though it mayn't be as urgent as that. It's about Limbrook. He owns that's his name. In the first place, he doesn't want us to withdraw the charge, and I've promised him that we'll apply for another remand tomorrow."

Superintendent Backwash had more confidence in his subordinate's discretion than he was likely to mention, and he saw that there was a tale to come. He might have recalled his own remark of a few moments before that you can never judge one fact till you have the lot. But it remained that it was a most irregular procedure to continue, even by consent, and by no more than delay, the prosecution of a man who was now known to have been wrongly arrested. He said. "I don't think you should have promised that. It's more than any of us has the power to undertake on our own."

But Inspector Cauldron took the rebuke easily. He knew that if he were to be condemned it must be on other grounds.

"I saw that," he said; "but it was something I had to risk. Perhaps you'll hear the tale, and then tell me if I was strong.

"To begin at the right end. Limbrook says that he knows nothing of the Houghtons, or of Miss Bingham. He never met them before, nor heard their names, as far as he knows. He didn't even know there had been a murder, having been too busy with his own troubles to read the papers.

"He hasn't the remotest idea why Charlotte Bingham should have pointed him out as Houghton, though when I showed him the photograph he admitted that there was sufficient resemblance to excuse the cashier's identification. He suggested that Miss then been too obstinate to admit it; but we can do our own guessing, and we shall have to think of something better than that.

"But the thing began to look really interesting when he told me why he had kept his name to himself, and let us charge him the way we did The fact was that he was in a jam between being forced into the dope racket and being put on the spot by Mildew's gang, and it seemed Heaven's own luck when he found we'd got room for him where he couldn't be blamed for not doing what he'd been told."

"That fits in with what you'd learned already about his recent associations."

"Yes. He told me that he got helped by them when he was starving in Cairo, and that they tried to make a tool of him after that; and when they found he wasn't their sort he'd learned too much for it to be safe for them to let him go. He's given me a lot of information, and promised more, on condition that we take care of him until we've broken the gang up, and that two men, in particular, are either run out of the country or safely jailed; and, for the moment, he can't see where he could sleep more safely than where he is."

"If he can put Mildew into our hands," Superintendent Backwash replied, "Sir Henry won't make any objection to the remand I dare say he'll even agree to his being convicted for Houghton's murder if he feels that he'll go on being safer with us. But we mustn't forget that there's a real murderer running loose. We can't arrest him while we've got another man charged with the crime in the same name.

"No, but we can keep him under observation. That is, when we find where he's lying up. We haven't done that yet."

"And thanks to the blunder we've made he's got an extra start. It has become one of those cases now where the Press helps. We ought to have that photo all over the world before this time tomorrow. And we can't do that, either, while this bogus prosecution's to be kept up."

"No. But, while it does, Houghton won't suspect that we're looking for him. That ought to be worth something.

Superintendent Backwash still looked doubtful, as though he were more conscious of the ambiguities of the position than of its contingent advantages. But his words, when they came, were more satisfactory than the tone in which they were spoken. "I'm not saying you're wrong. It all depends upon how much real help Limbrook's going to be. But you'd better get after the Bingham woman and deal with her. There's one there who isn't under any delusion as to whether we've got the right murderer. Not that she'll be doing any talking. Not till she's obliged. But if we keep Limbrook in jail, and start hunting Houghton again at the same time, we ought to know what her game was. And if you think she might double-cross us, you mustn't let her out of your sight till you've got her here."

Superintendent Backwash observed that the inspector had now risen, but stood hesitating, as though reluctant to go. He added: "I know what you want to say. You're afraid that this is getting too big for you, and is going to Tolbooth, or one of the other chiefs, and you want to ask me to let you have the biggest chance that has come your way.

"Well, I'm not going to promise anything. It doesn't entirely rest with me, as you know. And, in these matters, individuals can't be considered. It's the public service that has to be thought of first. But I shall tell Sir Henry that, so far, you've done well enough."

Inspector Cauldron thanked him for better words than he had expected to hear. But as to individuals not being considered! He wasn't *quite* young enough to believe that.... He saw that much might depend upon his handling of Miss Charlotte Bingham, and he lost no time in seeking her at the Old Jersey Hotel, where it was understood that she was continuing to reside. She was an American citizen, and English law does not allow of the "holding" of witnesses after the manner of her native land, where it may happen at times that, while the criminal is out on bail, the witnesses are closely jailed till the time of trial, for no further fault than being able to testify to his misdeeds; but she had given a voluntary assurance that she had no early intention of leaving England, and should not fail to be present at the trial of her sister's murderer, being not merely willing but anxious to bear witness against him.

None the less, the Transatlantic shipping companies had been warned that she was of interest to the Metropolitan Police, and requested to inform them at once if she should book a return passage.

Knowing this, Inspector Cauldron had some reason for supposing that he would be able to interview her without any prolonged difficulty. But he soon learned differently.

CHAPTER IX

Miss Bingham Was Not There

The reception clerk had a smile for Inspector Cauldron, of which he had not been prodigal on previous occasions, but it was one which the inspector did not entirely like.

He felt that there was going to be trouble ahead, and when he was briefly told that the lady was not in he had a correct opinion that the clerk could tell him more if he would. He asked: "You don't mean that she's left?"

The reception clerk, whose contacts with transatlantic visitors had made him more familiar with the American than the English tongue, replied that she had not checked out; her baggage was still there.

"Then why do you think she won't be coming in tonight?"

"I don't know that she's been about since the day you had her in court."

"You mean you know that she hasn't?"

"No. I couldn't say that. I can't see everyone who goes in or out. If a suite's engaged, it's not our business to watch how much it's used."

"But you know whether the keys have been left with you?"

The clerk glanced at the keyboard in a perfunctory manner. He said "Well Miss Bingham's got hers."

"I think I'd better see the manager."

The clerk told a page-boy to see whether Mr. Munro was disengaged, and next moment Inspector Cauldron was being shown into the manager's office.

Mr. Monro was one of those men whose skeletons appear to have been supplied to them a size too large. The bony hand which he extended had knobbly knuckles, the skin was drawn tightly over prominent cheek-bones, the light-blue eyes were recessed beneath craggy brows.

His manner was friendlier than that which Inspector Cauldron had been used to encounter in the reception lobby. He gave the impression of being glad to see him, as perhaps he was. He said: "Miss Bingham? I expected it would be about her. Half hour ago, I should have told you that she was still located here, though she's been away somewhere since Friday. But I'm afraid she's given you the slip. I had this by evening mail."

He passed a letter across his desk, written on the note-paper of a Paris hotel. The inspector read:

> Miss Charlotte Bingham begs to inform the manager of the Old Jersey Hotel that she will not be returning to England at present.
>
> She is sailing from Havre to New York on Saturday, and will be obliged if Mr. Monro will have her baggage packed and forwarded to her apartment at 47 Riverside Avenue, New York City, U.S.A., charges forward.
>
> She encloses a cheque for £20 on Chase's Bank (London) which will approximately settle anything for which she may be liable up to the receipt of this letter, if an account be rendered to the same bank, any remaining balance will be discharged.

Inspector Cauldron read this note carefully, twice over, but he knew that he was wasting time. Its meaning and its effects were clear. Miss Bingham had crossed to Paris on Friday, probably taking advantage of one of those weekend tickets for which no passports were required, and would now sail on a French boat, doubtless having selected one which did not enter British territorial waters. That must be checked too, but it also would be a waste of time. The fact was that Miss Bingham had bolted, and that perjury is not an extraditable crime.

He saw that, even if he should escape blame, he could have no credit for this. But he also saw that the investigation of the Houghton murder, which at one time had seemed simple enough, was only about to begin, after those most nearly concerned had gained a long start from the grip of Justice's outstretched arm.

"I'm afraid," he said, "that we may have been too quick to believe that she had had nothing to do with her sister's death." He reminded himself, as he spoke, that the manager, along with the rest of the world, believed that the dead woman's husband was in custody, and already being prosecuted for the crime, and that he must say nothing to remove that impression. He concluded. "I should like another chat with Janet if she's at liberty now."

"She's on duty now. You can have her down here, if you like."

I suppose it will be her place to have Miss Bingham's luggage packed?"

"Yes. You've no objection to it being sent on?"

"Probably not. But there's no reason for it to catch the next boat. I may have another word with you before it goes. Can I speak to Janet upstairs, after you've told her what you want her to do?"

Receiving a ready assent, he proceeded to the third floor, and met the woman coming along the corridor, a pile of clean linen upon her arm.

"Good-evening, Janet," he began. "I've just been told at the desk that Miss Bingham's out, and that we can have a look at how she has left her room."

The woman responded with the affability which he had previously discovered to be consistent with a severe abstention from random confidences. She opened the bedroom door with her master-key, and revealed a half-packed trunk which stood on the centre of the floor with a lifted lid. The keys of the rooms lay on the dressing-table. It was a simple deduction that Charlotte Bingham had left them there rather than hand them in at the counter, so that her departure should be as unnoticed as possible.

"I don't suppose," he said, "you thought you'd see her again."

"No," she answered, with more readiness than he had expected, as she picked up the keys, "you won't find much here that she didn't mean you to see."

"She couldn't have taken much with her, leaving as she did with no one to carry it down."

"She took her dressing-case when she went, and she'd taken a kind of suitcase—grip, she called it—out the day before, and not brought it back. And before then she sent Mrs. Houghton's things off to New York, and there wasn't overmuch left in this room when she'd done that."

"I see. Then she must have been planning a get away all the time?"

"I wouldn't say you're far wrong, if you think that."

"Well, I've got Mr. Munro's permission to look over what's here, and I should like you to give me any help that you can. But I don't think it's much I shall find."

"If that's what Mr. Munro wants done, it's not for me to say different."

Closing the door, perhaps with a natural inclination to prevent other guests observing this overhauling of a visitor's effects, Janet gave him the assistance for which he had asked. Her methods were of a characteristic thoroughness, and between them it is very unlikely that anything of importance was overlooked, but the result was just nothing at all.

Inspector Cauldron left the hotel with a realization that the C.I.D. in his person had been thoroughly fooled. It was his good fortune, rather than merit, that the event had developed in an unexpected manner, which might go far to obscure the blunder into which he had been led, even if it did not earn him some measure of praise.

CHAPTER X

Concerning the Missing Bullet

Inspector Cauldron reported next morning to Superintendent Backwash, who said no more than: "Pity we didn't have her a bit better watched" when he heard of Miss Bingham's flight. And then, with more consideration for the inspector's feelings than he had expected to get: "But if she'd said she was going to Paris for the week-end, I don't see how we could have stopped her. Not on the information we had then."

He added: "We've still got a clear week." He was thinking of how long it would be before Charlotte Bingham would pass out of French jurisdiction, and the narrow confines of an Atlantic liner, to the greater security and vaguer address of the American continent. He knew that, with the wealth she had at command, her extradition on anything less than a charge of murder, with good evidence in its support, would not be easily obtained; but the Sûreté officials in Paris had just received a favour from London which they would not be slow to return, if the request should be made in the right way.

Inspector Cauldron's mind moved on the same lines. He said, as though thinking aloud: "I wish I knew where that bullet is."

"You'll know a whole lot when you know that," the superintendent replied. But, as he said it, his eyes returned to his desk, and he had put the Houghton murder out of his mind. He was, in fact, far more interested in Mr. Limbrook's revelations, than in the manner of Mrs. Houghton's death, or the capture of her fugitive relations.

But Inspector Cauldron felt a more immediate interest in clearing up a matter with which he was more closely concerned. His mind continued to dwell on the mystery of that missing bullet. "If he knew—" Yes, of course. But how was he to proceed on the path of enquiry? He saw no hope in searching the Houghton suite again. Apart from the fact that it had now been put into order, and was in the occupation of other guests of the hotel, he knew that the examination it had received had been so thorough that there was no more than a negligible chance that the bullet could have escaped the search. And, besides, if it were there, the mystery and its significance went. He would be searching not only with the knowledge that it would be immensely improbable that the bullet was there, but also that, if he should find it, he would know, at the same moment, that it had not been worth the trouble.

It was better to assume that, in some way it had left the room, and to consider the implications of that, and where it could now be found.

If it were allowed that it could not have escaped the search which had subsequently been made, it followed that it must have been removed by human agency, for it was certain that, as the impetus of its flight had ceased, its own power of motion was gone. Might it not have been imbedded in some object that Charlotte, either because it was there, or for some other reason, had removed from the room? On her own statement, she had been first to enter after the shots were fired. She had had further opportunity during the fifteen or twenty minutes which divided the murder from when the police had taken charge of the room. Everyone else in the hotel who, with good reason or none, might have been there during that interval, had been exhaustively interrogated already.

His mind, circling round like a lost pigeon, came round to Charlotte again. As she had led him to arrest a stranger with that audaciously false identification, so she might have concealed something in which the bullet lay. To protect James Houghton? If he had been her lover, if their adultery had been at the root of the tragedy, it was a possible explanation. But there was a different one which appeared almost equally plausible. Suppose that the guilt were hers, and that he had disappeared rather than bear witness against her? In that event, she might have an even stronger and more selfish fear lest he might be found, he might care for her sufficiently to run away rather than give evidence which would be her death; but it did not follow that, if he were found, he would remain silent when in danger of execution for a crime in which he had had no part.

Had he had no part? That was to assume much. Suppose they had been involved in an equal guilt? The one bolts, by a common plan. The other hardly remains, points out an innocent man as a victim to content, or at least temporarily mislead, the law, and then retires at leisure—the befooled police making no effort to detain her. And as to the bullet—suppose it had penetrated something of hers? Something from which it could not be instantly withdrawn, and which would have been damning evidence that it was she against whom it had been discharged?

He felt that he had constructed a quite possible theory, but it was not one of which it was any pleasure to think. What was the word which had entered his mind to describe the part played by the police in this imaginary drama? Befooled? And the right word too! It is not by being befooled that promotion comes. When this case should pass on to the records of the C.I.D., it must deserve a better final description, or it would be well for him to send in his resignation, and look for a different job.

But one thing was sure. When Charlotte Bingham had told him that story about Houghton having said that it would be the safer course for a criminal to remain near the scene of his crime, she had not intended to assist his capture. It followed logically that no such opinion had been expressed, or that, if it had, she had good reason to know that the man was not practising his own theory.

The opportunity to identify a stranger was a chance she could not have foreseen. She could only have aimed to mislead the police in a more general way.

But that implied that she had definite knowledge that he had fled some distance away. Probably she knew where he was. As to that, there was only one guiding fact within the knowledge of the police. He had been a native of Preston. What more likely than that he should have sought refuge where he might have friends he could trust? Resolving that little time should be lost in intensifying the search in Houghton's native county, Inspector Cauldron turned his mind to his more immediate duty, which was to interview Mr. Limbrook again.

CHAPTER XI

A Chance for Inspector Cauldron

"You think Limbrook's straight?" Superintendent Backwash asked doubtfully. "Apart from the explanation he now offers, the case against him is rather black."

"Yes, I do. But it doesn't matter much to us whether he is or not, so long as he's prepared to give them away, and there's no doubt about that. The trouble is that I don't see how we can go very far on his evidence alone. He just confirms what we guessed—what we might say we knew—before. But there's not much he can swear to that any jury would swallow as legal proof. Not against Mildew, at least, nor any of the others that we're most anxious to get. We don't want to end up with two or three of the small fry in the dock, and the gang warned where we've been putting the ferrets down into the holes."

"And you think Limbrook's telling you all he knows?"

Inspector Cauldron was confident of this also. "He's got good reason to do that. If he gives them away at all, he wants us to put them where they can't take it out of him. We can't do that unless we get the heads of the gang. You can see how he feels by him asking us to keep him where he is now."

"It won't be easy to do that much longer. Especially if we should find where Houghton has gone to earth."

"We mayn't find that over-easy to do now, after the start he's got."

Superintendent Backwash was inclined to agree. "It mayn't be an easy job. He's got a long start, and there'll be no help from the press while we keep Limbrook jailed. He may be out of the country now, though it's more likely that he's up north."

"Well, I hope he won't be caught for the next fortnight, or a bit more. I thought at first that we ought to start combing Lancashire, but I've thought since that it may be wiser to go slow about that. I expect Sir Henry'd rather get Mildew behind the bars than any dozen murderers that have been hanged while he's been on the job."

Superintendent Backwash did not differ on that. They both knew enough of the wide-spread misery, physical and moral, which is caused by the sale of illicit drugs to understand that the murder of a single individual even from the basest of human passions, the greed of gain, is a venial error in comparison with the evil, callously caused, and with no better incentive, by these traffickers, with whom the law deals with such comparative leniency.

He said: "That's just how Sir Henry feels. And, I want you to understand this, Cauldron. You got on the track, and I've advised that the matter should be left in your hands. It's the biggest chance you're ever likely to have, and if you fluke it, heaven help you, for you'll get no mercy from me. And I'd like to know how you're meaning to go ahead."

"I haven't thought it out yet," Inspector Cauldron announced frankly, "not enough to say much yet. But I want to discover first whether they've any idea what's become of Limbrook. If they haven't it's a rather different proposition from if they have."

Superintendent Backwash considered this, in a mind that worked slowly, but with a subtlety that many criminals had had reason to curse. "Yes," he said, "so it is. How do you expect to discover that?"

"I haven't even thought out the best way for that yet. I might put Westbrook on to it, or have Beesley followed. But we want quick action, and those are ways that take time. The first thing that I've got on hand is a social call....

"It's a request from Limbrook I couldn't refuse. He's got a girl friend who would be expecting him to look her up when he got back from Egypt, and he hasn't gone near her for fear she should be involved in whatever trouble was coming to him.

"But he thinks she'll be getting worked up wondering what's happened, and as the explanation's hardly one that we should want him sending by letter to a young woman we know nothing about, I agreed to give her a call and explain as much as I think's safe for her to know, when I'm able to judge what she's like a bit better than I can now. It was a thing I couldn't refuse, considering how we arrested him in the first instance, and what he's offering to do for us now."

"No," the superintendent agreed, and added dryly: "You'd have been a mug if you had."

Inspector Cauldron did not profess to misunderstand. He said: "Yes. There's a chance, of course. Limbrook thought I should be a particularly safe channel of communication, because I'm not one that they would be likely to be following."

"No. They wouldn't be doing that. But they may be watching her house"

"I shall take all the precautions I can. But Limbrook doesn't see how they could be on her track at all, as he's been careful not to go there, or even to write, since he found the mess he was in."

"Well, we must hope differently."

The inspector did not dispute this somewhat obscure aspiration. He departed to prepare for his social call.

CHAPTER XII

At the Envoy Hotel

A man leaned against the Hyde Park railings opposite the Envoy Hotel in Bayswater Road. He was doing no harm, but when he observed the approach of Detective-Sergeant Porson, with whom he had a previous acquaintance, he moved slowly away, and would have loitered across the road as unobtrusively as possible, but the officer followed him with a more definite purpose, and a brisker step.

"Hello, Stokes," he said. "What were you passing to that young woman by the railings a few moments ago?"

"The man exclaimed with the indignation of one who, during an infrequent interval of innocence, is accused of his habitual crime. "Who? Me? Haven't as much as touched a young person's hand. Blast me to hell if I did."

"That won't go down with me, Tommy. When you're hanging about like that the show isn't far off, even in June. You'd better make off at a better pace if you want to sleep in your own bed."

"I tell you I haven't got a pinch on me. Search me if I have!" protested the indignant innocent, but Sergeant Porson, disregarding his reluctance to desert his post of observation, shepherded him firmly in the direction of Queen's Road Station, and watched him purchase a ticket for Moorgate, which would take him about half-way toward the bed that he had been recommended to seek.

It was hard on Tommy Stokes, who, after nerve-wracking weeks of precarious peddling, had been surprisingly told that he could earn his usual weekly remuneration by a more lawful surveillance of those who entered or left the Envoy Hotel during certain hours (after which he was to be relieved by a younger brother of Risky Tubbs), and who knew himself to be innocent of the passing of packets of any kind. But he also knew his record to be against him, and Detective-Sergeant Porson spoke in a voice of authority which he had good reason to fear.

And meanwhile Inspector Cauldron, relying upon his subordinates to have dealt with any posts of observation which might have been established around it, had walked openly into the Envoy Hotel, as it is seemly for detective-inspectors to do, and there requested to see the manageress.

"I should be obliged," he said, "if you would give me the number of Miss Billie Wingrove's room."

Miss Hounder looked at the card which had been placed silently before her. "I hope——" she began.

"No. Nothing at all. Miss Wingrove is a young lady for whom we have a particular esteem at the yard." The eyes of the manageress fell to the register. "Miss Wingrove," she said, "has just moved her room. Number 73 now." A sudden doubt disturbed her serenity. "She hasn't made any complaint, has she?"

"About being molested in the hotel?" It was a random shot, but it evidently went home.

"It was only during the last hour that she complained to me that she has been annoyed by the conduct of a Mr. Greaves who took the room next to hers a few days ago. There didn't appear to be anything very definite, but I told her that I should speak to him. I was intending to tell him that if I hear any further complaint he must leave at once. I've given Miss Wingrove a room on another floor."

Inspector Cauldron heard, and felt pleased. He had given Mr. Limbrook his word that he would take sufficient precautions to prevent his call being observed, and had kept his promise; but it was good news to him that Miss Wingrove was already receiving the attentions of the Mildew gang.

It told him two things: that they had become aware of her acquaintance with Mr. Limbrook, either in spite of the precautions he had taken, or before it had occurred to him that any concealment was desirable; and that they were unaware of his arrest on a charge for which bail is not allowed.

Obviously they regarded his disappearance as a defiance possibly preluding their denunciation to the police, and the organization had become active to trace him. Inspector Cauldron knew enough of their methods to anticipate how swift and ruthless, had their search succeeded, their vengeance (to which Cornelius Mildew would have given the milder description of discipline or merely business precaution) would have been likely to be.

A hunted man, unable to approach his own home, is likely to make attempts to communicate with his friends, especially if he suppose them to be unsuspected by those who pursue him. He may delay such a contact, according to the measures of caution or fear that control his mind, but it is merely a question of time. Mr. Limbrook's enemies might be seeking him by other means; but if those should fail, they had little reason to doubt that the watch they had set upon Miss Wingrove's hotel would ultimately succeed.

Well, that was how he had wished it to be! He heard the manageress repeat: "She's in Number 73 now. On the fourth floor. Shall I tell the lift-boy to show you up, or should you like me to announce you first?"

He paused a moment in his reply, as he considered the information she had given him. "No, don't announce me," he said. "I'll find my own way.... And, if you please, I'd rather you didn't say anything to Mr. Greaves. Certainly not unless I ask you to do so after I've seen Miss Wingrove. Young ladies are sometimes rather quick to take exception to things that aren't really meant. I shouldn't wonder if she decides to go back to her own room after I've had a few words with her."

"Just as you think best, of course," the manageress answered rather dubiously. "Mr. Greaves seemed a quiet, pleasant young fellow to me, or I shouldn't have given him the room I did. I don't want any trouble in the hotel."

"I don't think you need be afraid of that, if you'll just leave it to me. 'Least said, soonest mended,' you know, Miss Hounder. There's many a worse proverb than that.

He went up the stairs, knowing them to be less frequented than the lift of a lofty hotel, and arrived, without meeting anyone, on the fourth-floor landing. He had resolved to make use of the information he had just had to gain some acquaintance with Miss Billie Wingrove before disclosing the real errand on which he had come.

He knocked lightly on the door of Number 73 and called, "May I come in?" in his less official voice.

He thought he heard an exclamation of annoyance, and then a quick, light step, and the door opened a few inches. "What is it you want?" The tone was polite but not cordial. It was evident that he would not obtain a broader invitation to enter unless he should give sufficient reason.

"I am from Scotland Yard," he said. "Inspector Cauldron. I understand that you have had reason to complain of the conduct of a man on the floor below." The door opened a little more widely. A tall, slim, neatly tailored figure confronted him. Grey eyes almost level with his own—Inspector Cauldron is not a particularly tall man—surveyed him with a self-possessed but doubtful gravity. "I haven't made any complaint to the police."

"It might not have been unwise if you had."

She hesitated over this reply. "I don't want any trouble about it. I expect it will be all right now I'm up here."

"We shan't be making any trouble for you, Miss Wingrove. We just want to know what happened."

The fear of an unwelcome publicity may have led her to forget her first doubt of the authenticity of this unexpected visitor. She stepped aside from an open door. "You'd better come in," she said. "You'll excuse me being in rather a mess. I'm just moving up."

That was evident. Dresses and other garments, still on their hangers and cast over a chair back, were in process of being transferred to an open wardrobe. A vase of flesh-tinted gladioli stood on another chair, which could hardly be intended as its final location. Two pictures, and a photograph easily recognizable as that of Eustace Limbrook, lay on the divan bed. Miss Wingrove removed a hatbox from the third and most comfortable chair to accommodate her unexpected visitor.

"I wish," he said, "you'd tell me just what's happening."

She seated herself on the end of the divan as she replied: "It wasn't really anything much, and certainly not a matter about which I should have troubled you.

"But a young man, a Mr. Greaves, took the room next to mine a few days ago, and seemed to have nothing to do except watching me. He kept his door a little way open to see and hear all he could, and he listened to my telephone conversations. I proved that, after I'd thought it was happening, by waiting till he was talking himself, and then ringing a friend. I did that twice, and each time he stopped his own conversation at once, and came to the wall to hear what I was saying. Half the walls here are only thin wooden partitions, and I could hear his movements distinctly; and, of course, he could hear whatever I said.

"I tell you that so that you may know that it wasn't just a silly imagination; but I don't want you to think that it was anything really serious. He got the waiter to put him at my table when he first came—they're mostly little tables for two—but I moved to another, and since then he hasn't spoken to me more than to say good-morning when we've passed each other in the passages."

"I'm quite sure it wasn't imagination."

"Well, I shouldn't like you to have thought that. But so long as that's clear, I should like it dropped. I shouldn't have told Miss Hounder why I was changing my room if I had thought she would have called you in."

"You mustn't think she did that. I had reason to think this might be happening, and I came to enquire."

"I suppose you mean that Mr. Greaves has been making trouble before? Is he a bit wrong in the head?"

"Not exactly; except as far as all criminals are. But we have occasion to know his name. He's twenty-eight, and he's already spent about five years of his life in jail. Not that you need worry about him. He only does what he's told. That's a good photograph of Mr. Limbrook, if you'll excuse me noticing

"You know Mr. Limbrook?" There was a note of natural surprise, perhaps also of faint, puzzled apprehension, in the voice with which this question was asked. Billie Wingrove was too quick-witted not to perceive that the point of this visit was still to come.

"I saw him yesterday. He is engaged in a way which prevents him coming to see you, and has been so since he landed in England; but he was anxious that you should know that he is well."

"Do you mean that he is unable to write?"

"Not unable. But it would have been imprudent." He paused a moment, seeking to begin his tale at a point which would not sound more alarming than its conclusion, and she broke in, with some impatience sharpening the anxiety in her voice: "Don't you think you'd better tell me straight out what it all means? I'm not a fool, nor a child."

"Yes," he answered. "That was what I had decided to do. I will trust you with the whole tale. In fact, it was partly because we need your help that I am here now."

"Just one question first. Mr. Limbrook is not in any serious trouble?"

"Not of any kind you are likely to imagine. We have no complaint against him, and he is quite safe. He is endeavouring to render us a very important service. But if you'll listen to me, Miss Wingrove, and not assume anything, bad or good, till I've finished—"

"Yes. I'm quite prepared to do that."

He saw that her face had paled to a degree that revealed the naturalness of its previous colour, but she showed no other sign of discomposure as she cleared one of the loaded chairs to give herself a more comfortable seat than she had first taken. "If it's a long tale," she said, "perhaps it's a case for a cigarette." She offered one to her visitor, passed an ash-tray, accepted his offered light, and sat down to listen.

"I believe you know," he began, "that Mr. Limbrook, while in Egypt, found himself in some degree of financial difficulty?"

"Yes," she assented. "He didn't mention it to me in that way when he wrote—not as though he were short of money—but it was evident he must be, from what I knew. I actually replied that I would send £20, if that would be any use; but he wrote back that he'd got some help from an unexpected direction, and was coming home almost immediately. I had that letter some weeks ago, and I've not had a word since.

"I suppose he explained to you how it all happened?" she added, with more doubt in her voice than her words implied.

"No. He only told me that he had found himself hard-up in Cairo."

"That would be just his way. But I think you ought to know how it was. He is a constructional engineer by profession, and he came back to England from South America early this year. He'd had a two-year appointment there that hadn't been very well paid, but he reckoned that the experience would make it worth while.

"It was some months after that before he got any suitable offer, and then it was from the Rushton-Thornville Engineering Co., to manage their Egyptian branch. It was at a commencing salary of £1,200, rising to double that figure in five years' time. The only snag was that the salary was to be paid quarterly, and he had to finance himself till the first payment was due.

"I daresay you know what happened. Rushtons had had two bad years, but no one thought of such a firm being likely to fail. But it turned out that they were relying on getting a very large contract in Rhodesia, and when that went to a German competitor, the debenture-holders took action, and got receiver appointed.

"That happened just at the end of the first three months. Eustace wrote to me that he'd actually got the salary cheque, but couldn't cash it.

"I reckoned that he must be desperately hard-up, because I know that he'd only just expected to last out till he got the cheque, and he had mentioned in writing to me that living was a good deal dearer than he'd been told. But I'm hindering you from telling me what I want to hear."

"As you knew that already, Miss Wingrove, you'll easily understand what I'm going to tell you now.

"Mr. Limbrook had met a wealthy gentleman, a Mr. Cornelius Mildew, at a Cairo club. He is a man of very pleasant manners, and popular in social and sporting circles, both here and abroad, but we've known him for some years as one of the biggest dope operators in Europe, though we've never been able to get the sort of proof that a prosecution requires.

"Mr. Limbrook says that Mildew approached him just as he was on his beam-ends, and thinking of going to the British Consulate for advice, and offered him a loan of any amount that he might require.

64

He was surprised, as their previous acquaintance was so slight, and he knew that the idea that he was hard-up could be no more than a likely guess. But when you're penniless it's not the kind of chance that most men would be in a hurry to turn down.

"He said he would take £50, and Mildew insisted on making it a hundred, giving him a banknote for that amount, and saying that if it were never paid back at all he shouldn't mind, as the amount was nothing to him, and he was only too glad to be of some slight assistance to a fellow-countryman abroad—just the sort of tosh that such a man would talk, meaning to do what he did.

"Mr. Limbrook says that he insisted on writing an I.O.U., but Mildew tore it up, saying that paper wasn't required between friends. He was grateful, of course, and the next thing was that Mildew asked him to do him a favour which didn't sound much, and which, under the circumstances, it would have been very ungracious to refuse.

"He asked him to include some boxes of Egyptian cigars among his own luggage, and get them through the customs as his. There wasn't to be any attempt at evading duty. Mildew was emphatic on that. He said that the only point was that he was aiming to bring a large quantity to England to distribute his friends, and that the duty was lighter if they split up into several consignments.

"Limbrook didn't even know whether that were true. He naturally took his word. He declared the cigars, which were packed up in boxes usual for that class of goods, paid the duty, and got them through without difficulty.

"The customs officers opened one of the top boxes, just looked into it, counted the others, and shut down the lid on the lot. They weren't likely to do more in dealing with the luggage of an Englishman against whom there was no suspicion, and who had declared them frankly; more particularly so because they were busily engaged in searching for a consignment of dope that was known to be on its way here.

"They gave special attention to Mr. Mildew's luggage, though he's never been known to carry any of the stuff himself, because they had blocked a channel he had been using till then, and we had thought it just possible that he might rely on his clean record—he's always declared any dutiable articles most scrupulously—to bluff it through.

"Of course, nothing was found; and all we could say was that he'd been too clever for us again. But I needn't tell you that the dope was under the cigars of some of the lower boxes of the trunkful that Mr. Limbrook had brought in.

"The whole thing might have ended there if the man who called on him to collect the cigar-boxes hadn't assumed that he had known what he had been doing, and said some incautious words. He was probably frightened at what he had done when he realized his mistake and reported it to his brother criminals, who evidently concluded that there would be no safety for them after that, unless Limbrook were persuaded to join them. The result was that he received a telephone message asking him to meet two gentlemen in a private room at the Reader Grill, who would have a position to offer him.

"When he got there, he met two men who were strangers to him, and whose names he did not learn, who offered him a very liberal remuneration if he would undertake the reception of illicit drugs in wholesale quantities in this country, and the distribution of them to their major agents."

"With which, of course, he refused to have anything to do?"

"Not exactly. Indeed, I might say—"

"It's no use asking me to believe that."

"If you will kindly appreciate, Miss Wingrove, that I am simply giving you Mr. Limbrook's own account of an interview at which I was not present?"

"Very well. I'll try not to interrupt again."

CHAPTER XIII

Unpleasant Experience of Mr. Limbrook

"The appointment," the inspector went on, "was to last as long as he could handle the traffic without drawing suspicion upon himself, and even after that his financial future was to be protected, so long as he should remain loyal to the gang, and obey any instruction he might receive.

"There was nothing extraordinary in this proposal, nor in the liberality of the offer made. The profits of the traffic are enormous, and its security depends upon those who actually handle the drugs being people whom we have no cause to suspect. We catch the retail pedlars quite frequently, and occasionally one of those who distribute to them. It is a rare thing to get on the track of a man in such a position as that which they were offering to Mr. Limbrook. When we do, we may be able to seize stocks of several thousand pounds value, and you will see the importance to them of getting a man of good status, and previously unblemished character, to undertake it.

"But even making an arrest of that kind does little to hinder the traffic. Above them are the go-betweens, such as these two whom Limbrook met, who arrange everything verbally, and never touch anything but the money. And above them are those who finance and control the international operations involved, of whom we know Mildew to be one, though, as I have said, we have been unable to get the legal proof which would enable us to put him in the right place.

"Well, Mr. Limbrook declined this offer at first, as any decent man would. But after that their manner changed. They told him that he had gone too far to draw back. They professed to ridicule his statement that he had acted in ignorance of what he was doing, and pointed out that he had been paid in advance, and that by a banknote which could be shown to have come from the hands of a well-known drug-trafficker in Cairo.

"They laughed at his declaration that he had had it from Mildew, and told him that if the Egyptian who had handed it to him should decide to sell himself to the police, he would need to fake up a better explanation than that.

"They also hinted, in an unmistakably sinister manner, that those who had once come into the gang were not allowed to back out, and that refusal to undertake what was required might lead to a more sudden retribution than prosecution on a false charge.

"When he heard this, he saw the full extent of the trouble that he was in. It was easy to imagine an anonymous communication reaching us at the Yard, denouncing him as having brought dope into the country disguised as cigars. Enquiries would then disclose that he had been penniless in Cairo, and suddenly come into funds. The bank-note which he had changed with the P. & O. when he had booked his return passage would be traced back to some obscure drug-trafficker, who would appear to collapse under police inquisition, and offer to buy his own immunity by confessing what had occurred. False evidence is cheap and easily procurable in the East. Against a circumstantial narrative of how the bargain had been made, and the money paid, what could he oppose but an unsupported assertion that he had had it from Mildew, and been bamboozled by him? How could he expect such a tale to be received as anything better than the desperate lie of a cornered man?

"He says that he imagined Mildew going into the box and saying that he had met him at the club, but so casually that he hardly knew him by sight until he had come begging for help, and saying what a hole he was in, and adding, perhaps, that he might have given him five pounds out of charity. But a hundred? Was it likely, to a man he had hardly met? And, of course, if he had, it would have been by a cheque on his bank, and he would have had a proper receipt.

"He thought of himself as being sentenced to a long term, which might have been reduced somewhat in view of his previous good character, and the difficulty he had been in, but for the impudent accusation he had made against a gentleman who had befriended him. He didn't know that we already had Mildew under observation, or he might have regarded it a bit differently.

"But the only chance of being believed that he could see lay in getting to us before any accusation had been made against himself, and that mightn't have seemed quite as poor a hope as it did if he hadn't felt a doubt of whether he would have been left alive long enough to find out how it would work.

"So, whatever he might decide to do finally, he felt it best for the time to appear to be convinced that he had gone too far to draw back, and he said he had decided to accept their offer.

"He says that after that he did all he could to remove any doubt from their minds, and he must have acted well, whatever he really meant—"

Miss Wingrove, who had listened to this point in a resumed silence, which had allowed the smoothness of uninterrupted narrative, now interposed sharply:

"I wish you wouldn't put it that way again. Eustace would never have thought for a single moment of really going in with them."

"Well, I don't say you're wrong there. Anyway, we've got no complaint against him. But the way things turned out, he wasn't tested quite as he might have been. I only say that he must have convinced them thoroughly that they had got a recruit, for he wasn't followed when he left, which he certainly would have been if they had had any idea that he might be coming to us."

"How do you know they didn't?"

"Well, for one thing, if they had you wouldn't have been annoyed by your friend Greaves coming into the next room. They're trying to pick up a trail that they've lost. But that's where the tale takes a twist that you wouldn't guess.

"What happened next, which explains how he came to vanish in a way that's so puzzling to them, is the sort of thing that's more or less in everyone's experience, as far as I've been able to see—and we detectives see a good deal of life, and in some variety, whatever kind of mugs the rest of the world makes us out to be—not exactly a coincidence, but an unexpected development.

"Mr. Limbrook had come away from the Reader Grill with orders for the next twenty-four hours which, had he obeyed them, would have got him into it up to the neck, and he walked back to his own room trying to decide what he would do. He had taken a bed-and-breakfast room in Charmian Crescent when he landed, having nothing in hand but the balance of the £100, and not knowing how soon he would be picking up his next cheque, and he'd been going to one of the Atlas restaurant shops for an afternoon meal, where the cashier noticed his resemblance to a man we are wanting in connection with the Houghton murder, which is how the trouble, if that's going to be the right word for it, began.

"On the afternoon I arrested him there, he hadn't gone because he was hungry, he says, for he'd had a good meal at the Reader—he says it was the best he'd tasted since he left the boat, which just served to show him what he would be throwing up if he didn't take the easy course but because it bad become a habit to go there about that time, and he was sitting trying to think out what would be the

69

best course to take, when I sat down at his table, and offered him a solution he hadn't expected.

"It was the kind of mistake that isn't creditable to our department, and ought not to happen, but it's only fair to say Mr. Limbrook says it himself—that he didn't give us quite a fair deal.

"We charged him with being Houghton, who's wanted for wife-murder, and Mr. Limbrook said straightforwardly enough that he wasn't the man, but he wouldn't give his own name, as someone wrongly accused would be almost certain to do.

"He says now that, after the experience from which he had come, he was in doubt at first whether the whole thing were not some kind of a trap in connection with it, and he was asking himself at one moment whether I were a detective at all, and the next whether the dope gang could even pull the strings at Scotland Yard, and he were to be cleared out of the way by being prosecuted and hanged for a murder he hadn't done.

"But the thought that had most influence with him was that if he were arrested he would be relieved of the necessity either of carrying out the instructions he had received, or of incurring the vengeance of the gang for refusing to do so.

"They couldn't blame him for not doing what had become impossible, nor would they be able to get at him in any way before his release, by which time the whole thing would have become public, and they would know what had held him up. "

So while he was careful to deny that he was Houghton—he actually insisted on putting it into writing—he behaved in such a way that we didn't believe anything he said. But we weren't satisfied, all the same, and set enquiries afoot which proved to us, about forty-eight hours ago, that we had got the wrong man; so—"

"You mean you've kept him in jail all this time for something he told you he hadn't done? And in mistake for someone who wasn't he? I was wondering what it could be that you had to come to by such a roundabout road! Perhaps you'll tell me where he is now?"

"He's still in the same place, by his own particular wish."

"You really ask me to believe that?"

"He only told us the tale I've been telling you on the explicit condition that we hold him on remand instead of letting him out."

Billie Wingrove, being no fool, considered this with a gradually clearing brow. She said shrewdly: "Yes. I see. But it doesn't justify what you did. I should think you'll have to compensate him more than a bit. And all the more if he goes on staying there to help you get hold of this dirty gang. I can go to see him, of course?"

"Ye-es. You could. But it would be a very imprudent thing, and it might be that you wouldn't be able to help us in other ways, after you'd done that. What I was going to ask you to do was to go back to the room you left."

"I suppose I'm going to hear now what you really came for?"

"Miss Wingrove don't you think you're being a little unfair? I came because Mr. Limbrook thought you might be anxious if you heard nothing from him, and I promised him that I would let you know the facts in such a way that I shouldn't lead them on to your trail. I didn't even know you were being molested till I got here, though I can't say I'm surprised at that."

"I don't mean to be unfair. But when you tell me that he's being kept in jail for something he hasn't done, you can't expect me to look pleased! If Mr. Limbrook himself wants me to go back to that room, or anywhere else, you can count on me."

"I can't honestly say that he would wish you to that. His only anxiety seemed to be that you should not be brought into the matter in any way. If you do it at all, it will be without his knowledge, perhaps to help him, as I think it may, but mainly to help us in putting some of the worst of the criminal scum of Europe where they won't be able to do any more harm for the next five or ten years."

"You want me to go back to my own room without this man knowing that I've been trying to get away?"

"That would be the ideal way, if it's not too much to hope."

"It's just possible, if we both stop jabbering, don't care how anything gets crushed, and don't jib at carrying it all down the back stairs. That was the second dinner-gong that you just heard. Luckily, I've still got the key."

Inspector Cauldron understood that the decision had been made, and that the call was for rapid action and obedience to one whose knowledge of the conditions under which the manœuvre could be successfully executed was superior to his own.

The Envoy Hotel is one of those semi-boarding-house establishments which depend mainly upon regular guests, whom they take on weekly inclusive terms, which usually provide for morning and evening meals. The sounding of the second gong would draw together almost every living creature in the hotel except the lift-boy, the manageress in her ground-floor office, and the two porters in the hall. Even the chambermaids who were not off duty would be transformed into waitresses for the next hour.

The way to the front stairs and the lift from room Number 73 is much shorter than that to the emergency stairs at the far end of the passage, but the use of the latter avoided the danger of meeting some late arrival whose haste for the started meal would not be too great for a moment of observation at the unexpected sight of Miss Wingrove hurrying down with loaded arms, followed by an official-looking male, incongruously laden with a hat-box in one hand and a sheaf of feminine garments which there had been no leisure to pack cast over his freer shoulder.

While Mr. Greaves, seeing an unoccupied chair, reasonably assumed that Miss Wingrove was out for the evening, the two conspirators made the four journeys that the transit of her possessions required, having cause to congratulate themselves on one occasion, as they heard the whine of the ascending lift, that they had chosen the longer route. But they had good reason to think that they had been observed by no one in what they did, and, as their minds were otherwise less occupied than their muscles, there had been time for the inspector to make some suggestions as to the course of conduct by which she could best assist the forces of public order and the safety of one in whom she took an interest which the inspector, admiring a combination of brains and beauty such as he may not have had the good fortune to meet previously in so intimate a manner, was already disposed to envy.

At the end of the fourth journey he looked round on a room where Miss Wingrove's personal possessions had been dumped down in a manner which even he realized that their owner could not approve. "If," he said diffidently, "there's anything I can do to help you to get things a bit straighter?"

"No, there isn't," she answered, with some exasperation in her voice, as she lifted the shoes she had been wearing that afternoon off a chiffon dress. "I can manage much best by myself now. I know everything you want me to do. I even know the telephone number that you've told me three times! In fact, I knew it before. As though anyone who has a radio wouldn't know that! All I want is for you to go."

"I don't think there's any great hurry yet," he replied, conscious of something more than professional disappointment at this abrupt dismissal. "I shouldn't think even those who were punctual will be more than half through the second course." He had an uneasy doubt of whether she had realized sufficiently the seriousness of that which he had asked her to do. Even whether, in some circumstances, he might not be blamed. Perhaps a few further words, with less divided attention—

But he saw that she was regarding him now with one of those sudden flashes of anger which he had already experienced. "There mayn't be for you. Don't you think I want any dinner *at all*?"

"I beg your pardon," he said contritely. "I'm afraid I was forgetting that."

"Oh, it doesn't matter," she replied, with a quickly recovered serenity. "It's just what a man would overlook. But fancy criminals being afraid of you!"

She stretched out a friendly hand, but the next moment he found himself on the outside of a shut door.

He went down to Miss Hounder's office. "Miss Wingrove's moving back," he said, "to her old room. I've straightened that out. I think it might be wisest to hear any further complaint."

Miss Hounder agreed that that would be best, in a voice which had become indifferent to an ended topic. She had over a hundred guests to be polite to, to watch, to conciliate. She had the constant worry of the staff, the catering, the checking of the tradesmen's bills, the bookkeeping, the making out of the guests' accounts. Was it likely that she would go out of her way to talk of trouble which had been smoothed away?

Leaving the hotel, the inspector encountered a perturbed detective-sergeant. "I've just run Ratty Tubbs off," he said, "by the scruff of the neck. But I'm not sure that he didn't see you come out. He was hiding behind the Park gate."

But Inspector Cauldron was unperturbed. "I don't know, Polson," he said, "that it matters overmuch now."

CHAPTER XIV

Tea for Two at the Reader Grill

Left to herself, Miss Wingrove changed her dress and removed all traces of her recent occupation with impatient and yet scrupulous care.

She might be a hungry girl, with the knowledge that it was the only day in the week on which poultry appeared on a menu which, even in its variations, was of an unchanging monotony, but she did not intend, even for that, to lose a point in the game which she had agreed to play.

Mr. Greaves, now at the biscuits and cheese, observed her enter with a sideward glance, and became aware of a girl who was well groomed and cool and in the mood to exchange a smiling word with more than one of those whose tables she passed as she reached her own.

"I'd better give the soup a bye," she said. "Chicken still on, Phyllis?" She expected to have to put up with an alternative dish now, which she saw, with a renewed disposition to curse the dilatoriness of inspectors of the C.I.D., to be toad-in-the-hole, which she disliked. But the reply she got was: "Yes, miss. I didn't think you were out "

She observed without offence the implication that a portion had been inequitably reserved for her, to the detriment of less favoured guests. But she observed also, with less satisfaction, that the words would almost certainly have carried to Mr Greaves, sitting no more than three tables away in a thinning room.

Endeavouring to make gain of what threatened to go to the debit side, she answered clearly: "Yes. I was delayed on the telephone. I was hearing about someone who's been abroad."

After that she turned with good appetite to indifferent food.

It was about 9:15 P.M. when her telephone rang, and she heard the expected movement in her neighbour's room, and then Inspector

Cauldron's voice: "Is that you, Miss Wingrove? Do you think you are overheard?"

"Yes. That you, Clara? Tomorrow evening? Yes, that will suit me. And—oh, I say! I shall have something to tell you then. I've had a most amazing tale about Eustace. If it's true, it explains having heard nothing from him. But it's rather hard to believe." To which, after a natural pause, she added: "No. It's too long to begin now. I'll tell you then. Good-night, dear. Good-night."

Having replied politely, "Good-night, Miss Wingrove," Inspector Cauldron rang off.

Well, that was done! And it had certainly not been hard. When she heard from the next room the movements of one who puts on his boots, and then departing steps, she had reason to think that she had not fished in an empty pool.

She went to bed with a feeling of satisfaction which might have been more complete had she been sure that Eustace Limbrook's comfort was equal even to that which the Envoy Hotel provides for its less affluent guests. But she could not think of him as suffering any extreme hardships, now that the police knew that he was an entirely innocent man and one who was helping them. She had understood correctly that the modern prison system, even as it is applied to convicted persons, endeavours to exercise its punitive influences by torturing the mind rather than the body, and she correctly surmised that Eustace Limbrook was not being subjected to regulated indignities which it must be difficult for self-respect to endure.

Apart from that, the pulse of adventure stirred in her with the quick gaiety of her temperament and her youth, and her satisfaction was in no way lessened when she paused in the hall on her way to breakfast next morning and received her letters, among which she was quick to perceive one with a typed address and enclosed in an envelope of superior quality, such as her more frequent correspondents were unlikely to use.

Reminding herself that she was under the doubtless interested observation of her upstairs neighbour, she sat down to breakfast, and first opened a bill from Messrs. Swan and Edgar for the shoes which had been so badly misplaced on the previous evening, then glanced over a note from the friend whose name she had misused on the telephone, and finally opened the more official envelope and read the letter which it contained with an expressionless face.

It was typed on unheaded paper of good quality, and its contents, whether genuine or not, must be of substantial, though different, interest.

c/o the International Travel Agency,
26A Leadenhall Street, E.C. 3.

Dear Miss Wingrove,

I am requiring some research work to be undertaken for me at the British Museum, and your name,
with a very gratifying recommendation, has been
given to me by Sir Ranelegh James. "If you are not
already too fully occupied, perhaps you will kindly
call at the Reader Grill, Aldervill Street, W.1, at
about 4.30 p.m. tomorrow, the 14th inst., and ask the
waiter to direct you to me.

Yours faithfully,

Lawrence P. Ashbarton

She read this letter, and allowed a faint smile of gratification to
appear, such as its contents would naturally arouse in a research
worker who was (as the writer had probably ascertained) less than
fully occupied, having just completed commissions for two of her
more regular clients.

There was a bare possibility that it was a simple, genuine communication, meaning neither more nor less than it said; but this diminished as her eyes fell on the postmark of the envelope. Midnight.
And it had been about 9:30 when Mr. Greaves had left the hotel.
Certainly they were fast workers, if this were the result of the information he had carried! But a (presumably American?) gentleman
requiring the kind of assistance she would be able to render would
be likely to post his letters at an earlier hour. And the Reader Grill?
Wasn't that the place where Eustace had been interviewed previously? She had not memorized with care the name which the inspector had mentioned, her mind having been on the essentials of what
he said, but it had a familiar sound.

She would have liked to retain that envelope, which she thought
the police might be interested to see, but it was her custom to carry
her letters away from the breakfast-table and leave the envelopes for
the waitress to clear, and even in so small a point she would not alter
her usual routine. She gathered them up now—the two letters and
the bill—and said good-morning to Mr. Greaves as she passed out of
the room with just a shade more of affability than she was accustomed to turn in his direction.

Her previously unpractised art of dissimulation received its first testimonial when, speaking from a call-boy about an hour later, that gentleman reported: "Took it in like milk, if you ask me. Looked quite bucked after she'd read it. Oh, you can tell the boss that she'll be there, never fear."

She remembered that she had undertaken to ring up a universally familiar number as soon as she had anything to report. But had she? Well, scarcely yet! She might have more before the end of the day. She could leave it till then. But it would be a natural thing to telephone Sir Ranelegh James to thank him for the recommendation he had given. She did this after her usual midday meal in a Great Russell Street restaurant, and learned from him that it had been some time after eleven on the previous night when he had given her name in response to a telephone enquiry from a Mr. Ashbarton, a stranger to him, who had said that he had an introduction from a mutual friend in New York, which he would send on by post, but which had not so far, arrived.

The time of this enquiry enabled her to put the idea that she had received an offer of genuine work finally from her mind. Yet, whatever might be the intention with which she had been invited to call at the Reader Grill, she observed that the approach had been both skilfully and cautiously made. But for the information she had previously received, there would have been nothing in that letter to cause her a moment's doubt that it meant neither more nor less than it said, and even with all the illuminating knowledge that had been gathered at Scotland Yard, it might be a very difficult matter to assail its authenticity, unless she should first elect to go through whatever experience it might portend.

She had a moment of wonder as to how they had discovered that Sir Ranelegh would recommend her to them. But that was easily answered. Had he not expressed a generous gratitude for the assistance he had received from her in the preparation of *Contrasts of Cretan Art*, in the preface to that erudite volume? She had no doubt that, if he were asked, he would say that the enquiry he had received had not mentioned her, but merely asked for the name and address of a research worker he could recommend. It would have been made with a sure guess of how he would reply. But what proof could there be of that?

And the letter itself, purporting to be written from an address which hundreds of travellers would be free to use, and to which no answer need be sent, and giving no indication of the nature of the work required—it would be very difficult to prove that there were not a real vacancy for which she was invited to submit her qualifications.

Only, if at all, was there appearance of indiscretion in the selection of the Reader Grill as the place at which she was to attend, in view of the fact that it was there that Eustace Limbrook had been met before, and that she was being invited on the assumption that she was in—perhaps secret—communication with him.

But even this criticism shrank in her mind to its true proportion as she reflected that they might see reason to doubt the directness and minimize the extent of his communications to her, while they could have nothing more than a puzzled doubt as to whether the mystery of his disappearance indicated active hostility to themselves; and, besides that, the places where the members of such a gang could safely consort could not be numerous, so that it might seem the less risk to repeat the address of one the staff and management of which might be subservient to themselves.

Yet the reflection that the place to which she was invited was that in which Eustace Limbrook had been threatened with ruin, if not with death, sobered her to the point of deciding that it would be more prudent to inform the police of what she was about to do. It was four o'clock when she hesitated before the row of telephone boxes in Piccadilly station, entered one of them, and put in the call for which no pennies need be inserted. She asked to speak to Inspector Cauldron, but being told, after being kept waiting for some minutes, that he was not in, she hung up the receiver, on an impulse that she regretted a moment later, but would not reverse.

She booked to Hyde Park Corner, and walked the short distance back to Aldervill Street, arriving at the Reader Grill about ten minutes before the appointed time. The place had a look of quiet respectability, in a most respectable street. It would have made timidity seem absurd, even had she entered it with a more contentious purpose than was actually hers.

The fact that she was slightly early did not seem a sufficient reason for standing outside the door. She would enquire for Mr. Ashbarton, and if he had not arrived she could wait inside. But the head-waiter, a benign, fatherly man, who approached her obsequiously as she entered a long low room, at this hour almost empty of guests, replied to her enquiry that Mrs. Ashbarton would be pleased to see her, and led the way to a door at the far end, and then up a steep and twisting stair, so narrow that two could not nave mounted abreast.

She had not thought that it might be a woman whom she would meet, and the idea modified her conception of the encounter to which she came. It made an absurdity of the doubt she might other-wise have felt as she was led up three flights of those narrow stairs. There are a thousand of such old buildings in the West End. Do those who occupy them become criminal because they must make cramped approaches to little rooms?

The waiter half opened a door at the head of the third flight, for her to enter. He said: "Miss Wilhelmina Wingrove to see you, madam." The door closed, and Billie Wingrove's eyes met those of woman about fifteen years older than herself, expensively but qui-etly dressed, who rose with a pleasant smile, and an outstretched hand.

"You will like a cup of tea?" she said at once, rather as stating a fact than making enquiry. "I always have mine at this time. We'd better have it brought up now, and postpone our business talk until the waiter's out of the way."

The "cup of tea," being ordered, had the sound of a more sub-stantial provision than that with which Billie was accustomed to de-lay the assaults of hunger until she could sit down to the principal meal which was included in her two-and-a-half guinea contract with the Envoy Hotel.

"We might," Mrs. Ashbarton addressed the junior waiter who had come up the three flights in response to her ring more rapidly than the one who had conducted her guest might have felt equal to doing, "we might have some of those little toasted scones. And jam. Blackcurrant or strawberry? Well, perhaps both. And some cream. And some mixed cakes. With some of those little diamond-shaped short breads. And bread-and-butter, of course."

Billie judged that whatever inquisition she would have to face would be conducted with some regard for her physical comfort, and also that Mrs. Ashbarton was not ordering tea for the first time at the Reader Grill.

"I always like," her hostess explained, as the boy withdrew, "a good meal at this time of day. I think it must be the chilliness of the climate, of which temperature I have experienced little during the last ten or twelve years. That, and the rooms not being what I call properly warmed. I've been in Egypt for the last three months, and that makes me inclined to shiver in what you might call a warm place."

"In Egypt, have you?" Billie thought. Here was frankness, at least. Obvious connection with Mildew! And yet something puz-zlingly different from what she had expected to meet.

For the next five minutes they exchanged facts, and platitudi-nous reflections thereon, in the intimate smiling manner that women have, like two armies warily manœuvring for position before the peril of battle joins.

But when the waiter had retired, after placing a loaded tray upon the low table which he set between them, Mrs. Ashbarton came to her point with a directness that only interrupted itself for the inevitable query: "Sugar? Two lumps or one?"

"I was particularly glad," she said, "when Sir Ranelegh recommended you to me so warmly yesterday, because it wasn't the first time that I had heard your name, and I thought that you might be able to give me some information that a friend of mine is rather anxious to have.

"I'd better tell you first about what I hope you'll be able to undertake for me, because that will naturally be the more interesting to you. My husband died about twelve months ago, leaving a book unpublished, but complete so far as I am able to judge, on which—he was a good deal older than I—he had been working for over twenty years.

"Its subject is the Arthurian legends. I don't profess to know anything about them myself, but the manuscript is full of references, and quotations in Old English and Old French, and some other languages, which I should like to have verified, and typed out in a form more legible than they now are. I want the book to be generally prepared for the press in the best way that is possible when an author is no longer living."

"I'm not sure that I should be entirely competent for that. I've never actually—"

Mrs. Ashbarton interrupted with gentle firmness:

"From the recommendation I have had, I feel sure you would. And I should be quite willing to pay for any assistance you might feel it desirable to engage. I thought I would either pay you an agreed fee, say of five hundred dollars, with half that amount added for any expenses you might incur...or perhaps you would prefer to be paid according to the time which it would require? I should be pleased to pay anything that is usual...something, I suppose, from five to ten dollars a day?"

Billie Wingrove listened to this proposal, and felt puzzled. The offer had a genuine sound; and she saw that such a manuscript could not be faked. It would have been easy to invent an occasion for research work in connection with which such a difficulty would not arise. And, if she were listening to a genuine offer, it was the kind of work which she was anxious to secure.

"I don't think," she answered, "we shall be likely to fall out about terms, if I feel that I can undertake it. But could I have a look at the manuscript? I could tell better then how difficult it might be, and how much time it would be likely to take."

She thought this to be a crucial test. If the manuscript could be produced—

Mrs. Ashbarton made no difficulty about that, though the answer deferred, if it did not avoid, the proof. "It's in Princeton now," she said. "I should explain that, though I am English myself, my husband was a university professor there. But they are expecting me to send for it. I could cable this evening, and it should be here in ten days, if not less."

Billie thought: "It's not here, of course. That's what I might have supposed." And the thought must have brought a moment's blankness to her eyes, however quickly controlled, for Mrs. Ashbarton added: "Of course, I can't ask you to wait for it, if you have other work offering, unless I pay something to retain your service. Perhaps if I give you a cheque for £10 now?"

Her hand reached for a handbag of morocco leather from which a cheque-book protruded, but Miss Wingrove stayed her with a quick gesture. Doubting her as she must, she preferred to avoid the obligation which the acceptance of money imposes. And yet—how far did she doubt? If this lady were an agent of drug-traffickers, she was a most puzzling specimen of that fraternity. Perhaps, to Inspector Cauldron's more experienced eyes, she would be of an apparent criminality; but Billie Wingrove found it difficult to believe.

"There's no need," she said, "for that. I've got plenty to occupy me for the next few days. But what about the information that you said I might be able to give you—or your friend?"

She thought, as she put the question, that she showed some diplomatic adroitness in being the first to revert to this topic. Certainly, it would be likely to negative any idea that she suspected either the subject or good faith of the enquiry which was to come, or was conscious of anything concerning Eustace Limbrook which it was desirable to conceal. Mrs. Ashbarton answered her again with the naturalness and ease which had characterized her previous conversation.

"It is about a gentleman who was known to a friend of mine while they were both in Egypt, and who had mentioned your name as one with whom he corresponded here—a Mr. Eustace Limbrook.

"He has lost touch with him after what, I am told, was an absolute misunderstanding of a rather serious character, and he is anxious to get into communication with him again to clear it up. Mr. Limbrook is, perhaps, rather impetuous—rather quick to jump to conclusions?"

"No. I should say rather the other way."

"But perhaps he is one who might take something literally which was meant in another way—say, as a joke?"

"That would be—rather more possible," Billie admitted without conviction. It would be better to see where this would lead than to engage in futile discussion of the character of one whom Mrs. Ashbarton had not met.

"That is what Mr. Wellard thinks may have occurred. I believe he is rather fond of—well, of romancing, it might be called, and he may have been more realistic than he was aware."

"What is it you want me to do?"

"If you could let me have Mr. Limbrook's address, so that Mr. Wellard could write to him?"

"No," she answered, with a slow reluctance, for, put as it had been, it was not an easy request to refuse, "I'm afraid I couldn't do that."

Mrs. Ashbarton looked somewhat hurt, somewhat surprised, as at an unexpected rebuff. But she showed no sign of annoyance. Either transparently, or by excellent acting, she appeared indifferent, as one would be who had asked something on a friend's behalf which had been of little moment, even to him. She said: "Of course, it's not a matter that I can press, but I can't help thinking that you are making a mistake. You will forgive me if I am wrong, but I am told that Mr. Limbrook is in a position in which influential friends, who have the power as well as the will to help him, should be welcomed rather than—may I say, shown the door?"

"I'm sorry. I didn't mean to be rude. But I really can't give anyone his address."

"Perhaps if Mr. Wellard should see you himself?"

"Yes. I've no objection to that."

"Well, I'll tell him what you say."

With these words, Mrs. Ashbarton put the subject lightly aside. As the conversation had proceeded, they had both disposed of a good meal. Now she offered to refill her visitor's cup with an undiminished affability. She switched the talk back to her husband's manuscript, and mentioned that she was staying at the Old Jersey Hotel. That had the sound of an unlikely coincidence, but like most of its kind, it might be natural enough. The Old Jersey was large, an had many guests, and most of them were from the United States.

"Wasn't that," Billie; asked, "where the Houghton murder occurred?"

"Yes. Rather gruesome, wasn't it? But it wouldn't have been quite fair to Mr. Munro—that's the manager—if all the guests had walked out. He can't be expected to ask every man who brings his wife to the hotel for an assurance that she isn't being taken upstairs to be shot at the bathroom door."

"No," Billie smiled rather absently, "he couldn't do that." She was perturbed by a feeling that the interview was not developing at all as she had expected that it would do. Her refusal had been accepted too casually, with too great a readiness to return to the ostensible purpose of the invitation she had received, for it to be easy to think that it was the main object of the appointment, as she yet could not doubt it to be.

And now Mrs. Ashbarton had risen. In a leisurely manner she pulled on her gloves. "I'm afraid," she said, "I must be going now. I have a theatre engagement for this evening. I'll phone you as soon as the manuscript arrives; and, of course, you can ring me up at the Old Jersey at any time."

Billie Wingrove, seeing that the interview was about to terminate, asked herself what she had obtained that Inspector Cauldron would be interested to hear, and decided that it was not much. She had Mrs. Ashbarton's name, and the address of her hotel. She might be no more than an innocent decoy, or one of the minor cogs in the drug-distributing machinery, such as she had been told that the police found it little use to arrest. Beyond that, there was the name of a Mr. Wellard, which might be little or much. But her guess was that it would be known already, unless it had been assumed for this occasion. No, as a detective she had certainly not been a success.

And then, as she thought this, the telephone rang.

CHAPTER XV

Feminine Weakness of Billie Wingrove

Mrs. Ashbarton picked up the receiver. She said, "Yes, it's I," listened a moment, and then spoke with some petulance. "But I thought you were going to call for me at the hotel. And besides, it's so early yet." There was another interval of silence, and then: "Oh, well, if you're so keen about that! No...no, not to me. But I'm sure Miss Wingrove will be pleased to meet you. You'd better come up now."

She put the instrument down and turned to Billie to say: "It's Mr. Wellard. He was speaking from the ground floor. He seems quite anxious about Mr. Limbrook's address, so I told him he could come up. You won't mind seeing him?"

"No. Why should I?" It was the only possible answer, and the one which reason, if not feeling, approved. It was what she had come to do—to find out, for the information of the police, all that she could, while those to whom she would talk would think they were probing her.

But it was becoming a position she did not like, which she liked even less when she had been introduced to Mr. Wellard, a heavily built man, neither young nor old, with a plausible manner, who might be pleasant among his friends, but with hard, pitiless eyes and a snake-like smoothness in all he did, from which those of another temper might be disposed to shrink with aversion, if not with fear. She liked it least when Mrs. Ashbarton said: "I'm afraid I shall have to go. But if you'll call for me at the hotel in an hour's time?"

Mr. Wellard said that he would. Mrs. Ashbarton shook hands with Miss Wingrove in a friendly manner. Mr. Wellard held the door open for her He closed it again. He turned to say: "I understand you have Limbrook's address?"

She answered the abrupt attack with an equal terseness: "I have not said so."

He moved toward her, but keeping nearer the door "Well, you have," he replied. "Sit down."

He drew chairs for her and himself, still keeping, whether by design or not, between her and the door. "You will be acting very foolishly," he went on, "if you make trouble about giving us that. We are Limbrook's friends."

"I am not making any trouble," she replied, her eyes meeting his, not without effort, in a steady gaze, and showing the resentment natural to the manner in which she had been addressed. "I don't know you at all."

"There is no need that you should. All that I am asking is that you should give me Limbrook's address, which he will be glad for you to do."

The voice was persuasive, and might, to many, have been less antipathetic than it sounded to her. He had certainly shown little adroitness in the curtness of his opening words, but the fact was that he had misunderstood Mrs. Ashbarton's telephone intimation to indicate that she had met with a more obdurate refusal than had actually rebuffed the mildness of her request; while Billie Wingrove's sharp reaction was the result of an instinctive revulsion, such as some may feel for a large spider or the "harmless, necessary" cat.

"I don't see," she gathered courage to retort, "why I should give any information which is asked for in such a manner."

"I beg your pardon, Miss Wingrove," he answered smoothly, "if I've been a bit abrupt, but Mr. Limbrook's address is what it's necessary to have, as much for his sake as ours."

"If you can make me see that—" she replied in an altered voice, remembering that her purpose was to learn all she could. She must encourage him to talk, letting the result be truth or lies of whatever blend.

"Well," he answered, "it oughtn't to be difficult to do that. If you know much about him, you know he's broke and badly wanting a job, and that's what's waiting for him to take. A good job. One that he'll be glad to have. And I don't mind telling you that we're wanting him. We shouldn't bother except for that. We want a man with his qualifications and experience."

"Do you mind telling me what the job is?"

"I can't say more than I have about that. We want him for a confidential position. Not one to be talked about, even to his lady friends. But I'll tell you this. That was just how the trouble began. We had to test him, and one of us hit it up rather too high. He made out we were in a wrong line, and Limbrook took it for gospel truth, and we think that made him sheer off. So it's important for us to get in touch with him and put it straight. That's important to us; and the real job that we've got waiting ought to be important to him."

"If you can't tell me what you're talking about more clearly than that, I would prefer to have nothing more to do with the matter

"If she said this in anticipation of receiving a more dangerous confidence, it was an abortive manœuvre. Instead of that, it brought the crisis which she had instinctively feared from the moment when Wellard entered the room.

"It's not what you prefer," he replied, with a menace she could not mistake in the hard suavity of his voice. "This is real business, and you needn't think we're going to be jockeyed by you. You know where Limbrook's hanging out, and you won't leave this room till you've told me the last word that you know, and made me sure that it's true."

She rose at that, with angry eyes in a pale face. "I think this conversation has gone far enough," she said, with an aspect of courage she did not feel. Her thought was that she had failed, for she was getting nothing from him. And from the confidence in his voice she judged that he had spoken more than a bluffing threat.

She moved toward the door, but he rose quickly to interpose. He stepped to it, turned the key, and dropped it into his pocket.

"If you're not a fool," he said, "you'll know when the game's up

"With a quick movement she reached the telephone. Before he would have had time to silence her, she had called hurriedly: "Help! Help! On the third floor!" But he made no motion to interfere.

"You can save your breath," he said. "They take their orders from me."

In fact, she had had no answer at all; and, seeing his indifference, she gave up a vain attempt.

"I'll make it easy for you," he said. "If you'll be a sensible girl I'll give you a hundred pounds for what I could get from you at the price of a twisted arm."

"You wouldn't dare! You don't want to go to jail. Not even if you've been there before."

It was a random shot that went home. His cheek flushed darkly. He said: "Another word like that and you'll find out what I dare. It would be no more than your word against mine; and there are plenty downstairs to swear that I went out twenty minutes ago, besides describing the man who came up to you here.

"You're in my power, and if I should decide to want what young women like you call their honour, or break your neck, or just tickle you with this when it's not as chilly as it is now"—he picked up a short poker and thrust it into the red heart of the fire—"you'll find no one would look in here, even though you should screech till your voice cracked. But I'm not going to do anything of the kind," he added in an altered tone. "You're going to be a sensible girl and tell me Limbrook's address. Hang it all, there can't be such a secret in that! And I shall give you a hundred pounds. And after that he'll thank you for what you've done."

"I think you're the lowest cad that I ever met."

The words were scarcely spoken before he struck her backhanded across the mouth with a force which threw her against the chair from which she had risen.

"You'll learn to speak," he said as smoothly as before, "with a civil tongue. And if you don't want a real lesson you'll begin now."

"What do you want me to say?"

She asked this in a subdued voice, very different from that of a moment before. Her face was pale. She wiped blood from her mouth. It seemed that all her courage had gone with the impact of that brutal blow.

"Now that's talking," he replied, with a recovered good-humour. "There'd have been no need to treat you so rough if you'd used that tone all along. But you know what I want, and it's something that's soon said."

"I don't know that you'll believe if I tell you; and it's something about which I'm not too certain myself."

"I'll judge that when I've heard what it is."

"Inspector Cauldron says he's in jail for the Houghton murder."

Mr. Wellard stared, as he well might. It sounded grotesque. But he had the sense to see that she would have invented a more probable lie.

"That's nonsense," he said. "That's impossible. I mean it's impossible that he had anything to do with that murder. But I don't see how Inspector Cauldron could have left you in doubt. He must know whether he's got him in jail or not."

"He says they arrested someone they believed to be James Houghton, and he says he is Eustace Limbrook."

"Well, it ought to be easy to clear that up, one way or other."

"That's what they're trying to do. But he said it isn't as easy as it might sound. Mr. Houghton hadn't any friends in England who had seen him in recent years—and Mr. Limbrook—if it's he they arrested—is very similar in appearance. That was why he came to me, as one who would be able to say for sure."

"He wants you to identify him?"

"He wanted me to look at a photograph they had taken in prison and say who it was. Unfortunately, I couldn't recognize it at first. That was before he had mentioned who it was supposed to be. It wasn't a good likeness. Afterwards I felt sure. But it was too late to convince him then."

Mr. Wellard considered this. It was evident that he believed what she had said, and his mind was on its implications as it affected the only angle from which Eustace Limbrook interested those who had ordered him to make the girl speak. He said: "They'll be wanting you to have a look at him in the cells."

"He didn't say that. He didn't seem to trust me overmuch. He said I must be prepared to be called as a witness on the eighteenth— on the day of the next remand. They expect to have some information from America before then. The trouble is that Houghton's sister-in-law identified him absolutely, though they seem to think she was telling lies."

"Identified him as James Houghton?"

"Yes."

Mr. Wellard gnawed his underlip thoughtfully. He did not exactly doubt her tale. He still thought it to be such as no girl in her senses would invent as a plausible lie. And it accounted for the otherwise inexplicable way in which Limbrook had disappeared. But he felt that there was something queer about it. Devilish queer!

"I shouldn't have thought the Yard would be in a real tangle about that. Not for twenty-four hours."

"He said that one of the troubles is that the sister-in-law who identified him has gone back to America."

"You're sure it is Limbrook they've got? The woman couldn't make such a mistake as that."

"No. But she's gone. The inspector didn't say much about that. But I don't think they trust her. She may have misled them intentionally and then bolted."

Mr. Wellard considered this also. Several explanations suggested themselves readily to his criminal mind, one of which was not far from the facts. He asked: "What date was it when they ran him in?"

Learning that it was that on which Limbrook had disappeared, he put doubt from his mind. It was Limbrook, not Houghton, who lay in a prison cell; and a Limbrook who might still be loyal to the masters who had thrust themselves upon him.

"See here, Miss Wingrove," he said in his smoothest voice, "I'm sorry that I had to be a bit rough, but what you've told me shows that I did the right thing. If you're Limbrook's friend, you want him out of the mess, and you've come to the ones who can do that. We can do more than identify him. We can prove when he landed, and that he couldn't be the same as the Houghton who did the murder, because he was somewhere else at the time. I suppose, even if the police don't ask you to see him, that they couldn't refuse now, if you say you want to?"

"No," she assented doubtfully. "I don't see how they could. Not after coming to me."

"Well, I want you to see him tomorrow morning, and tell him that we're ready to get him out. That'll prove who his real friends are."

He paused, and then added, with a quiet but deadly significance: "Of course, if we weren't his friends, we could say that we'd never seen him before. We couldn't tell whether he were called Houghton or Limbrook or Percy Jones, because names can be changed and bandied about; but we could say that he wasn't the man who came home as Eustace Limbrook on the *Calcutta* a few weeks ago."

She rose, and this time he made no motion to hinder her. "I'll try to get to see him tomorrow morning," she said. "If you can help to get him released at once, I shan't bother about how you've treated me."

"Say nothing about that, and you'll have some good friends. Friends worth having. And that goes for him too."

He took the door-key from his pocket, and then paused. "There's one little thing to be done yet, which we mustn't forget. We're a firm that pays cash." From a hip-pocket there came a wad of one-pound notes which was thick, though they were new ones that lay close. "I don't suppose you'll want to count them," he said. "But you'll find there's a hundred there. And there's no need to tell anyone. We like to do our business quietly. And I'll expect you here again tomorrow evening. Say, seven o'clock."

She put the notes into her bag. He unlocked the door. He held out his hand. "No malice, Miss Wingrove?" he asked.

She raised her hand to a bruised chin and a swollen lip. "About this? Oh no. It doesn't matter at all."

She touched his hand without shrinking, and went out.

She left a man who thought that he had done well. A hundred pounds in her bag, and a chance of securing her lover's release! Most girls would forget much for such gains as those. He wondered whether, after fearing the loss of a valuable recruit, they were to have two. But pluck was needed for anyone to be useful to them. Had she got that? He had thought so at first. Afterwards he had been less sure. He interrupted himself in these reflections with the thought that he must lose no time in reporting what he had learned to those whose instructions he obeyed. He had a moment of doubt as to whether he might not have gone too far on his own initiative, in view of the most unexpected position with which he had to deal. But he thought not. He had some anticipation of praise, which would take the usual tangible shape. Anyway, he must report at once, even though one of his best customers, in the person of Mrs. Ashbarton, might be tapping an impatient foot in the lounge of the Old Jersey Hotel.

CHAPTER XVI

Billie Wingrove at Scotland Yard

Billie Wingrove took a ticket to Piccadilly station. Like Mr. Wellard, she had a report to make, and she was less sure than he that she deserved praise. She hesitated before the row of telephone boxes from one of which she had made that abortive enquiry some hours earlier, but there were several loiterers standing closely around. She had a needless fear lest she might be overheard, even in a closed box, and it crossed her mind that there are those who can read the lips. She left the station, and walked on through Leicester Square to the foot of Charing Cross Road, at the further side of which she came to a passage, wide and comparatively deserted, which had a solitary telephone box in its midst.

She entered this, and had the satisfaction, a moment later, of hearing Inspector Cauldron's voice, while she could look around on a clear pavement out side. She told him of the events of the last three hours with a particularity which took a longer time than might have been allowed to users of less official numbers. She added: "I'm afraid I did it very clumsily. I haven't had any practice at that kind of thing, and I hardly knew myself, once or twice, whether I were acting or saying what I really meant; and I kept thinking I'd gone too far either one way or the other. But I should guess it came off all right in the end, or he wouldn't have let me come away as he did, or given me the hundred pounds."

"I think," Inspector Cauldron replied, "you've done very well indeed. I'm not sure we shan't have to offer you a regular job. You'd better phone us in the morning, some time when you can be overheard, and ask if you can see Mr. Limbrook at once; and, of course, you'll get the permission. You won't forget when you're speaking that he's known as Houghton to us. But I needn't tell you what to say."

"Yes, I'll do that. What am I to do with the money?"

"Keep it, of course. If they like to pay a hundred pounds for Mr. Limbrook's address, there's no reason they shouldn't that I can see."

"Well, I'll think about it," she answered doubtfully. She was still in the same doubt when she reached her room at the Envoy Hotel. She turned the money out from her bulging bag. Clean, closely pressed, neatly banded together, the notes were a pleasant sight, being momentary wealth to her.

But she did not like the idea of taking money from those whom she did not intend to serve. It was only when she considered that they had been given to her, not in anticipation of anything she was expected to do, but for information which had been substantially accurate, that she finally decided that she could retain them without dishonour.

Decision reached, she unlocked her strongest suitcase to deposit them within it, and as she did so heard a clock in a room across the passage strike eight. And it was always slow! She would be late for dinner again. But against that she could set the substantial asset of Mrs. Ashbarton's tea.

The thought brought up the problem of that lady's good faith, and the question of the existence of a recondite work on the Arthurian legends, back to her mind, for which it was occupation enough for the period of the coming meal, though it remained one that she could not solve.

Inspector Cauldron was in the same doubt, but had better facilities for its decision. As the electric current outpaces the sun, there was still time to get a cable to New York, and for the police there to telephone Princeton University, before darkness came to the New World. By ten o'clock next morning he had learned that, unless the lady whom Miss Wingrove had met had been impersonating a more respectable character, she was all that she had represented herself to be. Certainly, a Professor Ashbarton had recently died. Certainly, he had left such a work in manuscript as had been described. His widow was known to be in England, and she had cabled the University, almost as the enquiry came through from New York, to dispatch it to her in London. The New York police were now anxious to know if this instruction were authentic, or did London wish them to hold up the package in the registered post, by which it would be consigned?

But the C.I.D. had no irregularity to allege. Enquiries made during the night in London had reduced the theory of impersonation to an extreme improbability. The lady had been known by sight to the manager of the Cockspur street branch of the Manhattan Trust for several years. He had known her to call in company with her late husband. Other evidences supported this assurance.

It remained only to investigate her more recent respectability and associations, for so far as the present enquiry was concerned there was nothing against her, except that she had acted as a decoy to draw Miss Wingrove into a most evil trap. And this might, or might not, have been innocently done.

As to Wellard, the name was new to the police, and most probably assumed, but the man should not he difficult to trace, with the assistance of Billie Wingrove's description, and a good guess might be confirmed by watching the Reader Grill during the time when she had been invited to call again. Nothing had been previously known to the detriment of that apparently most respectable restaurant. But that was to be expected. When such a place came under the notice of the police, it might still be used as a precarious centre by the dope peddlers, but for the aristocracy of the profession its use was done.

When Inspector Cauldron took Miss Wingrove's call, he had been in conference with his superior officer for the past half-hour, and the cable from the New York police had arrived a few minutes previously.

"You are," he asked, "being overheard? Then you'd better speak your piece, and after that I'll tell you what we have decided that it will be best to do."

But when he had listened to the expected request, he said no more in reply than: "You'd better come here. To New Scotland Yard. Ask for Superintendent Backwash, and you'll be shown straight up, and we'll talk it over then. You'd better thank me as though I've made some objection, but given way."

He had shortened that which he had intended to say in response to a warning from which his first statement had brought to the superintendent's brow, and now, as he laid the receiver down, he asked the meaning of that cautionary signal.

"I didn't want you," the superintendent replied, "to promise what we mayn't do."

"There's no reason she shouldn't see him, is there?"

"I'm not sure that it's the best way."

"You won't find Limbrook, or the girl, easy to manage, unless you let them run on a slack rein."

"No? I was thinking of that. We shall have to see what she says."

Half an hour later Miss Wingrove was announced, and being introduced by Inspector Cauldron, was received by the superintendent with a degree of affability less noticeable to her than it would have been to one more familiar with his customary manner. He offered a chair to his visitor. He cleared his throat. There was a pause of thirty seconds before he began.

"I think, Miss Wingrove, that Inspector Cauldron has already explained to you the serious criminality of these people whom, with your very valuable—perhaps I should say your essential—assistance, we are endeavouring to bring to justice."

"Yes. I understand all about that. I came to see Mr. Limbrook, and talk it over with him."

"What exact aspects of the matter—you will understand that, in anything I am saying, I am not refusing you that interview, nor making conditions respecting it, for it is not a request which I consider we have any right, nor, under the circumstances, any wish for a single moment to decline—but I should like to know what aspects of the matter, and to what purpose, you are thinking of discussing with him."

Miss Wingrove looked puzzled, for which she had some excuse. "I think," she said, "that I shall have to tell him what happened yesterday, and we may discuss how he can help you further, without too much risk for him."

"Or for yourself?"

"I wasn't thinking of that. I don't mind doing anything necessary. I got rather frightened yesterday, and I know I was clumsy in some of the things I said, but looking back at it, I thought it was rather fun."

"We think," the superintendent replied with deliberation, his eyes on a mouth that was made for laughter, and now showed a bruise that spread, wide and black, over the left side of the chin, "that you were a very plucky and clever girl. But will Mr. Limbrook be sure to look at it quite in the same way?"

Miss Wingrove looked doubtful. "If he understands how important it is," she replied, but with no confidence in her tone, "I don't think he ought to make any fuss."

"Mr. Limbrook regarded his own danger so seriously—and I don't say he was wrong: I think he was right in that—that he asked us to keep him here while we are smoking the nest. Do you think he'll he willing for you to be seeing them on his behalf, while we keep him here?"

"It seems to me that the question is what's best to be done to get them to give themselves away."

"So we think. But when he hears what you have been at, won't he want us to let him out so that he can deal with what is really his own mess in his own way?"

"I daresay he might."

"And you understand that we should be obliged to agree? We can't keep him now, against his own wishes, even though it might be much best for

"What," she asked bluntly, "are you wanting me to do now?"

"We've been thinking that it might be best if you don't see him. We could tell you what to say this evening just as well—perhaps better—than you could get it from him, and he wouldn't be upset by thinking that you are going into further danger on his account.

"I don't see that I should. It would be to help you catch some criminals of the worst kind."

"But would he look at it in that way?"

"I don't know. But I must talk it over with him. I'm not willing to go away without seeing him, if you're driving at that. It isn't reasonable to ask."

But Superintendent Backwash showed an obstinacy of purpose to equal hers: "Miss Wingrove, I understand how you feel, and if you think we're asking too much, it's for you to say. I may say we are in your hands. We need your help even more than Mr. Limbrook's. You may be able to do more for us than he possibly could, even if he were free. Indeed, the way things are going, he may be able to help us most by just staying where he is.

"You must understand that we are on the track of one of the worst gangs of international criminals, and we are bound to ask for the help of anyone who is in a position to give it, even at some personal risk; though I need not say that anything you may undertake will be with assurance that we shall be watchful for your protection."

"I've said I'm willing. What do you want me to do?"

"I'm asking you not to see Mr. Limbrook at present, for reasons which, whether bad or good, seem important to us."

"I wasn't asking you that. I meant, what do you want me to do to help catch these men?"

"We can't go very far along that line yet. We must feel our way. We are dealing with particularly powerful and wealthy criminals. Not the common type. Men with money and brains. All we know yet is that we may be able to get at them from a fresh angle through you. We want you to gain their confidence, if you can. You may do that if you convince them that you are Limbrook's intermediary, and that he has resolved to go in with them."

Miss Wingrove received this with a pause of silence, and Superintendent Backwash, whose patience could be equal to his pertinacity, showed no disposition to hasten her reply. But, as she thought her face had a stubborn look. She said at last: "I want to see Eustace, and I don't see any sufficient reason why I shouldn't; but I don't want him upset by hearing what happened last night, or have him arguing with me not to go there again. I'm willing to say nothing about that."

Inspector Cauldron interposed: "He'll ask how you got that bruise."

"Couldn't I have run into an open door in the dark?"

The two officers, who were authorities upon the damages caused by "blunt instruments" of every description, replied that they thought she might. They looked at each other in a doubt which both resolved in the same way.

"You'd better take Miss Wingrove to see him, Cauldron," the superintendent said. "She understands what she's doing, and I don't think that she'll let us down.

CHAPTER XVII

Interview in the Cells

Miss Wingrove sat in the police-car beside Inspector Cauldron, and said little, having matter for thought, which his discretion did not disturb. But when she spoke it confirmed his opinion that the C.I.D. had found a useful ally in their pursuit of the Mildew gang.

"You'd better not tell me," she said, "what you want done to-night—not till after I've seen Mr. Limbrook. I can't talk about what I don't know."

He answered: "I wasn't thinking of doing that."

"He doesn't know I'm coming?"

"No. It will be quite a surprise."

"I shall be able to see him alone?"

"Yes. We trust you for that."

She smiled her pleasure at this assurance, and added: "I don't think I told you that I might be in Egypt now, if that first quarter's salary had been paid. Mr. Limbrook wanted me to go out with him when he understood how long he was likely to be there, but it would have been very difficult, if not impossible to arrange, and so we agreed to put it off for three or four months.

"I'm glad now that I didn't throw up my work here. But I had been refusing anything that I might have been unable to finish before leaving, and that's why I should be glad of the chance of taking on Mrs. Ashbarton's book...if she's really got anything or me to do.

"So far as our enquiries go, the lady appears to be genuine. The manuscript certainly exists."

"Well that's how she struck me. But it's a fact that she was trying to get Eustace's address out of me on Mr. Wellard's behalf."

"Which may have been quite innocently done. But it doesn't follow that because she is Professor Ashbarton's widow and able to make a genuine offer to you that she isn't one of the Mildew gang. It's our greatest difficulty that there are so many well-connected and otherwise respectable people making money out of this traffic. But for that, we should be more successful in stamping it out."

He spoke with sincerity regarding what he regarded as a fifty-fifty doubt. He knew that even some of the most prominent social and political figures in the country are concerned in the protection of these vile but lucrative rings so that the police may be hindered by them even while they profess eagerness to help. But he saw also that such connections may enable them to enlist the unsuspecting services of other prominent and respectable people and in which category Mrs. Ashbarton should be placed was not yet possible to decide.

Billie Wingrove considered the same doubt from another angle. The book might exist. She would believe it was a genuine offer. That might be true even though Mrs. Ashbarton should augment her income by rendering services to a criminal gang. But if her own activities were to lead to the lady's arrest was it likely that she would be employing her on congenial work during the coming months? The improbability was extreme.

This thought led to others. She considered that while the officers of the C.I.D. were engaged in the highly interesting and proper pursuit of the Mildew gang they were free from anxiety as to whether they would be paid their salaries at the end of the week—or month, or quarter, or at whatever interval superintendents and inspectors expect such remuneration to reach their pockets. But Eustace and she were less comfortably placed. So far Eustace was in jail. Not uncomfortably, perhaps, nor being responsible for his own board. But it was not an address from which he was likely to do much business, nor to apply successfully for any vacant appointment. And, meanwhile, she was to be actively employed in doing herself out of a good job! She asked abruptly: "Inspector, where do I come in?"

Inspector Cauldron was surprised. He had already supplied her with the motive of helping one who, with superficial reason, he regarded as her fiancé, and the more altruistic one of helping to break up a nefarious gang. He had been concerned at the danger she might incur. He would not have been surprised had she shrunk from that, as many girls would have done. He had some scruples still as to whether she understood how great that danger might become, and a growing feeling of personal concern for her safety, which had led him to remind himself that her own interest was centred upon Eustace Limbrook, and that the dubious propriety of the action of the C.I.D. in keeping an innocent man in jail would not be improved if it should ultimately appear that a member of the force had misused the opportunity to make his fiancée's acquaintance and alienate her affections from him.

Beyond that he did not judge that those affections, being definitely placed, would be easy to turn aside. It was true that she wore no engagement ring—a fact which he had observed, with a futile satisfaction, at their first interview. But he knew that formal engagements have ceased to be an invariable prelude to matrimony, and the statement he had just heard, that she had been giving up her work to join Mr. Limbrook in Egypt, had been of a plain significance.

By every count Billie Wingrove was forbidden fruit, from which he had better turn his thoughts before they were tempted to the folly of a first bite. And actually he did not know her at all! He had not thought her to be one who would raise the question of payment for what she did. Not, at least, at such a moment as this.

"We can hardly settle anything about that now," he temporized.

"No doubt it—but we're almost there now."

"Oh, you needn't look as though—" She laughed. "I mean, I'm not going on strike. But if I'm not to talk things over with Mr. Limbrook! You know women are always more practical than men. And it just crossed my mind that it's the kicks that seem likely to come to us."

As she spoke the car slackened speed and drew up at the pavement.

Inspector Cauldron had spoken from a distracted mind, but he had not given so much attention to his own thoughts that he had failed to observe the slouching figure of Risky Tubbs obliterate itself up a neighbouring alley. So far, so good. It would, no doubt, be reported within the hour that Miss Wingrove had kept her word.

Eustace Limbrook was in a condition of *ennui* and discontent. The position of a prisoner on remand may be normally described as dull. Yet it usually provides at least one subject—the coming hearing—for anxious thought. Mr. Limbrook lacked even that.

He was bored with confinement and dissatisfied with himself. His stipulation that he should be retained in custody had seemed, when he had made it, to be no more than a prudent precaution, but, even so, his motive had been complicated by the idea that it might incline the police to believe his tale, and the innocence of his own actions, more readily than they might otherwise have been likely to do.

When he learned that they did not question his veracity, Mildew's character being already known, that motive disappeared, and there remained a growing dissatisfaction with himself, a growing restlessness at the inaction which he had chosen. What had appeared prudent in anticipation appeared ignominious in practice. He had resolved that, when Inspector Cauldron should appear—he had been told no more than that he was on the way—he would let him know that he had come to prefer the dangers of freedom to the longer contemplation of those blue-washed walls.

But when the inspector entered it was he who got in the first word: "I've brought someone to see you."

"Not Miss Wingrove?" he asked, making an instant guess at the only one it would be likely to be. To the inspector's surprise, he did not look pleased.

"Yes. She insisted on coming as soon as she heard where you were."

"Well, I'm sorry for that. I'd really rather not see her here. I was just going to say that I'd decided to ask you to let me go. Tell her that I shall be at Charmian Crescent tomorrow, and I'll explain everything there."

Inspector Cauldron hesitated before a proposition which would upset the elaborate plans formulated during the last twenty-four hours. "I'm not sure," he said, "that we could fix it up quite as quickly as that."

"Well, I mustn't be unreasonable. I know I asked to be kept here, though you can't say that I asked to come. Make it the first day that you can."

"It wouldn't be prudent to go back to Charmian Crescent."

"Possibly not. But I expect you could book a room for me somewhere else, and give Miss Wingrove the address. You've no idea how dull it is here."

"No doubt it is. But we were going to ask you to go out today. I mean for a few hours, so that you could do some observing for us, while, if they've traced you at all, they feel sure that you are shut up here. But I didn't want to alarm Miss Wingrove. I meant to talk it over after she's gone."

While he spoke he recalled that lady's blunt and unexpected question, "Where do I come in?" and it occurred to him that Mr. Limbrook might look at matters in the same way. He hastened to add: "Of course, we shan't ask you to this for nothing. Sir Henry was saying that you might be able to get damages from us for false imprisonment in one form or other, but we don't want all that to come out, and I dare say you don't either, if it can be fixed up in another way. Sir Henry would be willing to come to an arrangement with you that would put a decent sum of money into your pocket when we've run these wretches to earth."

"I expect he would," Mr. Limbrook replied rather coldly, "but what I said was that I don't want to stay here. However, I'll see Miss Wingrove, since she's come, and you needn't fear I shall say anything to alarm her. I only want to be sure she won't get involved in this."

Inspector Cauldron would have liked to reply that, if Mr. Limbrook were serious in that desire, he couldn't do better than stay where he was; but, knowing what he did, it would have been an impossible hypocrisy. He retired to fetch Miss Wingrove, considering that the ways of inspectors are hard, and wondering also whether the female is not only more deadly than the male, but, as that young lady had asserted, more practical also. Certainly the hint of reward which he had offered to Mr. Limbrook seemed to have fallen on stony ground. And now he had to introduce these two people, evidently accustomed to confide in each other, pledged or resolved upon opposite reticences, and leave them together in the hope that, when the interview should end, they would prove efficient and willing tools for the purposes which he had in mind. Well, it was not his; it was Superintendent Backwash's plan!

Billie Wingrove was not normally demonstrative. She was one of those young women who think that emotions should be under- rather than over-expressed—an attitude which is consistent with sufficient essential heat both for friendship and love. But she was of a sensitive sympathy also, and she understood without words that Eustace would have preferred to meet her in a different place and with a different tale.

It was true that the failure of the Rushton-Thornville Company was no fault of his, nor could he be greatly blamed for the trick which had made him a successful smuggler of illicit drugs. But it is the fact of failure which counts more than an analysis of its causes, and the fact was here. Billie saw it to be a position where there must be no absence of warmth on her side.

She came forward into the cell as the door closed, with outstretched hands, and lips which were no less ready than they, but she was received in a different manner.

There was no lack of pleasure in his eyes as Eustace greeted her entrance, nor was his voice cold, but the step he took was not forward, but back.

"I'm sorry," he said, "to have to meet you like this. I suppose they'll have told you what a mess I've got myself into?"

"They told me about the mess they've got themselves into. That was how it sounded to me."

"Well, I suppose they have rather," he answered more cheerfully, with some satisfaction at the position being put in that way. "But I was thinking of ourselves rather than them. I didn't want him to bring you here."

"If you're shut up here it's the natural place for me to come."

"It's nice of you to take it like that."

Billie Wingrove sat herself on the table edge, having already ignored an offer of the only chair that the cell contained. "Eustace," she said solemnly, "if you weren't so damned proud, we should always have got on better together. But I didn't think you'd call me a cad."

"You know I've done nothing of the kind. But I've got myself into an infernal hole, and I should have been one myself if I hadn't...."

"You mean," she interrupted, if you hadn't allowed for the possibility that I may have no loyalty and no guts. Well, if you think I'm to say thank you for that! But if you'll stop looking so glum I'll tell you something you never guessed. I've hated the very name of Egypt, and the idea of giving up my work, ever since I promised to join you if you thought you were likely to have a permanent post. And I should have hated about equally going back on anything I'd promised to do. So when I heard you were coming home, if I hadn't understood how sick you must be feeling about it, I should have said I hadn't often had better news.

"But I didn't know then that you were going to be clever enough to get those drug wretches to pay your passage hack, and then lead the police into the soup here in the way you have. Why, if you go the right way about it you'll have them eating out of your hand! When they say you've been here long enough you can just go on reading that Bible and quote St. Paul."

"Quote St. Paul?"

"Well, it may have been Peter or even Silas. I've learnt at my job that memory's a very treacherous thing. But didn't he get put into jail, and when they got frightened at what they'd done, and told him they were going to leave the key on the inside, didn't he get them all on the dither by saying he was quite comfortable where he was, and rather thought he'd prefer to stay?"

"I believe there was something of the sort."

"Well, look it up! There ought to be a lot of money in this if you handle it in the right way."

"As a matter of fact, Cauldron has just been hinting that a payment for compensation may be considered, but they want to call it a reward for information regarding the Mildew gang, and I suppose my pot may depend upon whether they get sufficient evidence for their arrest."

"I don't see why it should. And what can they expect you to do while they keep you here?"

"Perhaps that's hardly fair, it being what I asked them to do." He was on the point of adding that he didn't intend to remain there when he recalled the proposal that he should sally out later in the day, which he had promised not to mention. He ended vaguely: "I don't suppose I shall be here much longer."

"No," she replied, with mendacious truthfulness. "Inspector Cauldron talked about their having plans for you on his way here, but he didn't say what they were."

"You couldn't expect him to do that."

"No, perhaps not."

It was now—and it was evidence of the emotional stress under which the interview had commenced that he had not been more than half conscious of it earlier—that Mr. Limbrook's eyes became concentrated upon a badly bruised chin, and the natural query was met by the unavoidable lie; but from this point the conversation became of a more intimate and personal character, into which intrusion would only be justified so far as it might he essential to understanding of the events with which this narrative is directly concerned, as to which it may be sufficient to say that nothing further passed which it would have annoyed Superintendent Backwash to hear. They parted at last in mutual ignorance of the activities in which they were both likely to be engaged before midnight should come.

CHAPTER XVIII

Again at the Reader Grill

"If she tells the absolute truth about coming here and being taken to see him—about everything, in fact, except what passed when they were alone—and sticks to her tale, as I feel sure we can trust her to do, I don't see why she should be in any great danger," Superintendent Backwash had said during the afternoon, "unless they should have their suspicions aroused by some of our men being about. She may be actually safer if we keep them away."

"I've arranged to keep the place under observation from the other side of the street."

"Well, I don't think you ought to do more than that—not unless something's seen from there which gives you reason to interfere. Is this room they took her to front or back?"

"Back."

"So it would be. Still, it's a risk that she'll have to run."

"Do you think I ought to tell her that she'll be on her own?"

"No. It might make her nervous, and couldn't do any possible good. Of course, if the others should leave, or the place close, without her coming out, it might be necessary to raid it. But short of that—"

"And that might be too late to be any good."

"Possibly. But I've said that I don't see much risk for her. Not, anyway, for tonight. But I don't say it's a job I'd care to give to one of my own girls, and if she pulls it off she'll deserve quite as much as she's ever likely to get."

"She raised the question of what that would be rather pointedly this morning."

"What did you tell her?"

"Practically nothing. She seemed to speak on a sudden impulse, and let it drop."

"Well, it ought to be properly understood. She was right in that. Let her know that you'll be in a better position to talk it over next time you see her. You'd better give her the book of words now and let her go. She mustn't be kept here longer than she can explain."

This conversation took place while Billie waited in an adjoining room for instructions concerning her second interview with Mr. Wellard at the Reader Grill. Ten minutes later she was able to leave, for they were soon said. To interpret them circumstantially and convincingly must rest with her, at no less than a deadly risk, but she had some confidence that she would not fail.

Having disposed of her, the inspector went back to interview Mr. Limbrook, to whom he proposed what was neither a difficult nor a dangerous occupation. There are premises almost opposite the Reader Grill which can be approached from the back, through the Carew Mews, in which a vacant fourth-floor room had been secured by telephone from the estate agents without any officer of the C.I.D. appearing upon the scene.

It was an improbability of many thousands to one that the private car which pulled up in Thomas Street would be observed by any adherent of the Mildew gang as Eustace Limbrook left it in company with Inspector Cauldron and two other plain-clothes officers and went through the Mews, by a back-stair entrance, to the attic room from which it was possible to observe all who left or entered the Reader Grill.

It was 3:30 P.M. when the watch began, and it was fruitful almost immediately. A man came out whom Mr. Limbrook identified with certainty. "That," he said, "is one of the two whom I saw there."

"That," Inspector Cauldron replied with equal confidence, "is the man Miss Wingrove knows as Wellard." He felt that this identification alone justified all the trouble which had been taken to secure that post of observation, for though neither of the narratives which either she or Eustace Limbrook would, so far, be able to give would be of much weight without corroboration, yet the two together, being attached to the same man, had a very different value. The only trouble was that, though it might be pleasant to put Wellard in a secure place, the net was spread for those of more importance than he.

The watch continued until a few minutes to seven without further result. It was an experience by which Mr. Limbrook was neither disappointed nor surprised. He had been successful in identifying one of the men, and it appeared mere luck that it had been during the first few minutes rather than the last. Inspector Cauldron could say nothing of the reason he had had for expecting that they might be passing in toward the end of the time. But as seven approached he felt—though he had impressed upon Miss Wingrove that she must be after rather than before her time—that he could risk no more. He said that the hours during which Mr. Limbrook had maintained that unrelaxing watch were as long a period as he could ask him to occupy in such a manner, and that the car was now waiting to take him back. Tomorrow they would discuss what further was to be done. Mr. Limbrook said that it couldn't be too soon for him. He went back with one of the officers, and Inspector Cauldron, with the other, resumed the watch.

Now that the hour of Miss Wingrove's appointment approached, it was reasonable to suppose that Wellard would return to meet her; but that did not occur. At a few minutes after seven she entered. But Wellard did not appear, nor did any other known or suspected member of the Mildew gang, nor anyone who was otherwise under the notice of the police. Neither, as the hour passed, did she come out. Eight-thirty came, and this position continued...nine o'clock...ten.

Could there be another exit? Another entrance? Inspector Cauldron felt sure there was not. There was the main door to the shop, and an entry immediately beside it, which led to a kitchen door. He felt confident that there was no other approach.

Yet he could swear, and Sergeant Porson was as sure as he, that Wellard had not returned, nor Miss Wingrove left.

At ten-thirty the Grill closed and the staff were observed to leave. "If it should close and she should not come out—" Superintendent Backwash had said. Inspector Cauldron went round by Thomas Street, after telling Sergeant Porson to remain at the post of observation until he should see him reach the door of the grill, when he was to follow. At ten-forty they went up the side entrance together and picked the lock of the kitchen door, which was quite easily done. They examined premises of most innocent appearance, which were dark, vacant, and quiet. They searched thoroughly. They identified the room in which Miss Wingrove had been interviewed on the first occasion. They found no trace of her or of the clues which criminals are supposed to leave with monotonous regularity on the scenes of their evil deeds. Observation suggested that the room had been occupied by several people, and it was clear that cleaning-up operations were deferred till the morning hours, but there was no crime in that. They found no back exit from the premises.

Inspector Cauldron went back to Scotland Yard dissatisfied with himself and more disturbed in mind with fears for Miss Wingrove's safety than a hard-headed inspector of the C.I.D. should have permitted himself to be. Anyway, it was a poor tale to tell to the superintendent, who, with Chief Inspector Tolbooth, was waiting to hear the result of the evening's enterprise.

"I couldn't even," he ended disconsolately, "get any clue to what happened. There must have been three or four people together in that room where they had her before, but you can't make much out of that. There hadn't been any attempt to hide anything or clear it away. Not that we could see. And in the whole place we could find no trace of a struggle or excessive disorder of any kind."

"You don't even know," Chief Inspector Tolbooth remarked, "that she went to that room at all."

"We don't know anything except that she disappeared.

"How long would it take you," the superintendent asked, "to run Wellard in?"

"Porson says he could probably have him in a few hours."

"That would be unless he's on the alert. He may have some exceptional friends. But our first trouble would be that there's no evidence that he's been concerned in this. All you seem to have done is to provide two witnesses that he wasn't there. But there's one thing quite certain. If they've taken the risk of making away with Miss Wingrove, they must have known that she was playing a double game: and, if they know that, they must know also that it was in conjunction with us, and that we shan't be likely to take such a thing lying down. They wouldn't try it at all without having everything organized very thoroughly and feeling confident they could pull it off without too much risk for themselves."

"Well, they've taken the first trick. I thought I ought to let you know before I did anything further. But I don't see what I can do better now than to go back and have a more thorough search."

Chief Inspector Tolbooth broke into the conversation again: "You might telephone Miss Wingrove's hotel first and ask whether she's in bed there."

"It doesn't seem to be much of a chance. Not if you think that either Porson or I have any eyes in our heads. But it's worth trying, of course."

"I suppose," the superintendent asked, "there's a night-porter at the Envoy?"

"Yes. Of some sort. I believe there is."

Superintendent Backwash glanced at a clock that ornamented the opposite wall. It was one A.M. He picked up his desk telephone and gave instructions that he was to be put through to the Envoy Hotel, but without mentioning that it was a police call.

A moment later he passed the receiver over to Inspector Cauldron, with the remark: "You'd better take this. You know the ropes there better than I."

The night operator appeared to be of a sleepy or incurious disposition. Being asked for room Number 73, he made the required connection without troubling to reply, or enquiring the name of the midnight disturber of a lady's peace. With mingled astonishment and relief Inspector Cauldron heard a voice he knew reply, with some sharpness of irritation: "Yes. Miss Wingrove. Who's that?"

"It's I. Cauldron. I just wanted to know that you got back safely."

"Look here, Clara," came the angry response. "It's past a joke ringing me up at this hour. I never promised. I only said if I could. I've been busy tonight."

"I suppose that means that you're overheard?"

"What do you think? Anyway, I don't want to be waked up at this hour. I'll probably ring you some time tomorrow—that's today now. When I'm in Great Russell Street, more likely than not. I'm not going on talking now. It's too cold."

"Then we'll hear from you in the morning?"

Inspector Cauldron found himself cut off. "I expect," he said, "you think you'd better put someone else on to this job."

"What did she say?"

"Nothing. She was evidently afraid of being overheard. She'll ring us tomorrow."

"Wise girl."

Superintendent Backwash chewed the top end of a pencil in a contemplative manner. "Someone," he said, "has been rather a fool. But it's too soon to say who. Anyhow, we've put our foot into it with a splash. How many people saw you trespassing at the Reader Grill?"

"No one that I'm aware of. We got in quietly enough. Of course, if they were watching—"

"Which is improbable. You'd better get back and obliterate every sign that you broke in or looked things over inside. Everything—Miss Wingrove's safety, in particular—may depend on how you can do that."

"Yes. We'll do that, if it takes half the night. I can't help wondering what sort of a mug I've been."

"Or, perhaps, I? You had orders from me to break in if you didn't see the lady come out. But we can discuss that better when we know what happened. By the way, we've just had a report in from the Preston police. They haven't made any progress. They've combed the whole district without finding Houghton or anything more to the point than some old photographs, which we no longer need."

"Well, we don't want him just yet."

"No. But we soon may."

Inspector Cauldron did not dispute that. He had, indeed, little disposition to dispute anything, his own incompetence least of all. He went hack to the Reader Grill to remove the traces of his invasion, wondering the while what the true explanation could be, and in what guise of incapacity he might have to appear on the next day.

CHAPTER XIX

Mr. Mildew Upon the Scene

Mr. Catsgill, of Timbrel, Timbrel, and Catsgill, was the only surviving partner of that old and highly reputable firm of solicitors, who had carried on a lucrative business for five generations in the vicinity of Lincoln's Inn Fields.

It was about six years earlier that Mr. Catsgill had been faced by sudden and disastrous financial difficulty. Stock Exchange speculations, which had at first been moderate in amount and conservative in character, had become gradually bolder with a monotony of success, and then encountered an overwhelming reverse. Faced by the alternatives of holding on to a falling market or selling at almost ruinous loss, he had resolved to back his own judgement further and ride out a storm which he thought would be quickly done. In the result he had found himself in a position in which, without speedy help, he must be ruined indeed. He had many affluent clients, but to disclose his rashness to one of them would have been, even though compassion had brought relief—which was an improbable eventuality—to have committed financial suicide in an altered form. Men do not commonly entrust their monies and mortgage deeds to solicitors who gamble beyond their depth. The reputation of his firm for cautious probity was of an importance he dared not risk. In this extremity, almost incredible to himself, he had thought of Cornelius Mildew a wealthy and genial club acquaintance who was no client of his, and of whom he had heard a tale of large-scale generosity which gave him courage to put his own trouble before him.

The immediate result had been better than could have been reasonably anticipated. A note to his brokers over Mr. Mildew's signature had kept his account open and mitigated the severity of losses it was no longer possible to avoid. An ample loan had re-established a banking account which had become, not merely exhausted, but dangerously overdrawn.

What had the generous saviour required for this essential assistance? It had seemed, less than nothing at all. He had made opportunity of the occasion to transfer some of his legal business, which had been in the equally respectable hands of Messrs. Miller & Talkingbooth, to Mr. Catsgill's office. This business had been of a quite innocent character, such as is normally incidental to the transactions of wealthy men, but, after a time, the solicitor's benefactor had confided to him that a proportion of his wealth was derived from transactions in "chemicals," of international magnitude, which it was sometimes necessary to conceal from the greeds and jealousies of the European governments through whose custom-houses they would, under normal circumstances, be allowed to pass.

Mr. Catsgill understood vaguely that his client was interested in substances which might be useful either in peaceful industry or in the production of munitions of war. He might not approve, but his opinion had not been asked. Mr. Mildew had a manner which inspired confidence. He obtained important legal advice which was, at first, more or less legitimately given, and of much advantage to him in the illicit transactions that he controlled.

At a later date, Mr. Catsgill came to suspect, and subsequently knew, that he had received no more than a partial and misleading confidence, and had been advising upon matters of definite criminality, Mr. Mildew, being challenged, admitted this with an engaging frankness. His previous reticence, he said, had been solely out of consideration for Mr. Catsgill. He defended his occupation with the facile and specious arguments common to those of his kind, who maintain an outward front of respectability, and have not yet passed through the solving process of a criminal cell. He instanced the wealth of brewers, for which a peerage is a frequent reward, as though the distribution of alcohol were a particularly meritorious activity. He urged that, if he should decline to handle the traffic, it would still go on, and its profits would pass into worse hands. Offered to one who had benefited so freely from his generosity, it was an argument difficult to decline.

Mr. Catsgill may not have been convinced, but he was talking to a man who had done much for him, and to whom he was still heavily indebted. Indeed, more heavily than at first, for compound interest accrues, and Mr. Mildew had put all talk of settlement easily aside, until the markets should recover to a point which they showed no disposition to reach.

Gently, imperceptibly, but definitely at last, Mr. Catsgill became aware that he was actively assisting with all the resources of his legal knowledge a gang of traffickers in illicit drugs, with no more remaining subterfuge than the discreet obliquities with which it was customary among themselves to conceal the nature of what they did.

That he should himself be criminally involved would have seemed as wildly improbable as—till it happened—that he should sink himself in speculative a liabilities beyond his power to honour. Even his new clients, he had many occasions to observe, acted with such aloof discretion in what they did that the menace of the law only rumbled in their ears faintly, from far below. But the moral weakness of a man to whom prosperity had come by a path which had trained character less than brain, acted a second time as it had before.

"There is a little matter arisen," Mr. Mildew had said, as he took his familiar seat in the solicitor's private office, during the afternoon of the day which was to end for Inspector Cauldron in so unsatisfactory a manner, "on which I should like your advice, and possibly some assistance also. But perhaps I should hardly call it a little matter. I don't know. The fact is its either nothing at all, as seems most probable since yesterday, or the most dangerous problem with which our organization has had to deal since I took control more than ten years ago.

Mr. Catsgill was a man of some presence, and a typically legal cast of countenance, excepting only that he wore a short beard, formally trimmed. Now he looked properly concerned, as such a preamble required him to do, but it was no more than a professional attitude. He was used to hearing the troubles which occurred from time to time in controlling the operations of his client's lawless retinue, or outwitting the customs and the police of a dozen lands. Dangers that were remote to his client could not be knocking at his door. But he recognized Mr. Mildew's tone as being more serious than he remembered hearing from him since the catastrophe which had left £13,000 worth of drugs in the hands of the French police, and might have meant worse things than that, had not a certain Jules Moreau been most opportunely killed at the level crossing which he appeared to have been using at an unfortunate moment.

Also, he had heard a word which he did not like. Advice? Yes. He was used to giving that. Even criminals are entitled to consult their solicitors. And it would be hard, indeed, to show that he had gone beyond what the law allowed. But *assistance*? That was a vague word. It might mean little or much. Certainly he must show no sign of objecting, in advance of hearing what it might be that his client had in mind.

"I expect," he said, with a pleasant, carefully graduated gravity, "that you'll he equal to dealing with it. But let's hear what it is." He settled himself to listen with attention to a tale that was fully told.

"Yes," he said, when he had heard all. "I see what you mean. I should say it's nothing at all. You bought the man before he was taken up, and, in any case, he'd gain nothing by saying he'd been drug-smuggling a fortnight before. It wouldn't be listened to, more likely than not. And he's got his own trouble to think of, without bringing in that. It looks to me as though you've got the chance of making him grateful by coming to the rescue now; and after that he might be very useful to you."

"Yes...we shall know more of that when we hear what the girl has to say."

"Probably it will come out all right. But it was certainly a queer thing that he should get arrested the way he did."

"So I've been thinking ever since I heard it yesterday. Still, queer things do happen. And it explains what's been baffling us for the past week—the way that he disappeared"'

"Yes. It's always best to know what the trouble's likely to be. You think Wellard's fit to handle the girl?"

"No. I'm quite sure he isn't. I've called him off. It's absolutely vital to know whether she's been got at by the police, or being loyal to us. The fact is, that's the point I wanted to talk over with you. I want you to see her yourself tonight."

The solicitor heard this with an expressionless face. He asked: "Do you think that would be wise? Are you proposing to bring her here?"

"No. I can arrange it so that she won't know who you are; and she won't be seen with you at all."

"I suppose you will be there?"

"No. There will be no occasion."

Mr. Catsgill became silent. It was evidently a proposition, he did not like. Mr. Mildew did not appear to observe that, but he added in explanation: "It is a place to which I have never been. It is not commonly used, and is not under the observation, of the police."

"You are sure of that?"

"Sure. The way by which you will enter and leave has been prepared against such an occasion as this. We have prudence—and means—to provide against storm while the skies are clear."

Mr. Catsgill may have been impressed by this, or he may have had other thoughts. But he made no further objection.

"I will see the young woman," he said, "if you will tell me how I should best proceed."

Mr. Mildew laid a small key on the table. "This," he said, "will give you entrance to the offices of Sutor & Sutor, in Ryder Street, Number 22, on the fourth floor.

"They are a respectable firm of consulting engineers. The police take no interest in them, which they have no reason to do. The offices are on the top floor. There is no lift. At the hour you will arrive, Sutor—there is only one partner of that name alive now—and his clerk will have left. You may find Wellard there, or he may arrive a few minutes later. He must be present on this occasion, as it will be best that the girl should meet someone she already knows. But after that he will not be needed. He can handle the riff-raff pedlars, but for a matter of this kind he has shown himself to be no more than a clumsy fool."

"I have not had the pleasure of Mr. Wellard's previous acquaintance."

"No. And there'll be no need to mention names now. You'll know he's the man, because he'll be recognized by the girl. He won't be told your name, and I don't suppose you'll ever see him again. He will know no more than that someone in higher authority than himself will be coming to hear the tale the girl has to tell."

"Well, I will see her."

Mr. Mildew heard this with satisfaction. He had not doubted that his request—it might be called his order—would be obeyed; but he had anticipated encountering a more pronounced reluctance. He could not suppose that the solicitor would render him the dubious services he received but for the financial fetters which he had fastened upon him. And yet even that must be no more than conjecture, so reticent had Mr. Catsgill always been, so frugal of word or look.

He might be satisfied that their mutual discretion was sufficient to guard him from any possible danger. He might consider the financial advantages which he received to be most easily earned, and the first business contact with this wealthy client as his fortunate day.

Even now, he might recognize the request that he should interview Miss Wingrove as an additional evidence of the scrupulous care with which every element of risk was examined, and, if necessary, removed from their most respectable paths.

But, whether he went reluctantly or with a ready will, Mr. Mildew was confident that he would make no mistake. Lawyers are used to judge the characters and motives of those they meet. His scrutiny of the young woman, his methods of handling her, would be very different from the crudity of those which Wellard had used with such needless violence, and doubtful result. Mr. Mildew showed no less than his usual soundness of judgement when he concluded that the experienced lawyer should be more than a match for the girl who would have no knowledge of the calibre of the man she met.

There remained only one thing to do.

"If," he said, "you will kindly let me have a half-sheet of paper, I will make out a receipt."

Asking for no explanation of this inconsequent remark, Mr. Catsgill supplied his client's request. Mr. Mildew produced a fountain-pen.

He wrote out a receipt for three months' interest upon the considerable sum of the lawyer's liability to himself, dating it for the next day. He handed it silently to Mr. Catsgill, who read it with the same absence of remark, blotted it with care, and put it into a drawer of his desk.

They both understood without words that he had received a very substantial fee for the work to be done that night. He had also been reminded, without the offensive crudity of words, of how entirely his reputation was in Mr. Mildew's hands.

That gentleman, who did not waste words when his business was concluded, now rose and left, saying that he would call tomorrow at the same hour.

Mr. Catsgill drew out his private cheque-book, and wrote a cheque to himself for the amount of the interest for which he had just taken a receipt. He did not intend that his books should fail to confirm the payment which he was supposed to have made. His hand stretched to the bell, and then paused.

He sat for some time, looking at the cheque, with his mind in an indecision he had often felt before, but always resolved in the same way.

He did not like the errand he had undertaken. Curiously, he disliked it because he felt it to be an affront to his dignity, even more than for any danger it might hold. Normally, it was the etiquette of his profession that others—even important and wealthy clients—would come to him, as Mr. Mildew had just done. That had not always been so. In earlier centuries, the lawyer had commonly been expected to ring the bell at his client's door. Perhaps this fact renders men of his profession more tenacious of this recent dignity than they would otherwise be.

Anyway, he resented the idea of going after his usual business hours to an office where he was to sit waiting till this man Wellard might appear. It seemed not only to emphasize his bondage to Mildew that he should have been required to do this; but to be of the nature of a threat for the future years. What might he not be asked to do tomorrow, if he should do this today?

If he should inform the police! How often he had considered that. They might give a substantial reward. He supposed they would, if the information should be important enough. But to the extent of the debt which was upon him? He thought not.

Nor could he consider that even the conviction of Mildew would relieve him from the liability to discharge it. It was possible that it might. Actually, it was still law that the property of a convicted felon passes to the Crown, and it was a debt which the Crown might not oblige him to pay. But here was a double doubt. The severity of that law is seldom enforced against the rights of innocent dependents or heirs. And the debt was for money legitimately lent. It was fairly due. No, he could not be sure of relief. It might be ruin to inform the police, even if he should otherwise escape the vengeance of Mildew's powerful and ruthless gang.

And all this was on the assumption that he would be believed! That was always the point at which he put such speculations aside. It was astonishing how little evidence he could produce: how little he knew. He had always been consulted in privacy. Nothing had been upon paper. Nothing known to a third party. Little mention of dates, or names, or places.

All this had had the aspect of a prudence which he approved. But it cut with a double edge. He might do no more than make statements the police would discredit on enquiry. He did not know that Mildew was already under suspicion.

But he knew that he would be a lost man if Mildew should have any suspicion of him. There would be no impartial trial, no opportunity for defence, no jury to be convinced. The judgement might be delivered without his knowledge: the sentence merciless, certain, swift. No, the path of safety lay in loyalty to the man from whom he received more benefits than the police would be likely to bestow.

And, after all, if Mildew did not control this traffic, someone, else would. It might easily be in worse hands. His hand reached out to the bell.

"Smailes," he said to the clerk who entered, "I want this cashed in pound notes. Yes, the whole amount."

When the money came he locked it in his own safe, but an entry in his private cash-book would show it to be paid to Cornelius Mildew tomorrow as interest on his debt to him. His creditor had called upon him today, demanding a payment on account of interest which was overdue. Being put off, he had said that he would call again tomorrow. After that he had decided that it must be found, and drawn it in readiness for the second call. What could be more natural than that?

It gave a reason for the calls, and it showed Mildew in the light of a dunning creditor, rather than as one who bribed him to illegal acts. This observation of how cunningly Mildew acted might promise security while they walked on the same road, but it held no encouragement to attempt betrayal. Mr. Catsgill directed his mind to how he would deal with the girl.

CHAPTER XX

Another Way to the Reader Grill

At 6:30 P.M. Mr. Catsgill mounted the stairs of 22 Ryder Street, knocked twice upon a door which bore the name of Sutor and Sutor, and, receiving no reply, inserted the key which Mr. Mildew had given him into the lock and entered an empty room. He saw a clerks office, small, but, to his experienced eyes, showing signs that a regular business was carried on. He passed through it to an inner room, better furnished, and being evidently that which was occupied during the day by the surviving Sutor. He saw no door except those through which he had come.

Mr. Mildew had been vague as to how he was to be joined by Wellard, but there had been an implication that there was a private passage through these offices to the premises of the Reader Grill. Mr. Catsgill looked round with natural curiosity for a door which he could not see. He concluded that there must be a passage outside, and probably a door, which Wellard would be able to show him. In the meantime, should he lock that through which he had entered? He considered this, and decided to do so. If Wellard were to come that way he would presumably have the means of entrance, while, if Mr. Sutor should unexpectedly return, it would be about equally difficult to explain his presence whether the door were locked or not, and a turned key would prevent less legitimate intrusion. But he did not anticipate Mr. Sutor's return. He knew Mr. Mildew's methods to be less bungling than that.

So he went back to the outer office, locked the door, and returned to find a man facing him who had obviously entered where a revolving bookcase had turned, showing a gap in the wall, beyond which was the room where Billie Wingrove had been fed by Mrs. Ashbarton, and struck by the man who was now before him, on the previous evening.

"Mr. Wellard, I presume?" he said, without cordiality, seeing a man whose appearance he did not like.

"Yes. I suppose you've locked the door?"

The question was unceremoniously put, but with no assurance in the speaker's voice. Mr. Wellard knew nothing of the identity of the colleague who had been thrust upon him or of his status within the gang. He was prepared to bully or cringe. When he found that this bearded stranger, of professional aspect, and whom he recognized to be better, though not more expensively, dressed than himself, made no reply, and looked at him with no friendliness in his eyes, he altered the manner of his address.

"If you'll come this way, sir," he said, stepping aside to allow Mr. Catsgill to precede him through the gap. "Miss Wingrove may be here any time now."

When they had passed through it he swung the partition slowly back into place. It had a similar bookcase upon the farther side, so that it was heavy and hard to move, smoothly mounted though it might be.

Mr. Wellard, as one trying to make conversation, went on: "It can't be moved at all from the Ryder Street side. Only from this. I don't suppose Sutor knows anything about it. I didn't till I had instructions this afternoon, though I suppose I'm the only one who's been making regular use of the place. It took me some time to get it to move, hut it should work more easily now."

He looked at Mr. Catsgill narrowly as he said this for a thought came that, if he were high in the counsels of the gang, he would probably have been better informed, but otherwise that he might be only another who, like himself, took orders from principals whom he never met. But the lawyer made no reply. He asked, as though he had not heard what was said: "When is the young woman due?"

"Seven. But she might be a bit earlier."

"Tell me what you thought of her, if there's time before she arrives."

Mr. Wellard, after unlocking the door of the room, which he had secured while he had opened the panel, though there had been little reason to doubt that his orders to be left alone would not be strictly obeyed, answered readily enough.

"She's a good-looker and seemed sure of herself at first. Quite a cool hand. She turned Mrs. Ashbarton down cold. I thought there'd be more trouble with her than I had in the end.

"She was cheeky, even when I got her alone, till I showed her we weren't going to stand any nonsense, and then she gave way so quick that I saw she'd been pretending pluck that she hadn't got. ... And after that money talked, as it always will."

"You didn't tell her anything of the business Mr. Limbrook had been asked to undertake?"

"I said no more than I was obliged, beyond letting her know that we were prepared to get him out of his present mess, and give him a good job after that. Of course, there's no knowing what he'll have said to her now."

"No...nor the police."

"They can't guess anything if he hasn't blabbed. And even then she couldn't add much to what they'd have heard from him."

Mr. Catsgill felt less sure about that. He knew that the legal value of a statement—especially if it be of an improbable character—may be much more than doubled if it be confirmed by a second witness. He thought, indeed, that it had been imprudent to interfere at all, whatever fear might have urged. He had a passing doubt that Mildew might have shown less than his usual judgement in this, until he recalled that there had been no remotest reason to think that Limbrook had been in the hands of the police until the girl had disclosed it, and that this unexpected development had been handled by Wellard in his own way, which Mildew had not approved—had shown how gravely he doubted its wisdom by enlisting his own services in this exceptional manner. Well, he must keep an open mind till he should see her and hear what she had to say. And after that he would act as the occasion required. There was a sound of light, firm steps ascending the stairs.

Billie came up quickly, conscious that she was a little late, and she showed some colour, and even a slight shortness of breath, either from the steepness of those narrow stairs or the excitement of what she did.

She looked at the man she knew and—with more satisfaction—at one whom she did not.

The latter had risen at her entrance. He placed a chair for her. He was quick to speak, not wishing to give his companion an opportunity of offering to introduce him, and having either to give or refuse his name.

"Miss Wingrove, is it not? So I supposed. You know Mr. Wellard already. We are hoping that you bring good news of our young friend. But there is no hurry. The stairs must be—are rather steep."

The words put Billie more at ease than she would have been with Wellard, now seated farther away, and leaving the conversation to the lawyer, as he had been instructed to do. That was well, and yet she felt, with a sudden fear, that it might be harder to lie convincingly to this stranger than to the man she had met before. It is less repugnant to deceive a foe than one who has the eyes of a friend.

"Oh," she said, "I'm not as breathless as that. Though there are rather a lot of stairs. But I don't know that you'll call it good news. Of course, Mr. Limbrook will be glad for you to help him. I thought that was good news for him rather than you. He seemed rather surprised as well as glad. He thought you mightn't like to get mixed up with a police matter."

Mr. Catsgill looked at her keenly as she said this. How much did it imply that she knew?

"I don't quite understand what you mean by that," he said quietly. "Giving evidence of identity to secure the release of someone who has been arrested in error is what no decent man should object to do."

"If you don't understand, I'm sure I don't. I thought you might. But Mr. Limbrook didn't say anything definite. I think he was afraid something might be overheard which would do more harm than good. But I may have been wrong about that. It was just a guess.

"You mean you only saw him in the presence of the police?"

"Not exactly. I was supposed to see him alone. But there was a policeman not far off, so that you couldn't be sure. But I got the idea that he didn't come to you before because he was afraid that you might deny knowing him now that he's got into this mess, and, if you had done that, it would have made his position worse."

"If he thought that, it wasn't very complimentary to us. But now, if we identify him, they'll let him go?"

"Yes. How can they do anything else? They know he isn't Houghton already. I feel certain of that. I believe they knew it even before I identified him. I think it's they who are in the mess now.

"They took me back to Scotland Yard after I'd seen him, and went all over it again. But they'll be glad if Mr. Mildew will identify him as having come from Egypt in the same boat. They say that will be final, and I think they'll be glad to have some evidence which they can say Mr. Limbrook ought to have mentioned before."

"What name did you say?"

"Mr. Mildew."

Mr. Catsgill looked at Mr. Wellard with some interrogative surprise, and that gentleman looked blankly puzzled, as, in fact, he was. Actually he had never before heard Mr. Mildew's name mentioned in this connection, Mr. Limbrook, at his interview with him, having said little and listened much. "I didn't mention any names," he said.

"No," Billie agreed readily, "but Mr. Limbrook

"What did he say?" It was Mr. Catsgill who asked.

"He said that Mr. Mildew had been very kind to him before they sailed, and had offered to get him a position before they landed, but he didn't know that he'd feel the same after hearing that he was in jail, however it might have happened."

"Then will the police be communicating direct with the gentleman you mention?"

"No. I told them to leave that to me."

"And they agreed?"

"Yes. After I'd seen Mr. Limbrook and I told them that was how he preferred it to be."

"He wished you to arrange it through us? He hadn't met Mr. Mildew here?"

"No. But he said it was through Mr. Wellard and his friends that everything had been arranged since he landed. I understood that Mr. Mildew is the one who can prove he was on the boat and that I could get in touch with him through Mr. Wellard."

"You told the police that?"

The questions had been asked with a quiet rapidity which inclined Billie to answer with a similar readiness. If she paused now it was for no more than a second which might have no significance. But it was a second which did not escape the notice of the one who had questioned her with such quick persistence. "I didn't go into details with them if that's what you mean. I didn't see why I should. I told them that I could arrange for Mr. Mildew to identify Eustace and they could leave that to me."

"The police usually prefer to make such enquiries themselves."

"I dare say they do. But I suppose they're not usually in such a hole. They may think it best in this case to fall in with what Mr. Limbrook wishes."

"Yes. So they may. When do they expect to hear from you again?"

"I told them I'd ring them up. It might be tonight."

"And Mr. Limbrook will be willing to take up work for us when he comes out? I suppose you'll be glad to feel he's making money again?"

"He said he was on your business when he was arrested. But he didn't seem to wish to talk about that. It seemed to me that it was because he thought something might be overheard, so I didn't say much."

"I can see that you are a young lady of discretion. You can ring up here tomorrow about this time, or earlier, and I will undertake to have a message of some importance ready for you. You'd better ask for a message from Mr. Wellard. There'll be no need to give your own name if you do that."

Mr. Catsgill rose at this, making it clear that, on his side, there was no more to be said. Billie rose also, well content in the belief that she had won the confidence of these difficult and dangerous men. At least, it seemed, she was to be allowed to go safely away. There was to be no second bruise on the jaw.

The one she had had was still black, and she had observed Mr. Catsgill's eyes upon it while they had talked. Did he know how it had been given? Probably so. And yet, possibly not.

She would have felt less satisfaction in what she had done, and less confidence in her own security, had she known his thought:

"She is not a girl who would become docile because she was struck like that. This man Wellard must be a fool. It is he who was bamboozled by her."

This conclusion became certainty when she had shown that second of hesitation in answering the question to which those before had been intended to lead. She had hesitated because she had a momentary doubt as to what it would be wise to reply. Evidently she was not stating facts: she was simply repeating what she had been told to say, or what she had thought they would like to hear. Now he saw that she had left her bag on the floor by her chair, where she had placed that inevitable companion of the modern pocketless woman when she sat down. He supposed that she did that deliberately, as an excuse for intruding upon them again, to overhear something not intended for her. Or perhaps it might contain something designed to mislead them further.

On this point he was wrong, attributing to her a subtlety which she had not used. Actually, she had overlooked the bag, which is an indication of the measure of her relief upon finding that her tale was accepted, and that she was free to go, the significance of which any woman will understand. She was down the first stairs before she became aware of her oversight and then stood in a moment's reluctance, gathering courage to return.

Meanwhile, Mr. Catsgill, having followed her to the door, and closed it after her, turned to say: "Well, that sounds all right." And then: "If you'll swing the partition again I'll go back the same way."

He spoke to one who was in the good humour of self-congratulation, which these words confirmed. Mr. Wellard might be truculent in his general attitude to his fellow men, but he had a genuine fear of the unknown heads of the gang to which he belonged. If no worse should follow, a blunder might mean an end to the easy living he now enjoyed. And even that might be too much to hope.

He had not heard of anyone leaving those unlawful ranks with a mere dismissal and loss of the emoluments he had been receiving. They either rendered satisfactory service—or disappeared.

And he had judged, by the manner and speech of this stranger who had been thrust upon him, that he had not come as a comrade to assist, but rather as an inspector to assess, and perhaps condemn what had been done.

Now he felt confident that he would be exonerated, even approved; and to have done well in a matter of such delicacy and importance would mean reward, which was always given with liberality.

He was readily obedient to the direction to open the way to the Ryder Street office. He did not even delay to ascertain that the door was locked, as it would have been prudent to do. The nameless stranger was at the door, and should see to that. Mr. Wellard merely obeyed the instructions which he received.

The swivel moved slowly upon a pivot well mounted, but long unused. The gap had not become wide enough for Mr. Catsgill's passage when the feet of Miss Wingrove were heard remounting the stairs.

"You'd better close that for a moment," Mr. Catsgill easily, "I think Miss Wingrove's coming back."

"But the door's locked, isn't it?" Mr. Wellard gasped, straining to reverse what he had done, and failing to close it before Billie, with no opposition from the solicitor, entered the room.

She paused, staring, in a natural surprise, at the gap in the wall, where the bookcase from the opposite side had commenced to show. Mr. Wellard, seeing that it was too late for concealment, had ceased a useless exertion, and stood ready to execute any order for violence he might receive. But Mr. Catsgill was unperturbed.

"I think, Miss Wingrove," he said, "you forgot your bag when you left rather abruptly. I suppose you have come back for that. It will give us an opportunity of showing you another way down. If you will be good enough, Mr. Wellard, to make it wide enough for us to pass, we will all go together."

Mr. Wellard, with some shortness of breath, he being a man who did too little, and ate too much, widened the gap through which they were to leave, and Billie, scarcely conscious that she had picked up the bag, looked on with a bloodless face.

Had they expected her return? Did they now plan her end? There was a vague, horrible suggestion of the methods of Sweeny Todd in the widening gap of the wall. She had an impulse to run.

Had there been any movement to intercept her, there would have been a scurry of flight which one at least of those she feared would have been energetic to block. But the quiet authority in Mr. Catsgill's voice, which assumed rather than ordered, kept her on the side of panic at which convention will still rule. Her heart beat fast. Her instinct feared. But her reason was not sufficiently moved to rouse her will to the point of active opposition. She saw no movement to detain her, no sign of resentment at her discovery of that unusual method of exit.

Mr. Wellard, having opened the way, stood back. He had expected to leave by the stairs, after letting Mr. Catsgill through, and closing the gap. He was mystified by the course of events, and the casual manner in which Mr. Catsgill had taken Miss Wingrove's inopportune return. He wondered: had he seen the bag? Had he expected her to come back? Had he purposely omitted to lock the door? Quietude of manner was, to his experience, no assurance that treachery or violence might not lurk behind the suavity of his speech.

But he saw it as a matter in which he had ceased to have any responsibility, except to obey: to be watchful for word or sign.

Mr. Catsgill asked: "You can close it from the further side?"

"Yes. But not open it again."

"Very well. There will be no occasion for that. This way, Miss Wingrove, if you please."

He led the way into the further office, and Billie followed him, wondering whether she were not committing a folly for which even her life might pay. Mr. Wellard, in almost equal doubt, though without her occasion for fear, came last, and, with the same exertion as before, though this time with the assistance of Mr. Catsgill's rather perfunctory hand, closed the aperture.

They went down the stairs in the same order, and without words, until they came to the hall, where Mr. Catsgill paused.

"It will be best," he said, "that Miss Wingrove should leave first. Wait here a moment, Wellard. I will return."

He walked with her the short length of the hall. Mr. Wellard heard him say: "Miss Wingrove, you will understand, of course, that what you have seen is not to be mentioned to anyone. If we could not trust each other in so small a matter, it would have the most serious consequences, not only for yourself, but for—"

The end of the sentence was lost, but its meaning was plain. There were a few more words which were beyond hearing, and then Mr. Catsgill came back. The previous note of authority was more evident in his voice as he said: "Wellard, it is essential that you should not mention what has occurred to *anyone*. I mean that literally. It is not a matter for your discretion. You will do well to put it from your mind as though it had not been. It is a test of the girl's good faith—and of her fitness for what we may require her to do—and if it should fail, we must know *absolutely* that it could have been revealed through no lips but hers. I shall report that you have done well."

With these words he left, showing his usual face to the world until he gained the shelter of his own home; but after that, to his wife's eyes, he had the look of an ageing man, and in the night he slept ill. It was clear that he had no pleasure in that which he had resolved to do.

CHAPTER XXI

Mr. Mildew Has a Bad Night

Mr. Mildew also had a bad night, though it would be too much to say that he had become seriously alarmed. He thought the risk of any disclosure which could reach himself to be very small. But it was a small risk of what, to him, would be an incredibly dreadful thing. He was rich, respected, securely placed (he believed) beyond even the faintest suspicion of the police. The indignities of prison walls, the loss of all he valued in life, were too remote to be readily accepted as actual fears. For such as he, they would be impossible, unbelievable things. At the worst, his wealth, his lawyer's confident action, the extreme prudence with which all his operations had been conducted, would stave them off. But he could not tolerate the thought that it might come to that. He had always considered his precautions absolute. He would not easily allow himself to think otherwise now. Yet here was a vexatious incident to be watched, the end of which was not plain to see. How had he gone wrong?

There had been, first, the planting of the drugs in Limbrook's baggage. Even now, he could see no error of judgement in that. It had been soundly planned, either for success or failure, and, in fact, it had succeeded; and the customs officers had been fooled again, as they always were.

But, even had it failed, it should not have come near to him. Limbrook, financially stranded in Cairo, had found means to get home. Who would have believed a tale that he had not known that he had the dope? Who would have believed that he had borrowed that £100, against Mr. Mildew's own denial, and the testimony of an Egyptian who would confess to having paid him the banknote, and from whose bankers it could be proved that it had been obtained?

There might have been more danger (though not much) had Limbrook been likely to say that he (Mildew) had paid him to do the smuggling. But he would not think to allege what was not true, and would incriminate himself. There could have been no more than a bare assertion that the money had been borrowed, which he would have denied, and what good could such a desperate plea have done to Limbrook, or harm to him? Even had it been fantastically believed, to lend money is not a crime!

There had been the indiscretion of the man who had revealed to Limbrook the nature of the smuggling which he had been tricked to do. That was bad; and it was there that the whole trouble began. But he had been dealt with in such a manner that his mistakes were ended. Beal had made sure of that. And where was the security on which he relied, if it could be destroyed by a subordinate's blunder?

He had issued orders, when he had heard of it, to lose no moment in either enlisting Limbrook in the gang, or else silencing him for ever. Those orders had been fulfilled to a point which would have removed the danger in a few hours, one way or other, when Limbrook had disappeared in a manner so incalculable, so inconsequent, that no man could have anticipated that it would occur to defeat his plans.

But, even so, the danger was vague, remote, difficult to exactly define. Was he losing nerve? Was he in danger of allowing himself to be drawn into personal interference with the work of his less intelligent subordinates?—A mistake which had had disastrous consequences for his predecessor, and led to a damaged organization coming into his more capable hands.

He vexed himself with such thoughts in the solitude of the night hours, while rain beat drearily on window and roof, but he slept at last, and waked to a world of sun. When he drove from his Palace Gardens residence to Mr. Catsgill's offices, he had recovered his normal spirits and self-control. It is humiliating to remember how much we may vex ourselves in the night with unreal fears!

Mr. Catsgill received him with no more than his usual gravity. He also had taken counsel with weakness and fear, and had found fortitude in the night. He had regretted some of the impulses, revised some of the judgements, which had first risen as he had listened to the answers his questions to Miss Wingrove had brought on the previous evening.

Now he narrated what had passed with a lucid accuracy that was sparing of needless words. If, as is probable, he had intended, when he ordered Wellard to keep silence, to conceal an indiscretion which Mr. Mildew would be unlikely to approve, he had put the thought aside for a franker disclosure; if he had doubted Miss Wingrove's loyalty then, he expressed an opposite opinion now.

Mr. Mildew listened, and was relieved on the main issue, accepting the solicitor's assurance that he had little reason to fear betrayal either by Mr. Limbrook or the girl; but he heard with some difficult patience and self-control, more than one thing which was of a contrary kind. It was not his habit to give more confidence, even to his legal advisers, than the occasion required. He saw that it was natural that Limbrook should have mentioned him by name. He had anticipated that he might be asked to give personal evidence of identity on his behalf. There need be nothing in that to raise suspicion, so long as the police had no knowledge of the drug-smuggling episode, which now seemed a reasonable certainty. Little, even then, if they were not aware of the advances which had been made to Limbrook after his landing in England...perhaps not much if they were.

He was more perturbed that his name had been mentioned before Wellard. *That* would have to he dealt with in a conclusive manner, even to the elimination of an otherwise useful man. He saw a danger that, though the police might make no guess, the public evidence he might be required to give on Limbrook's behalf might expose him to his subordinates as the leader of the gang, whose identity had been a mystery until now. Why had not Limbrook had the sense to ask the police to apply to him direct, and simply as one who would identify him as a fellow-passenger on the boat? Probably that was all that would be required now, but it was the channel through which the request had been made which disturbed his mind.

The other matter—the exposure to the girl of that melodramatic exit, a device of the former leader of the gang, which he had not approved—was a different affair. He said of that: "Wellard should have locked the door. It is a blunder such as I am not quick to forgive."

Mr. Catsgill wished to be fair. "It is only justice to say that it was I who let Miss Wingrove out. He must have thought that I had attended to that. And I gave him the order to open the gap."

"Then," Mr. Mildew said, "the fault was not his." He omitted saying whose it must therefore have been. He added: "But when she had seen, you acted wisely in taking her down. It was boldly done. And it will make it more likely that she will be faithful to us."

He rose to go.

"She will expect," Mr. Catsgill reminded him, "a message from you this evening."

"So you told me before."

Mr. Mildew's tone was sharp. Did Catsgill think himself to be taking control? Or that it was needful to repeat what had once been said?

He went with some abruptness, and the lawyer walked to the window, and looked down on the traffic two floors below. He would not have been greatly surprised, and certainly not annoyed, had he seen a police-car waiting to invite his client for a less comfortable ride than it was his habit to take, but there was no vehicle at the pavement except Mr. Mildew's own luxurious limousine, which he watched him enter. It moved smoothly away, and Mr. Catsgill turned to other business which he had already neglected till too late an hour.

CHAPTER XXII

The Real Houghton Is Found

Billie Wingrove came down to an early breakfast. It was a meal from which she usually returned to her own room, but this time she came prepared to go straight out, though she contrived that there should be no difference from her usual appearance as she sat at the table.

She had nearly finished as Mr. Greaves, who had heard her movements from his adjoining bedroom, took his own place. She rose as a plate of egg-and-bacon was laid before him, went straight out, and boarded a city bus a few yards from the hotel entrance. It was certain that she would not be followed by him, for he would expect that she had gone upstairs, as was her usual routine.

Yet she got off the bus at Lancaster Gate, and continued her journey by the Underground. She was sure that she was not followed then, or when she changed at Oxford Circus for the Piccadilly Line. She got out at Piccadilly Circus, and went into one of the telephone boxes there. She felt certain that she was unwatched, and as to being casually overheard in that underground bear pit—so far, good. She felt she had won the first trick in a risky game.

She was fortunate too in being put through to Superintendent Backwash without delay. She said: "I want to see you at once. If I come, can I be shown up to you without waiting? I don't want to be seen, if it can be avoided."

The reply came slowly. "We don't want you to keep coming here, Miss Wingrove. Where are you now?"

"Piccadilly Circus. At the Tube Station."

"Then you can speak up. Say what you want to now. It's far safer than coming here. You won't be overheard. You're having a long talk with a woman friend. Most women use telephone boxes for that."

"I've got a lot to tell you, and it's too urgent to leave. But I hardly know where to begin."

"Begin with the urgent part. We may not be too dull to fill in the gaps."

"I didn't think you were dull. I've got a message for you. It says: 'Follow Mr. Mildew when he goes to Mr. Catsgill's office this morning, and arrest him for drug-trafficking when he comes out.'"

"Who gave you that?"

"I don't know. That is, I don't know his name. It was a man I met last night."

"Who's Mr. Catsgill?"

"I've no idea. I suppose, if you have Mildew followed, you'll find out."

"Bright girl! Well, we'll do that anyway. Wait a moment.

Within ten seconds Superintendent Backwash was speaking again: "Now you'd better tell me the whole tale. Take your time, and be accurate. I've put you on to a second line, and I'll have it taken down. Now go ahead."

On this direction, she gave a full and reasonably accurate account of the events of the night before, including the episode of the forgotten bag, and her descent to another street than that by which she had entered the Reader Grill.

She told it without interruption beyond the excusable comment: "And when you did that you gave Inspector Cauldron one of the worst headaches he's ever had." She ended with a repetition of the message already given, which Mr. Catsgill had whispered as they parted at the entrance of the Ryder Street offices.

"Well, that's plain enough," the superintendent commented, at its conclusion, "and you've done far better than coming here. Now listen, Miss Wingrove. We don't know what may be happening, nor how fast, and we don't want any trouble to come to you. What are you proposing to do next?"

"I thought of going to the British Museum. To the reading-room."

"Well, you should be safe there. But don't go out to lunch."

"You don't want me to starve?"

"No. But get something first. Enough to last, if you're a wise girl. When you do go out, we shall be keeping an eye on you. You can ring Wellard up about seven tonight, as you've been told to do, take his message, and ring me up to let me know what it is. I'll let you know then what to do next."

"But won't Mr. Limbrook be expecting to see me?"

"No. We'll tell him you won't be here."

"There's just one thing more you ought to know. I'm rather frightened. There's a man been watching this box for the last five minutes."

"How do you know that?"

"Well, hanging round."

"Has he got slovenly clothes, and a dead flower in his coat?"

"Yes."

"Then you needn't worry. We put him on to you, as soon as you said where you were. He won't be far off till you phone us this evening."

With these words the superintendent cut off unceremoniously, having to deal with other matters which would not wait. Five minutes later, Inspector Cauldron was in his room with a typescript of Billie Wingrove's narrative.

"It sounds good enough," he said. "She's got a cool head in her own way, considering how little practice she's had."

"It's astonishing," Superintendent Backwash agreed, "what some girls will do when there's a man to be helped, though I can't see my missus doing much in that line for me. It all makes good sense, as you say, except that hole in the wall."

"That does sound rather tall. You can't imagine any sane crook going to so much trouble for any use it would be likely to be. But it led us a dance last night. We've got to admit that. And we should have had two good looks at the gentleman who sends messages, and doesn't mention his name. What do you intend to do about that?"

"Nothing yet. How can we? I should like to arrest Mildew, of course. But I can't do it merely because a nameless gentleman suggests it, and tells us he'll be driving to an office we don't know."

"We've got Limbrook's evidence, and that of Miss Wingrove, besides that of the man who sent us word, and evidently means to give him away. We don't know how much that may be worth."

"Nor how little. We've got some evidence, as you say. But against Mildew it's next to nothing. Nothing a clever lawyer wouldn't brush aside like a lot of cobwebs. You know that as well as I do. But we've got to work quick, all the same, if we're to lay him by the heels before we let Limbrook out. I heard from Preston just before you came in. They've found the real Houghton now."

"Not arrested him, have they?"

"Not exactly. They're sending him for us to interview here. The man's made them believe that he's innocent, more or less. Anyway, they wouldn't arrest him till they were sure that was what we wanted."

They continued discussion of the two different criminalities which had become so curiously intertwined, until the information came through, from a police-box phone, that Mr. Mildew had driven to the offices of that highly respectable firm of solicitors, Messrs. Timbrel, Timbrel and Catsgill, which he had not left when the report was made.

"There, you see!" the superintendent exclaimed, with some disgust. "You can't arrest a man for calling on a firm like that. They may be his own solicitors."

"They probably are. But we weren't asked to arrest him, for going there, but only after he'd been."

"We can't arrest anyone on a mere hint from a man we don't know."

"We've got to do something, all the same. The only question is what. I might interview Mildew about giving evidence for Limbrook, and see how he reacts.

"So you may. Though there are two objections to that. It is what Miss Wingrove is supposed to be the recognized medium for arranging, and it's probable that Mildew would prefer it to be any way but through her. And now that Houghton's been found it has become a mere farce to call on him at all."

"Which he won't know, and I shouldn't be likely to mention. I might go for him now, and then we could wait to learn what message Miss Wingrove gets, and what we can make of that. And try to find the man who questioned her last night. He ought to be the trump card, if we can only get him into the pack. He must have his knife pretty deep into Mildew to send a message like that."

"Yes. But he's probably thinking first of his own skin. He'll hang back all the more when he sees that we're not prepared to act on a word from him. I take it he doesn't mean to speak till he knows Mildew's inside a locked door."

"We shall know all that when we find him, and a lot more. We'd better have Miss Wingrove look over the portraits here. But I think I'll get along now.

Inspector Cauldron, rightly interpreting the superintendent's silence as consent to, if not approved of, the course he preferred to take, went out, and that gentleman turned to Chief Inspector Tolbooth, who had been a silent listener to the latter part of this conversation as he had been on a previous occasion. There was nothing unusual in that. Silence was as natural to Chief Inspector Tolbooth as speech is to his fellow men.

But he was an officer of long and varied experience, now near to the age of retirement, generally allowed to have arrested more murderers, and to know more of the intricacies of international criminality, than any other detective officer in the civilized world, and his opinions, when they could be extracted from him, were proportionately valued.

"Sir Henry," Superintendent Backwash observed, "is a bit doubtful whether this thing isn't getting a bit too big for Cauldron to handle. He's really left it for me to decide. If you'd care to have it, you could pass over anything you've got on hand. Or Bradley might take it on."

He paused for a reply that he did not get, and went on: "It isn't only that Cauldron hasn't had the experience of one of you older men. He may be right about seeing Mildew himself. I'm not sure, and I let him have his own way. But I don't think he was thinking about the best way of handling the case, so much as of keeping that girl out of danger."

Chief Inspector Tolbrook said non-committally: "Yes?" And then: "One-man girl, if you ask me." He indulged in a further pause of silence, and added: "Cauldron does well enough."

"I shall tell Sir Henry," Superintendent Backwash replied, "that you agree with me that Cauldron is handling the case with ability and discretion, and that it will be well to leave it in his hands for the present."

Chief Inspector Tolbooth heard this liberal rendering of what he had said, or declined to say, without protest, or, indeed, without comment of any kind. Inspector Cauldron went on his way to Mr. Mildew's residence in happy unconsciousness of how nearly he had lost one of the greatest opportunities that a young detective-officer can dream to have, and Superintendent Backwash turned his mind to consider the most damning questions which he could contrive for Mr. James Houghton, from the answers of which his "voluntary" statement would almost certainly be composed.

CHAPTER XXIII

Mr. Mildew Is Willing to Help

Inspector Cauldron had no difficulty in finding Mr. Mildew, for that gentleman's movements had been closely followed since he left Mr. Catsgill's office, but for some hours he was so occupied that he judged that it would be inopportune to obtrude upon him. He lunched with two gentlemen of unimpeachable character, one of whom was a nephew of the Prime Minister. Even Inspector Cauldron's sceptical mind could not consider them as possible accomplices of the importers of noxious drugs.

After lunch, they drove together to one of the oldest and most famous of the great political clubs, where they entered the bridge-room and readily found a fourth for a game which occupied them for the afternoon.

The inspector considered the advisability of interrupting the game, and rejected it, seeing that he might be put off with a quick word of consent to the request which he came to make, or promised an interview at a later hour, thus allowing Mildew an opportunity for prior consideration, which he would prefer not to give. Vital though he knew the factor of time to be, he restrained himself to wait until that gentleman drove back to his own home, where he could be seen alone, and at the leisure that (to Inspector Cauldron's mind) the occasion required.

It was slightly after six when he arrived at Palace Gardens, and sent in his card with a message that he wished to see Mr. Mildew on a matter of some urgency.

He was shown into a comfortable smoking-room, and had not been in the house more than three minutes when its owner appeared.

He came forward with a smile, and an outstretched hand. "It was good of you to come," he said. "I scarcely thought you would be so extremely prompt. But I can see that our fiction-writers do not exaggerate the efficiency of the C.I.D."

136

The inspector did not understand this, beyond recognizing that he was ignorant of something he was supposed to know. It was an ignorance which he could not conceal, if he would.

"I am afraid," he said, "that that is a rather ambiguous compliment. Writers of fiction sometimes represent us as being even more stupid than we are. But I am not sure that there may not be some misunderstanding. On what business do you suppose me to have called?"

"I have no doubt that you have called in connection with the Houghton murder, and in response to a message I sent you scarcely more than an hour ago."

"It is in connection with the Houghton murder, but the message you mention had not come to my knowledge."

"Well, that doesn't matter, so long as you are here, and I can talk to you direct."

"Perhaps you would tell me what the message was?"

"It was in reply to one that I had this morning, which said that a man named Limbrook, whom I met on a P. & O. boat a few weeks ago, had been arrested by you in mistake for the Houghton murderer. It asked me to identify him. It said that the request came from the police. You will know better than I whether that were true."

"It might be put in that way."

"Very well. It might or might not be genuine, but it placed me in an embarrassing position.

"On the one hand, I knew Limbrook, though only in the casual way that shipboard acquaintances are made, and half-forgotten before the Customs are cleared. If he is in real trouble, I don't want to refuse to give him any help that I ought, and I don't think I should have any hesitation in telling you, one way or other, whether he's the man that you've got.

"On the other hand, the request came to me in the name of a man I met years ago, in a way that I didn't like, and who has tried to thrust his acquaintance upon me several times since. And the whole thing sounded fishy to me. I couldn't see why Limbrook (if it's really he that you've got) didn't tell you at once that I could identify him. I couldn't see why you didn't come to me direct.

"So, after thinking it over, I telephoned from my club, scarcely more than an hour ago, to say that I wasn't prepared to do anything unless I had a direct request from you."

"You telephoned from the club?" Chief Inspector Cauldron repeated. As a fact, he knew that Mr. Mildew had not been near the telephone since lunch. It was the first point which he could check, of the statement he had just heard, and it did not appear to add up correctly. But Mr. Mildew turned it aside, without appearing to notice the dubiety in those echoed words.

"To be exact, I instructed the porter to do so, as I was leaving the club. You will see that, short as the time is, I naturally supposed that you had received the message, and called upon me in consequence."

Faced by this plausible statement, Inspector Cauldron realized the subtle cleverness of the man whom it was his duty to expose for the scoundrel he could not doubt him to be. To have accepted the underlings of his drug-trafficking organization as a natural medium for communicating with Scotland Yard, would have been as dangerous as to have denied all knowledge of Wellard's existence might have been in another way. But he had done neither. He had taken the attitude which would be natural to one who was approached in such a dubious manner, and he had admitted a degree of knowledge of the man who had been selected for a channel of communication which might be very near to the truth, in view of the distance which he maintained between himself and those from whom his wealth was derived.

With no perceptible pause, the inspector answered, using the pseudo-frankness with which he had been met: "Yes, I can see how it looked to you. But we did what Limbrook asked, in his own way, which seemed fairest to him. As a matter of fact, it was a girl, not a man—a Miss Wingrove—through whom the request was to be made."

"In the first instance, yes. So I heard. But I know nothing of her. It was through a man that it came to me, and one with whom I have no desire to have dealings of any kind. To be quite frank, I heard talk some time ago—but it was no more than gossip, and may have been quite wrong—that he dabbled in prohibited drugs."

"Perhaps you wouldn't mind mentioning his name?"

"Do you think I ought, after what I have said? I think I would prefer not."

"You can be sure that it will go no further with us."

"Well, I suppose, in any case, you'd find out after what I've said if you wished to do so. I don't see why I should make any mystery about it. He's named Wellard. I couldn't describe him accurately, if you asked me to do so. But my memory is of a rather coarse, heavily-made man, with the manners of a cheap bully."

"Just one other point, Mr. Mildew, if you don't mind, Mr. Limbrook mentioned that he had borrowed money from you. It would be a point in his favour if you could confirm that."

Mr. Mildew paused a moment, as though searching his memory for a forgotten fact. "Yes," he said. "I believe he did. Indeed, I feel sure. But a good many people do. And if I lend with good will, I don't bear it in mind. It wasn't money I expected to see again. But if he says so you can call it a bull point for him."

"Could you tell me the amount of the loan?"

Mr. Mildew thought again. "No, I'm afraid I couldn't. It might have been a tenner. Or more. The fact is, it was the kind of thing I forget as soon as it's done. I'm not a poor man, and to keep account of anything I give to a man who's short, it would be—well, almost like counting your change. But let me know when and where Limbrook—or let us say the man you've got—is to be seen, and I'll come round at once. Any time tomorrow will do. I suppose, if I recognize him, you'll let him go?"

"It may be necessary to bring him up for the next remand. That will be for the Commissioner to decide."

"But you wouldn't need me in court?"

"No. I can't say certainly. Probably not."

"Well, I shall be glad to avoid that, if I can."

Mr. Mildew rose. "You'll take something," he asked hospitably, "before you go?"

Inspector Cauldron excused himself. He left with a feeling that the honours of the encounter had not been his. For a moment he even wondered whether Mr. Mildew might not be a maligned man. "It would be almost like counting your change." He knew that he always counted his with scrupulous care. He supposed most people did. But he could see how a very wealthy man might regard it differently. He did not really believe that Mr. Mildew had forgotten lending that £100 note. But he had evaded either admission or denial in a plausible way. Certainly not a man to be arrested on an anonymous verbal denunciation.

It looked to him at the moment as though this opportunity of breaking up the Mildew gang, from which he had hoped so much, might fizzle out, as others had done before. Mildew would be too clever for them again. There would be two or three bodies fished out of the Thames, including those of Limbrook and Billie Wingrove more likely than not, and after that the inquests—the open verdicts—the additions to London's record of unsolved crimes—and the drug-traffickings would go on as before. He must try to bring it to a better ending than that.

There remained one question. Why had Mildew mentioned Wellard by name, and attributed to him the illicit activities in which he was doubtless engaged? Had it been simply to give verisimilitude to his own narrative, and would the man now be withdrawn from his usual haunts, or ordered to live a blameless life until suspicion should turn aside? Or did Mildew think that he would close the hungry mouth of the law by throwing it a sufficient meal? Or, finally, had the man offended or failed to a degree which caused him to be betrayed? Suppose Wellard, being arrested, could be induced to talk? It was a possibility—but only on the presumption that he could have nothing important to say.

With these questions vexing a doubtful mind, Inspector Cauldron arrived back at Scotland Yard, just as Billie Wingrove alighted from a taxi before the door.

"Anything fresh?" he asked, remembering that the superintendent had not encouraged her to visit the headquarters of the C.I.D.

"I don't know. I was just sitting down to dinner when I had a message asking me to come here at once."

"Then you'd better come upstairs with me."

He led her to Superintendent Backwash's room, and was greeted by that usually self-controlled officer with more evidence of perturbation than he had often seen him exhibit.

"Anything wrong?" he echoed irritably. "I should think there is! We've got this Houghton murderer—or not-murderer—according to how much of his tale is true, and how much he's cooked up while he's been hiding away. We've got his statement, and we've wirelessed to hold the Bingham woman on the French boat. The Houghton case is going all right. Though I wish to heaven our Preston men hadn't been in such a hurry to send him here. ...

"But as to Mildew, it's put us in the soup up to the neck, or a bit deeper than that. It's blown the whole thing right open. By this time tomorrow Mildew'll *know* that we've been playing with him. He'll be doubly on his guard, and what more can we hope to do then?"

"What's the trouble exactly?"

"The trouble is that Blades has got hold of the tale, and, unless we smash his presses, it'll be in the *Plain Talker* all over London tomorrow."

Inspector Cauldron whistled, as his habit was at such crises as these, and it was not on a cheerful note. The editor of the *Plain Talker* had attracted the unfavourable notice of the police two years before, and, through their officious interference, he had spent nearly nine months in jail.

Twice already, since he came out, he had retaliated by exposing their mistakes in unkindly ways. Now, from the day when the man accused of the Houghton murder had denied his identity from the dock, he had kept his reporters on the track of events on the bare chance that he might come upon a more ample revenge, and he had been aware, even before the news had reached those who had official right to receive it, that James Houghton had been found, and was on his way back to London. Tomorrow morning there would be placards about the streets asking: "How many Houghtons?" and perhaps even more directly impertinent suggestions concerning the inefficiency of the C.I.D.

Well, that could be endured. It could even be countered to some extent by a prompt statement to the press which would be assured of prominent space in the columns of the morning papers. That would be decided at a conference which the Assistant Commissioner had already called for a later hour. But its effect upon the Mildew investigation was a quite separate matter. If the police had been actively searching for another James, it was an easy deduction that they had not been in much genuine doubt concerning the identity of the man they had first arrested. If they had found the real James twenty-four hours before, Mr. Mildew could conclude with certainty that Inspector Cauldron had not called upon him from any real desire that he should assist them in that way.

Faced by this fact, a man of far less acumen than he had shown himself to possess might conclude that their real interest had been roused by statements that Limbrook had made, and that their enquiries were directed upon something quite different from the Houghton murder.

It was impossible to guess that, on that discovery, he might think it necessary for his own protection to do; but it was certain that he would be restrained by no higher consideration than that of his own well-being, and that he controlled those who would be ruthless to execute his commands, even though they might have no knowledge of from whom they came.

The safety of Billie Wingrove under such circumstances had been Superintendent Backwash's first thought, and to ring up the Envoy Hotel and tell her to come straight to the Yard had seemed the first and obvious step to take. That had been simple. But the next was less easy to see.

"There's one chance," Inspector Cauldron said with stubborn refusal to resign a game which he had determined to win. "There's that man who gave Miss Wingrove the message to us."

"Yes. If we can find out who he is—and he's still alive."

"What about fetching in Wellard, and having a few words with him?"

"And what charge would you prefer? He's done nothing that we can prove except bruising Miss Wingrove's chin."

CHAPTER XXIV

Houghton Gives His Account

This is not the saga of James Cadell Houghton, or of the natural consequences of the abrupt decease of his wealthy but otherwise somewhat unsatisfactory wife. It is rather the story of matters of more importance which had become grafted upon it, like a more expansive bloom on a wild rose stock.

But as the Houghton tragedy was used by a capricious fate in that inconsequent manner, we can hardly refuse to listen to a tale which the one most closely concerned had become anxious to tell.

Statements obtained by detective officers from accused persons have been subjected to adverse criticism which has not always been undeserved, but that which was written down in Superintendent Backwash's office, though it had the common defect of being composed in the jargon considered appropriate for such documents rather than in the words of the suspected man, was at least of an entirely voluntary nature.

Being arrested after a fortnight of precarious hiding, and being informed of his sister-in-law's flight, he had become anxious to make a statement which, true or false, represented him as having had no responsibility for Isabel Houghton's death.

Preferring his own words to those to which they would ultimately be transformed, we may choose to listen to the narrative as he gave it under the direction of the skilful interrogations of the police.

"You know, Mr. Houghton," the superintendent began, with more courtesy of address than he always thought it necessary to use when questioning suspected persons, "you're not under arrest at present. We are willing to listen to anything you may wish to say, and I needn't tell you that we are quite open-minded, and only want to get at the truth. But, all the same, the circumstances of your wife's death, and your own subsequent conduct, put you under the gravest suspicion, and it is my duty to warn you that anything you say will be taken down and may be used in evidence."

"I don't mind that. I want to tell the whole tale. Charlotte can't expect anything else, now that she's got safely away."

"You mean that Miss Bingham was concerned in your wife's death?"

Mr. Houghton was a small neat man, of somewhat nondescript appearance, normally alert of manner, but having fallen to an aspect of listless dejection, under the influence of his recent experiences. But, as he told his story, animation revived, and the ready emphasis of his answers impressed the little group of attentive and habitually sceptical auditors with a probability that they held at least a large measure of truth.

"I should say she was! They just shot it out together, and you know what happened."

"You mean you saw Miss Bingham kill your wife, and made no effort to interpose?"

"I had a fat chance of that, being the other side of the corridor! How long do you think those shots took to fire?"

"And you made no effort to bring the murderer of your wife to justice? You just ran away like a guilty man?"

"Yes. You'll say I did. I don't say I was right in that. But there wasn't much time to think. And I shouldn't say anyone murdered Isabel. She'd have been a lot more likely to murder us."

"Still, she was the one who got killed, and consequently can't speak for herself. But you'd better tell us what happened, in your own way."

"That's what I'm trying to do. The trouble was that Isabel was jealous of Charlotte. I don't say she had no cause. But it was her own fault at the start, and she didn't go the right way to make things different. She was always jealous, and she was worst when she'd had a glass or two more than she should.

"But I'd better tell you how it all started. It's more than I want to say, especially now Isabel's dead, but it doesn't make sense if I hold it back.

"I married Isabel for the most natural reason a man can have. I knew I could have had Charlotte. She'd made that clear, more than a bit. But I liked Isabel better.

"It wasn't till after we were married that I found out what she was. She was spiteful, and jealous of Charlotte long before she had any cause at all. She used to drink more than enough—I'd say we all did that, more or less—but when she'd had her last glass she'd let things out of the sort that can't be unsaid.

"Once she said that she'd only had one reason for marrying me, and that was to give Charlotte one in the eye, and I knew her well enough by that time to see that it might be literally true. Unfortunately, Charlotte heard her say it, and after that there was no keeping peace between them.

"Isabel's tongue used to make hell when she was a bit excited with drink, and if I paid her back in the same way, she'd get violent, till she didn't care what she did."

He bent his head as he said this, separating the hair to disclose a long white scar. "A bronze elephant did that. A fair weight it was too. It came the full length of the room. You wouldn't have thought she'd have had strength to throw it. I ducked, but I was too late. It was meant for my face, and it cracked along the top of my head.

"You'll say I'm giving you lots of reasons why I might have killed Isabel, but such a thought never came into my head. I'm telling you the truth, as well as I can, and you'll see now it worked out.

"Isabel always got up late, which I didn't like. I'm an early riser myself, and she didn't like anyone else to have breakfast till she was ready for hers.

"When she'd been up late, she might sleep half the morning, and I'll own by this time that I'd lost whatever love I used to have for her, and got to prefer Charlotte, who was honestly fond of me, so far as either of them could think of anything but themselves.

"I used to be up for hours in the morning while Isabel went on sleeping, and I'll own that, at those times—well, I used to go to Charlotte's room. It was the only time we had when Isabel couldn't have been certain to know.

"We had no reason to think she suspected that, jealous as she was, till the day before the trouble came, and even now I don't know whether she knew anything, or only made a good guess. But there's a girl, Doris, at the hotel, who Charlotte thought had been making mischief with her tongue.

"Well, she made one of the worst scenes that we ever had, saying that I had been unfaithful to her with her own sister, which was no more than the truth, though, of course, we both swore blue that we'd never had such a thought in our minds.

"She made out she believed us at last, and we went to one or two night-clubs together, but Charlotte and I both saw that it couldn't go on, and we may have encouraged her to drink, thinking that it would give us an opportunity next morning to talk things over, and decide what it would be best to do.

"I went to Charlotte next morning, and we decided to go off together, but it meant going back to New York first, to get funds, which was what the three of us had already planned to do on the next boat.

"We couldn't decide whether to give her the slip at once, or try to make things go on as they were till we all got back to America together, and while we talked the time passed more than we were aware.

"When I went back to our rooms, and entered the bedroom to see whether Isabel was awake, and hoping she hadn't heard me coming through the outer door, she sprang up like a wild cat, with the gun in her hand. She screamed out: 'You've been with that sneaking something again!' I couldn't catch what the word was.

I was in too much hurry to back out of the room.

"I went back to Charlotte, and we agreed that there'd be no safety for either of us while she had that gun in her possession. But Charlotte didn't think there would be much trouble in making her lay it down. She said: 'I'll get it off her now. She won't try any tricks with me.'

"I tried to persuade her not to do anything rash, but she wouldn't listen. She said: 'Nonsense. I'll get your gun first. She'll sing a different song when she sees that. She knows I can shoot straight, and she can't.'

"I said, 'Anyhow, don't do it now. Let her cool down'; but she said, 'Work herself up, more likely. I know Isabel. You just leave her to me,' and she pushed me out of the way.

"She knew where my gun was, in a drawer in the dining-room, opposite the bathroom door, and she must have expected to be able to get it, and then go to the bedroom, and perhaps talk to Isabel through the door, and let her know she was armed. But it didn't happen like that.

"Isabel was in the bathroom, and must have heard Charlotte enter the dining-room. She opened the bathroom door, but whether she meant to kill anyone when she did that is something you can guess, if you will, but I don't see how we can ever know.

"Anyway, she had her own gun in her hand, and she was just in time to see Charlotte take mine, and when she saw that she fired without saying a word. She fired twice, and the second bullet hit Charlotte somewhere—I've wondered whether she kept you from knowing that—"

"It hit her," Inspector Cauldron interposed confidently, "in the left arm."

Superintendent Backwash looked surprised, "You might have mentioned it before," he said reasonably, "if you knew that."

"I didn't know it till now. But I remember how she was all the time pulling down the sleeves of her dressing-gown the first time I saw her in bed. And it wouldn't have been the right arm. Not if Mrs. Houghton really fired first."

"Charlotte wouldn't have fired at all if she hadn't," James Houghton replied confidently, and his opinion received logical confirmation from Superintendent Backwash: "She fired first, whoever it was at, because she couldn't have done it after she was hit where she was. We can give you that."

"Well, that shows how it happened. And when anyone's being shot at across the breadth of a room, they haven't got much time to think out what's best to do. They shoot back, if they've got any use for living, and think it out when they've got more time.

"That's how it looks to me, and I don't blame Charlotte at all. I ran in when I heard the shots, but, of course, I was too late to do anything. I found Charlotte wiping my gun with her handkerchief. She was wonderfully cool, as she always would be when there was a row. She just said: 'I think I've killed Isabel. I couldn't help it. She fired first. She got me in the arm. You'd better go at once. I shall have to say it was you. But I'll make time for you to get off, and when I'm back-home you can let out what really happened.' Then she gave me the gun and said: 'Put it down somewhere on the floor. It won't matter where.'

"I scarcely knew what I was doing. She was so cool and quick, and it was such a sudden shock. I did what she said, and then she added: 'But, of course, you'll need money.' She went back to her own room very quickly, and got her handbag. I met her in the passage. She pushed £200 in notes into my hand—we always had plenty of money lying about—and she got me into the lift just as I heard one of the maids coming along the passage. I think that's all that you want to know."

"You've made a very clear statement, Mr. Houghton," the superintendent replied, "and it won't be many minutes before we have it ready for you to sign; but there's just one question I should like to ask, and one fact I should like to tell you.

"The question is: did you ever express an opinion to Miss Bingham that a criminal would be wise to hide near the scene of his crime, rather than attempt to get further away?"

Mr. Houghton looked genuinely puzzled. "No," he said. "I daresay it's a good idea, but I never gave it a thought. I never expected it to be of any interest to me."

"Miss Bingham may have thought you would go to Lancashire?"

146

"She may. I didn't say so. But she'd given me enough money to go a good distance away."

"Yes. She is a clever woman. The fact I wanted to tell you is that she isn't in New York yet, and I don't know that she will be. We hope to get her back here."

"Well, anyway, it's the truth I've told, and I did what I could for her, running off like I did."

"I am inclined to agree. But, on your own statement, you were an accessory after the crime, and you have no one but yourself to blame for any inconvenience you suffer now. When you have signed your statement, it will go before the Assistant Commissioner, and subsequent procedure will be for his decision, pending which you will understand that we must detain you here."

Mr. Houghton made no objection to that, which he was hardly in a position to do.

CHAPTER XXV

What Is to Be Done Now?

The Assistant Commissioner received Mr. Houghton's statement, and was not pleased. He saw that it bore upon the decision
which must first be made, and which had become a matter of instant
urgency, if any statement were to go out to the press that night.

They had already got one James Cadell Houghton in the cells
who should not be there. They had now detained a second, and, if
his statement were to be believed, he must be relegated to the same
category. A third possible culprit was now on a French boat, approaching the American coast, where, if she were permitted to land,
she might be for ever beyond their reach. He saw the case as one
that might become a classic of cumulative blunders in the annals of
the Yard. Was it wonderful that, in addition to assembling the best
brains of the C.I.D., he had sent an urgent summons to the prosecuting solicitor, Mr. Otbury, to be present, so that they would have the
benefit of his experience and of his knowledge of criminal law?

"The first question," Sir Henry said, after he had read the
Houghton statement to his assembled advisers, "is whether we are to
take this document seriously or as the invention of a cornered man."

"He doesn't," Mr. Otbury remarked, "present himself in a favourable light."

"A man in his position," Sir Henry replied, "can't afford to consider that."

"No. But if he were inventing he might have improved it a good
deal in his own favour."

"He may have thought it would be less plausible if he did."

"Well, he would have been right in that. It is very nearly what I
was meaning to say."

Sir Henry saw that Mr. Otbury was disposed to credit the statement with at least an important percentage of truth, where he would
have preferred to hear convincing arguments of its worthlessness.
He changed his point of approach, to ask: "What do you think of the

chance of getting the woman back? We've already cabled for her to be held, but I can't say I've got much confidence in it being done?"

"It depends mainly upon the goodwill of the French Sûreté and how promptly you act.

"She's a U.S.A. citizen on a French boat, and perjury isn't a crime for which you could get her extradited, even if she were a native of this country.

"Of course, short of murder, we might frame a charge of manslaughter, or, alternatively. if you are not dropping the case against Houghton, of her being an accessory either before or after the fact, in such a form that the French extradition treaty would cover it. But if the boat docks in New York Harbour I should say, if the woman's still on the boat, you've lost her, more likely than not. With a United States' citizen as wealthy, and with as much influence as she's certain to have, the ship wouldn't be docked for a couple of hours before they'd have a Habeas Corpus order for the captain to deliver her up, and where would you be then?"

"You mean she's already out of our reach? We can't expect a liner to turn round and come back without landing her passengers or cargo, just to oblige us. Nor to discharge them outside the three-mile limit."

"No. But they might discharge *her* if there's another French boat coming out that would take her over."

"Or an English one?"

"Or an English one, of course, if you can get over the difficulty of her being surrendered before the formalities of extradition have been gone through."

"I'm afraid we couldn't ask for that."

"No. That's why I said a French boat."

"Gentlemen," Sir Henry said, his eyes upon the circle of intent faces which had listened silently to these exchanges, "you can see that the woman may not be easy to get. But the first question is, do we want her, and, if so, on what charge?"

Chief Inspector Ribber answered with the entire confidence in his own judgement which would have been less irritating had it not been so often right: "When you boil it down you'll find it all hangs on whether she were wounded or not. And you won't know that till you get her stripped."

"That's how it seems to me," Superintendent Backwash agreed gloomily. "And another thing that's equally sure is that we shan't get a verdict against the man unless we can get the woman either in the witness-box or the dock."

"You mean you wouldn't proceed with the prosecution?" Sir Henry asked sharply. It might be necessary to drop it, but that would make a poor statement for the Press, put it how you would!

"No. I'm not going that far. We're not proposing to proceed against him on the facts as they stand now. There's the warrant already issued. If that were taken out before we'd heard what he had to say, whose fault is it but his? He's got the way he bolted to thank. I should take a remand tomorrow and move heaven and earth to get the woman back."

Sir Henry said that unfortunately he couldn't move heaven and earth. The only things you could hope to move were the French Bureau de Sûreté and the liner's captain. But he found that there was a consensus of agreement with the opinions already given, and a quarter of an hour later the following statement had been drafted for general Press distribution, while Chief Inspector Tolbooth had left the room to see what could be done on the Paris phone:

> Owing to false information supplied to the police under circumstances which are now being investigated, a gentleman who declined at the time to disclose his identity was arrested as James Cadell Houghton. The police, not being satisfied, continued inquiries which resulted in the true James Cadell Houghton being traced to Wigan. He was brought up to London today and will be formally charged tomorrow morning with the wilful murder of Isabel Houghton.

This statement, while accurate within its own narrow limits, contrived to suggest that the police had acted with particular sagacity rather than the blundering folly which had allowed the woman who was, in all probability, the real murderer, to escape after befooling them into the arrest of an absolutely innocent stranger to the crime. It would be read by everyone (and how many do not?) who looks through a morning newspaper, and introduce the matter to their minds from this desirable angle before the *Plain Talker* would be likely to come to their notice, however largely it might be sold on the streets during the day.

Having issued this, the Assistant Commissioner felt that he had done all to support the credit of his department that the position allowed. But there remained the no less urgent and far more serious question of how this disclosure would affect the possibility of uncovering the identities of the Mildew gang.

CHAPTER XXVI

Dinner for One

Billie Wingrove sat in a comfortable room eating a much better dinner than that which she had left untasted at the Envoy Hotel. A liberal selection of women's magazines had been provided for her amusement when the meal was done. She could not fail to observe that Scotland Yard was treating her as an honoured guest. Yet, while she peeled a pear which deserved to be received in a better mood, her eyes frowned, and her mouth set in a mutinous curve, as she formed a resolution which even Superintendent Backwash's patient pertinacity might not find it easy to change. She had done all that she had agreed. She had telephoned Mr. Wellard from a call-box near the British Museum at six-fifteen, being as late an hour as was consistent with her being back at the hotel for dinner, which she did not intend to miss, and she had received a rather curt message from him that Mr. Mildew was dealing with the matter himself and that nothing further would be required from her The substance had been substantially accurate, but the tone in which it had been conveyed had been Mr Wellard's own. It had reflected an uneasy irritation in his own mind—a doubt of whether he were to be rewarded or flung aside—which had followed the telephone conversation with one of his immediate superiors a few hours earlier. That he had allowed it to appear may be accepted as additional evidence of his unfitness for anything requiring more finesse than a bully is likely to have.

Billie had hung up with a feeling that, for good or evil, her part was done. Had she been invited to join the gang, she might have consented, with the dangerous purpose of betraying them to the police, for she was one of those who, having tasted the excitements of intrigue and hazard, do not readily put them aside for the dullness of safer living; but if she were bluntly told that her further services were not required, what more could there be to do? To force herself further upon them would be a reckless and almost certainly an abortive attempt. It is not by such methods that sudden confidence can be won.

As she had hung up the receiver, she had felt, with a curiously mixed reaction of disappointment and relief, that her part was finished. So far as she was concerned, her only remaining interest would be in the question of whether Professor Ashbarton's manuscript was destined to reach her hands. And, had she been thinking only of herself, it is quite likely that she would have met Superintendent Backwash's invitation with a firm refusal. She would have said with finality that she was just about to have dinner and couldn't come.

But there was Eustace to consider, as well as herself. There was getting him out of that horrid cell without further delay. There was his safety after he had come out. There was the question of some substantial recompense for what he had undergone in consequence of that blundering arrest.

When Superintendent Backwash, without even troubling to enquire what instructions from Mildew she had received—which might have been no more than a prudent reticence, knowing from where she spoke—had asked her to come to the Yard at once she had replied readily that she would. She saw that that over which she would have worried during the dark hours was likely to be sooner resolved.

Now she understood that a conference of the higher powers of the C.I.D. was being held, as she supposed, to decide a line of attack, in which Eustace, and presumably herself—or why had she been so hurriedly summoned here—would be blind pawns in the game; and she resolved, with a stubborn set of the mouth which was still black and yellow from the impact of Wellard's hand, that she would do nothing more, nor should Eustace if she could present it, until there had been a frank disclosure between them of the parts which both had already played. The methods of the police were their own concern, but confidence between Eustace and herself was more important to her. They might hesitate as to how far it would be wise to take them both into official confidence, or how far either might dissuade the other from taking the risks which such criminal chase requires, but these were doubts that she was not likely to share.

So her thoughts went, as the skin of the pear fell in one long unbroken spiral upon her plate from a knife which moved in a firm hand; nor did her resolution weaken during the long two hours that she spent in turning over the pages of *Good Housekeeping* and the *Woman at Home*; but when at length Inspector Cauldron entered the room she found, as will often be, that her resolution had been no more than to force the lock of an opening door.

"I'm sorry, Miss Wingrove," he said genially, "that we've had to leave you alone so long, but we've had one or two rather difficult points to decide; and we haven't had an opportunity yet of asking you what message you got from Mildew this afternoon, though I might be able to make a good guess."

"If you only asked me here so that I could tell you that," Billie answered, with an equal smile for one whom it had seemed natural to regard as a friend since he had carried her clothes (and how!) down the back stairs of the Envoy Hotel, "I'm afraid you won't think you've got much for the dinner it's cost you. He just told me that my further assistance was not required."

"Yes, so we supposed. But we didn't ask you here to learn that. It was for your own safety, in view of developments which are certain to occur during the next twenty-four hours."

"You mean you're going to make some arrests, and they'll think it's I who have given them away?"

"No. I didn't mean that. I don't know whether we shall or not. But they'll know that our request to identify Limbrook hasn't been genuine, and with less brains than they've got—"

"You're not going to ask *Mister* Limbrook to do anything dangerous while you keep me shut up

"I beg your pardon. Mr. Limbrook, of course. We shan't ask him to undertake any risk he won't understand, any more than we should ask you. But I can't say what we shall do yet. There's nothing settled at all."

"Then I'd better say this at once. I shan't do anything more, and Eustace won't if I can help it, unless we all understand it thoroughly. I haven't liked that sort of thing going as far as it has, and I'm determined it shan't go further on the same lines."

Inspector Cauldron heard this and looked keenly at the speaker for a long moment of speculative silence before he replied. But after that he said easily: "I don't quite see how we are to fall out over that, Miss Wingrove, because we both look at it in the same way.

"We've just ended a long conference on the Houghton murder, which wouldn't have been of any particular interest to you, and we've adjourned for an hour, because even policemen must eat; but after that we're going to meet again to see what can be done regarding the Mildew gang, and I've got the job of seeing both you and Mr. Limbrook before then and giving you a fair choice.

"If either of you feels you've done all we can fairly ask, it's O.K. with us, and we'll give you all the protection we can; but if you, either or both, are willing to go on, I'm to invite you to be present, and you'll hear everything that's discussed."

"And Mr. Limbrook will be told what I've done already?"

"Yes. I suppose he will. Anyway, that's your matter. We don't object. It mightn't be very easy to avoid."

"No. I don't think it would. You're going to see him at once when you leave here? Before I do?"

"Yes. At least, I was going to ask you to do one thing first. But—yes, so I shall."

"Then you can tell him all that I've done, so long as you make it clear that I've wished him to know."

"Yes. I'll do that. And am I to understand that you're still willing to give us any help that you can? I don't know what it would be. It might be nothing at all. But you'll see that it might alter how we should plan if we should be counting you out."

The silence which followed was not more than five seconds long. She thought of Eustace. She saw that her answer might involve his danger—perhaps his life—just as much as her own, for she could not think that he would stand back from a risk which he watched her take. But, in any case, would he stand back? She thought not. For a moment she may have thought of a bruised chin. For a moment the spirit of adventure may have stirred her heart to a quickened beat. For a longer second she thought vaguely—for she had little exact knowledge—of the ruin of lives from which the Mildew gang drew its wealth. At this thought she forgot to ask, as she had once done, what recompense for that danger would come to Eustace or her. She said: "You can be sure that I'll do anything that I can. I don't think I shall mind the risk if you tell me it's worth taking and you think I can pull it off. But, so far, I haven't done very well. I didn't deceive that man yesterday, or he wouldn't have said what he did. But what is it you said you were going to ask me to do now?"

"We think you did very well indeed; and you must believe that we're not bad judges."

"You just think," she answered, with a sudden smile, which relieved the seriousness the conversation had taken, "that you'll give me more self-confidence if you tell me that."

He smiled admission of that he could not deny. "Well, perhaps I did. But I meant it, all the same. It was about that man I was going to speak. We keep a lot of photographs of our—special friends—in a room not far from here. If you could identify him among them, it might be the greatest service you've done for us yet."

"Well, of course, I'll try. But he didn't look that sort to me."

"Possibly not. Though you'll be surprised at what a good-looking album we keep. But, in this case, I haven't much hope myself, though we're bound to try."

On these words they parted. The inspector went off to interview Eustace Limbrook, with somewhat more duplicity to confess, and somewhat less confidence in the way he would be received; and Billie to spend a useless half-hour in looking for a portrait which was not included in the extensive collection to which she was introduced.

CHAPTER XXVII

An Interview of Some Difficulty

Inspector Cauldron had not been mistaken in his anticipation that the second interview would be more difficult than the first.

Eustace Limbrook was of a sensitive pride, which had become no less alert because it had been hardly treated in recent days.

He was not blind to the fact that, whatever might be said in defence of the way in which he had accepted that mistaken arrest, it had been a singularly undignified part to play, and he had not been free from the thought that he was being used as a tool by the police, with a lack of ceremony for which the initial responsibility was surely his. And—there was no comfort in this reflection—it was precisely how that scoundrel Mildew had used him before. His observation of life had taught him that some men appear destined to play the game, and others to be the pawns which they push about, but, until that disastrous failure of the Rushton-Thornville Engineering Company had thrown him on the rocks in a foreign land, it had not occurred to him that he was formed for the ignobler role.

Now he had to learn that the care for his own safety, which had led him to accept that blundering arrest, had introduced a girl whom it should have been his first thought to protect to the very dangers he had been prudent to shun. He had to learn that she had united with the police to deceive him in what she did. And finally, and perhaps not the least hard to endure, that it was she who, even in this, had played the more dangerous, more important, more spectacular part.

Twice already she had ventured her safety, perhaps her life, among these villainous, ruthless men, while he had done no more than identify one of them from an attic window, with a policeman to protect him on either side! She had been actually struck on the face and had gone into the same danger again, be-fooling him with that lying tale of an open door, which he had swallowed while Inspector Cauldron had doubtless smiled at the ease with which he could be deceived.

He had been in a mood to quarrel—to have a proper under-standing was how he had phrased it in his own mind—when the in-spector entered the room where he had been kept waiting since seven o'clock, with no explanation of why he was fetched there at so late an hour, and the tale he not heard with such belated frankness added fuel to what was already a lively fire.

"I don't say," he replied, after he had listened in a morose si-lence to the inspector's apologetic narrative, "that I won't give you any help I can, providing, of course, that you don't let Miss Win-grove get mixed up any more in what you know very well isn't a girl's work; but don't you think there are one or two things that ought to be straightened out before we talk about that?"

"I'm afraid we couldn't make any bargain about Miss Win-grove. I've told you already that her help is promised to us. I may say that I'm as anxious as you can—I mean we are all anxious that she shouldn't take any serious risk. But in a matter of this impor-tance we may have to put personal feelings aside and sometimes ask members of the public to help us in dangerous ways, of course being made fully aware of the nature of what they do."

"That's all right for me. But Miss Wingrove's a different mat-ter."

"Well, it's for her to decide, and what she says is that she'll give us any help that we think she can."

"She may talk differently if I ask her not to."

"She may, of course. But I think better of her than that. If you say that if she does you won't, it might please her rather than not."

Eustace Limbrook had some excuse for frowning over the im-plications of these remarks. He saw that the police did not regard her assistance as of less importance than his; and he saw, if that were so, that what he had said was no more than that, if Billie Wingrove con-sented to risk her life, he would take all the more care of his. Cer-tainly he hadn't meant that!

"You know perfectly well," he said, "that she's an inexperi-enced girl, and that, for your own purposes, you are asking her to incur risks that no one in her position should be allowed to take. Keep her out of it, and I'll do anything, and agree to anything that you like, and you know that that's offering more than a little. It wasn't what I meant to say a moment ago."

"No. I got an idea of that. Mr. Limbrook, I'll be absolutely frank with you, and you must decide as you will. Speaking not so much for myself as for the C.I.D., I want you to understand that we're not indifferent to Miss Wingrove's safety. Far from it. Per-haps, from a different angle, we're almost as much concerned as yourself. But it's true that we look at something else, even before that.

"We've got a chance—it's beginning to look a poor one, but it's a chance still—of running in some of the heads of a gang of criminals who do more harm in a single year than all the murderers who have been hanged in England since we were born, and if any citizen, woman or man, as a public duty, or with any other motive, will help us in that, we've no right to say no.

"We won't ask them to take any risk they don't understand, and, so far as Miss Wingrove and yourself are concerned, I don't know that we shall ask you to do anything at all. It all depends upon the programme on which we decide tonight. But I don't say we shan't. We only want to know, first, whether we can count on your help or not, so that we can make our plans accordingly. And I ought to tell you that they must have been waiting for us about ten minutes now."

"Well, you've got me beaten. You know that. So far as keeping Miss Wingrove out of the game, after what she's done, and if you've been talking to her on the worse-than-murderers line, as I've no doubt you have, I don't suppose there's a chance now. And if she's in it, it's not likely that I shall want to be hanging back. And, apart from wanting to keep her out, you can't suppose I should be sorry to see Mildew end up at the right address, or to give him a push that way. But as to keeping your friends waiting, I can't say I'm much concerned. They may have worried about me sitting here for the last three or four hours, but I think not."

"Do you mean you've been neglected? You should have rung for some dinner to be sent in. I'm real sorry about that."

"Well, I didn't. I didn't recognize that it was a hotel. And I didn't know, from minute to minute, when I might learn why I had been brought up here."

"Well, I'm sorry. I can't say more. I can't be everywhere. Sergeant Pope will hear something he won't like about this. If you say you want a meal now, I can't object."

"I'm not saying that. I'm not feeling as hungry as I did two or three hours ago. But what I want to know is how the whole matter's going to end. You can't expect that I want to spend the rest of my life here.

Inspector Cauldron might have replied that his detention had been prolonged at his own request. But his mission was not to irritate but placate. And besides, though he might have secured a point of debate, he knew that the issue was essentially less simple than that.

"I've no authority to say more than this," he replied, "that you're free to leave practically at any moment you wish. If we didn't want you to go, we couldn't possibly keep you against your will, now that the real Houghton is in the cells.

"But you can see for yourself that the position has changed in another way. Yesterday we knew we'd made a mistake, and we might have been glad to have it forgotten with no further publicity than we couldn't avoid, but we know now that it's all got to come out When the *Plain Talker's* on sale tomorrow you'll find that everything we've done will be represented in the worst light, with some extra frillings that don't belong, and we shall have to turn our own cards face upward to show the truth's no worse than it is.

"And when we've done that there'll be no question of coming to terms with you to hush anything up. And though we made a mistake in arresting you—you can make the most of that, which we can't deny—it's mostly your fault that you weren't released in a few hours or even sooner.

"At least, perhaps 'fault' may not turn out to be quite the right word. It might be put as important cooperation with the police. It seems to me that it all turns on what we're able to do with the Mildew gang; but perhaps you can figure it out a different way.

"Yes, perhaps I could."

Mr. Limbrook's reply was no less curt because he saw the force of the argument. He could certainly put the case differently, but would he, in so doing, "figure it out" more accurately than the inspector had done?

The doubt, perhaps illogically, increased his disinclination to put himself at the disposition of the police without a better understanding of what his position would be at a later hour. It was too nearly like being a convict on ticket-of-leave, whose good conduct might earn further relief! Inspector Cauldron, leading the way to the conference which he supposed had already begun, felt that he had said the wrong thing, but could not see how to better it by addressing further words to a silent man. It may have been fortunate for the event that Mr. Limbrook's problem had been engaging the attention of others who had more power, if no better will, to deal with the difficulties which it presented.

Sergeant Pope met them in the corridor. "Beg pardon, sir," he said, "but Sir Henry wants to see Mr. Limbrook in his private room. Yes, sir. Alone. That was what he said."

Inspector Cauldron went on to the conference room to engage with his colleagues in informal discussion of the case until Sir Henry should appear.

CHAPTER XXVIII

Compensation for Mr. Limbrook

The Assistant Commissioner greeted Mr. Limbrook with a cordial smile and an outstretched hand.

"I wanted," he said, "to have a few words with you before I ask you to join us at a conference we're about to have concerning the Mildew gang, because I don't want to mix up two separate things. We made a mistake when we arrested you—a mistake for which, from your point of view, there was no excuse—and we want to put that matter right. The Home Office has authorized me to offer you £2,000 compensation, and I hope you'll agree that that is not treating the matter in an ungenerous spirit."

"No," Mr. Limbrook answered frankly, "I think it liberal."

"Then I'm to ask you one thing that we don't stipulate at all. It's for you to agree or refuse; but if you can see your way to agree it will be an obligation to us. We don't want this payment of compensation mentioned publicly. We shall much prefer that you say no more than that you've been cooperating with us and have no grievance, leaving the public—and the Press—to guess where the blunder ended and the cooperation began, or even whether there's been any real blunder at all."

Mr. Limbrook, who had expected a request of a different kind, agreed readily to this. "But, of course," he said, "Miss Wingrove will have to know "

"Yes, we recognize that. But if you ask her not to mention it, I'm sure she can be depended upon. And now, if there's nothing more to be said, we'll see what can be done in this Mildew matter."

The Assistant Commissioner rose as he spoke, and led the way to the adjoining room. Eustace Limbrook followed him with a tighter heart than had been his from the day when the cheque for his first quarter's salary had been refused by the Cairo bank. It was not merely the promise of £2,000, though that could not fail to be a source of satisfaction to a penniless man, whose professional pros-

160

pects held no immediate promise. It was the feeling that the right thing had been done in the right way, and that the ground was clear, with no complication of motives, for him to give the police such assistance as was in his power.

He was not too dull to observe that there might be other motives than a liberal justice actuating the offer which had been made. Criticism of the undeniable blunder of his arrest would be disarmed by the fact that he himself would profess to have no complaint. It was no more than the right thing done at the right time, in the right way, both to silence a coming attack on the C.I.D., and to put him in the humour for anything they might ask him to do. But how often is the right time chosen for doing the right thing in the right way?

It was doubtless true that compensation given with this quiet promptitude produced a position more favourable to the metropolitan police than could have resulted from a public payment made at a later date in response to public clamour or his own insistence; but, if the right course be taken, it is not an occasion for adverse criticism that its results should be satisfactory! Mr. Limbrook felt that the spontaneity of this gesture on the part of those toward whom he had felt no goodwill ten minutes before had removed the stigma of his arrest, and enabled him to put its ignominy out of his mind. It was in the spirit of equal and willing comradeship that he followed the Assistant Commissioner into a room that was dim with tobacco smoke, and loud with voices that fell as their entrance was observed.

Billie Wingrove, whose attention had been divided restlessly between the discussion which was proceeding around her, and anxiety as to how Eustace, whose coming was so ominously delayed, even after Inspector Cauldron had appeared, had taken the news of her own activities, needed but one glance to assure her that all was well. It was not merely that his eyes met her own without reproach, as he made his way toward her over outstretched legs. It was a subtle change in himself, reminding her of the days when he had been preparing to take up his Egyptian appointment, planning for her to join him there, and confident in himself and his advancing place in the profession he understood.

"We'll talk after," she whispered hurriedly. "Listen now."

He nodded assent, taking a chair she had kept vacant at her side. Unobtrusively, their hands met. Trouble might be behind, and danger before, but she was more conscious of a present in which all was well. "You might tell me first," the Assistant Commissioner was saying, "if you've come to any agreement as to the best line to pursue."

"No, sir," Inspector Cauldron answered, "we haven't come on anything very luminous yet. There seems to be only one promising line to take, and that's to find the gentleman who interviewed Miss Wingrove, and expressed anxiety for Mildew's arrest.

"But she couldn't spot his photo among our little collection here, and the only chance of tracing him seems to be to fetch Wellard in, and try to make him talk by letting him think that Mildews given him away.

"How quickly could you do that?"

"Within an hour, or a bit less. At least, we know the hotel where he's putting up, and he's gone in, and up to his room. We had that information an hour ago, and the place will be shut and locked for the night by now. They don't keep a night-porter. Wellard is a gentleman of regular habits, and likes to stay in a quiet place—except now and then, when he's on a spree.

Sir Henry glanced at his watch. It was after one. He said: "Very well. Fetch him in." If Wellard were destined to have a short night's sleep, there would be even less for some who were assembled there. "And that," he went on, "is the best suggestion we've had yet?"

Chief Inspector Ribber spoke in the faintly satirical tone which at one time had disinclined his colleagues to receive his suggestions kindly, until they had learned, by one most unhappy experience, that they were not safely to be ignored: "Except the one thing which we've all thought too obvious to mention, that Mr. Limbrook might give Mildew a morning call."

The remark produced a moment's silence, while those to whom the idea had not been obvious gave it the puzzled but serious consideration that a suggestion from such a source could not be denied.

"What," the Assistant Commissioner asked, "would be the object of that?"

"To thank him for offering his help, and to tell him that it won't be needed. It would be a very natural for him to raise objections, to look at a pro- He knows that Limbrook must be already aware that he's one of the gang, even if he doesn't know he's the boss, and the fact of his paying such a call the moment he gets free will make it appear that he's ready to go on working with him."

"Wouldn't the fact that he knows so much make Mildew anxious to get rid of him?"

"Yes. It might. Or it might incline him to offer him a confidential position, at a very high salary. It would depend upon how sure he could be made to feel that he could trust him, and how much use he would be likely to be."

Sir Henry looked dubious. "If," he said, "Mildew's suspicions should he already aroused, it would be a very dangerous as well as useless thing to attempt."

"But I don't see why they should be by then, sir," Inspector Cauldron, who had been quick to see the possibilities of the suggestion, interposed. "There's nothing in the paragraph we've sent out to the press to show the hour of the day when we got the real Houghton identified, and it's a thousand to one that Mildew won't see the *Plain Talker* before he goes into the City—even if he does then. If he should feel any doubt when he reads the morning paper, the fact of Mr. Limbrook calling so promptly should put it out of his mind."

"You needn't leave it to that to make his mind easy," Chief Inspector Ribber pointed out. "He could have a letter from us by the first post."

"How," the Assistant Commissioner asked, "will this affect the question of Wellard's arrest?" It was natural for him to raise objections, to look at a proposal sceptically from every side, for though others might get the credit of success, the responsibilities of error were his to bear.

"I think," Superintendent Backwash was first to reply, "it ought to help rather than not. Probably Mildew won't have heard of it by then, and it will make no difference at all. But if he has, he'll think we acted on the hint he gave, probably having had some suspicion of Wellard, or evidence against him, in our hands before. The fact that we've arrested Wellard, and haven't arrested him will confirm his belief that he bluffed Cauldron successfully when he saw him this evening."

The Assistant Commissioner looked at Eustace. "What do you say, Mr. Limbrook?"

"I'm quite willing to go, if you think that's the best course to take. Mildew lent me money, he got me to smuggle dope under his cigars, he must know that I should take the proposals I got afterwards as coming from him, and now he's offered to identify me. He's been a friend, in his way; and now that I'm released, unless I meant to break with him entirely, it's more natural to give him a call than to keep away. Yes, it seems a thing I might be expected to do. I don't see that it should be dangerous at all. Of course, I don't know how much I shall be able to get him to say."

The Assistant Commissioner still hesitated. He looked at Chief Inspector Tolbooth, whose opinion he valued no less because it would be slow to come. "That the best we can do?" he said, in the tone of one who would welcome an alternative which he could not see.

"I don't like the idea of Mr. Limbrook going alone.

The Assistant Commissioner looked slightly surprised. If Chief Inspector Tolbooth thought the risk to be too great, why not say so in plain words? It was evident that Limbrook must go alone, if at all. Mildew would not be very likely to talk with a detective standing at either side!

"I don't see how that's to be avoided. If the risk's too great, we must proceed on other lines."

"I wasn't thinking of risk. I don't think it's so great that Mr. Limbrook need worry much about that. I was thinking that, if Mildew does talk, two witnesses will be about twenty times better than one. I think Miss Wingrove should go along, if she doesn't mind."

"Of course, I'll do that."

"I'd much rather she didn't."

The two voices came at office, but it was Billie's that went on. "Nonsense, Eustace. You've just said that there's no risk about it. What do you think could happen?—at midmorning, in Palace Gardens! And if he believes we've gone there to trap him, he mayn't talk, but he'll be all the more careful how he behaves, because he'll think the police won't be far away. And if he wanted to play any tricks, two people would be much safer than one. Surely you can see that."

"I can see that your mind's made up," Eustace smiled. He had said no more than he thought when he had put the risk of such a call aside as a negligible idea. After all, Mr. Mildew wasn't a gangster with deadly weapons sticking out of every pocket. Whatever deeds of violence he might incite, he was most unlikely to stage them in his own house. Possibly, it might be the one place where his worst enemy might feel secure!

He accepted, without further protest, that which he would have been unable to change.

At a later hour of the night, Mr. Wellard, a sullen and frightened man, was brought in.

There came a time when, being easily persuaded that Mildew had given him away, and then, with much greater difficulty, that anything he said would be dealt with in such a manner that his betrayal would not become known to the man whom he feared much more than the police, he became willing to talk. But, unfortunately, he had little of any value to say. The names of a score of retail pedlars already known: two other names of men in positions similar to his own: a description of the man who had interviewed Billie Wingrove, which was only important as confirming the accuracy of her own memory—they had hoped for something better than these, which they did not get.

CHAPTER XXIX

Mr. Mildew Has a Morning Call

It was far past the hour of the midnight collection when the Assistant Commissioner dictated a brief, but courteous intimation to Mr. Mildew that, as the real James Cadell Houghton had now been traced and identified beyond doubt, it would no longer be necessary for him to supply identification of Mr. Limbrook, whose release would take place immediately. Sir Henry thanked him for the assistance to the course of justice which he had been willing to render, and remained his obedient servant.

It made no difference to the time of delivery of this letter that the last collection of the night had been gathered in. A special messenger to the G.P.O., and a short telephone conversation with its presiding functionary, secured that Mr. Mildew would find it among his morning mail.

He read it with satisfaction. He would have done anything which might have been necessary with a bold front, but he disliked contacts with the police, of whatever kind; and to have appeared in court in that connection might have had consequences hard to assess, but certainly best to avoid. The letter, coming before he read the press announcements, also averted any sinister doubt which might otherwise have disturbed his mind. It was with a conscience at peace, and in a spirit of good-humour with himself and the world, that he ordered his car to be ready to take him to the City at 10:30 prompt, and by so doing almost missed his morning visitors, who had selected that time as the earliest at which it would be reasonable to intrude upon him. He was descending the steps of the portico of his dignified residence, and the watchful chauffeur had already alighted to open the door of the limousine, when a humbler taxi drew up behind it, and two people got out.

Eustace turned to pay the driver, and Billie, who had not met Mr. Mildew previously, paused on the pavement, presenting to that approaching gentleman an attractive, but quite unfamiliar figure.

"People," he thought, "come to beg for a hospital subscription, or to sell tickets for a charity ball." As a professional philanthropist, he was accustomed to such interruptions, of which he disposed with a generous cheque-book. And it was astonishing what attractive young women would give their time and seductive airs to such begging appeals! Probably, he thought, with a cynicism not entirely contrary to the fact, they received a pleasant compensation for what they did. But the taxi in which these people had come, and the fact that they paid it off, were hardly suggestive of professional canvassers, who would come on foot, or in a private car, according to the level on which they worked. It was with a faint stir of questioning interest that Mr. Mildew's mind came to this point, and prepared him for the sight of Mr. Limbrook, whom he remembered perfectly, as he turned to greet him.

"I hope," Eustace said, holding out a hand which he would have preferred to employ differently, "that I haven't called at an awkward time. But I felt bound to thank you as soon as I was free to do so, and Miss Wingrove agreed that it would be the right thing.

Mr. Mildew met this with a blank look, and a hesitant acceptance of the offered hand. He heard the name with a puzzled frown, which cleared almost instantly as though an effort of memory had recalled it to him. "Miss—" he began. "Oh yes. Miss Wingrove, of course. And you are Mr. Limbrook? You must pardon me that I did not know you at once. I knew your face, but I could not place it. We meet so many when we are travelling abroad! But I should have identified you all the same. I am glad that it has not been necessary. I heard by this morning's post that the police have admitted their absurd mistake. It is really no thanks to me."

"I must thank your goodwill, all the same," Eustace replied, with the best appearance of that quality which he could contrive to bring to his own face. "I might have been dependent upon it, if the real Houghton had not been found."

Billie Wingrove, watching for a chance to interpose in a natural manner, thought: "Eustace is too formal, too stiff. He will get nowhere by that attitude. Any moment the man may close the interview by getting into his car, and the chance will be gone."

Mr. Mildew did not do this, but his next words seemed to show that his mind was not free from suspicion. "I have wondered," he said, "that you didn't apply to me more promptly."

"Perhaps I should have done," Eustace replied boldly, "but I wasn't sure that you would welcome it. I couldn't even be certain that you wouldn't deny knowing me; and where should I have been then?"

Mr. Mildew gave him a hard glance, showing how thin was the veneer of geniality which he practised to wear. Then he answered as smoothly as before. "Why should you have feared that? It wouldn't have been a very creditable thing to do. But we needn't stand talking here. You must have a glass of wine with me before you go. Andrews, you can take the car back for half-an-hour. I'll let you know when I'm ready."

It was clear that Eustace's last reply had led him to resolve on a further talk. He let himself into the house with a latchkey, and preceded his guests to a smoking-room at the far end of the hall, without calling a servant. When they were seated, he forestalled Eustace, who had resolved to stake the success of the call upon a further bold drive into the enemy camp, by saying bluntly: "Mr. Limbrook, I appreciate your motive in calling upon me, though I neither asked nor expected thanks for consenting to identify you under such circumstances that I suppose no decent man would have hesitated. But when you appear to suggest that I might have refused to recognise you, even though—as an extreme possibility—your life might have been at stake, that is a discourtesy—to use no stronger word—even more pronounced, and with even less occasion for it, than the gratitude which you have professed; and you can hardly be surprised if I ask you to explain your words."

"Yes. That sounds reasonable," Eustace agreed amicably. He felt more at ease now that the battle was joined, and the mere fact that he had got Mildew to talk seemed to bring him more than half-way home. "But there will be no difficulty in giving you the explanation."

Mr. Mildew leaned forward to touch the bell, pressing it three times. Then he settled himself back in his chair to listen.

"You'll remember, in the first place," Eustace began, "that when I was broke in Cairo you were kind enough to lend me £100 to enable me to come home, which I did on the same boat as yourself."

"I remember," Mr. Mildew interrupted, "lending you something, but I shouldn't have said it was as much as that."

"Well, it was. After that, you asked me to bring some cigars in for you with my own luggage. You said that you were willing to pay the duty, but that they would get through the customs at a lower rate if they were split up into several lots.

"I didn't know whether that were true. I don't now. But I took the cigars—under the circumstances I could scarcely refuse—I paid the duty, for which you had given me the money, and got them through. After that, I learned that the top boxes only had contained cigars, beneath which there had been a consignment of noxious drugs."

Mr. Mildew looked surprised. He asked gravely: "And you thought that I had been a party to that—clever trick?"

"It seemed evident. It explained the cigars, and it gave a motive for the loaning of such a substantial sum to one whom you had only casually met."

"And that's how you and Wellard got together?"

"Wellard introduced himself with a proposal that I should join the drug-smuggling gang."

"Which you naturally refused to do?"

"No. I agreed."

"Intending, doubtless, to inform the police?"

"No. I can't say that. I had no other means of income. I was in a desperate position."

Mr. Mildew had the look of one who controls contempt. "Yes," he said drily, "we must allow something for that."

For some moments he smoked in a thoughtful silence. Then he asked: "Do you mean me to understand that Wellard mentioned my name?"

"No. I can't say he did that."

"I should not have been greatly surprised. Mr. Limbrook, you must excuse me saying, in the presence of this young lady, that, though you may be an excellent engineer, outside your profession you are an exceptionally simple man.

"In the first place, I am not poor. I have ample means. The assistance which I was able to render to you may have been of great value in the unfortunate position in which you were placed, but it was literally nothing to me. It was no more than I would do for any countryman stranded abroad, and forget it in the next hour. It was as though you should pay a bus-fare for a man who had changed his clothes, and left his money at home.

"With the wealth I have, there could be no temptation to engage in that nefarious traffic, even if there were no moral objection, and if I were foolish enough to risk the legal penalties which it involves. Did it never occur to you to consider the far greater probability that the drugs had been concealed there by smugglers whose identity would not be traced, even though discovery should be made?"

"Yes, I thought of that. But you will remember that you arranged to collect the cigars, and it was your own messenger who disclosed the true nature of the consignment.

"Which, had he been the man I had actually sent under such circumstances, you might have been quite sure that he would not have done."

"I thought he took me for one of the gang."

"Probably he did. It may occur to you that a messenger from me, under the circumstances you have imagined, would have been better informed."

At this moment a telephone, which was on a low table at the side of Mr. Mildew's chair, rang. He took up the receiver, listened a moment, and answered, in a tone of casual friendship: "No, Bill. Not just now. I'm engaged. Give me a ring at the club sometime this afternoon."

Meanwhile Billie and Eustace had exchanged glances of silent interrogation. It was plausible. Could it possibly be true? After all, what *was* the evidence against this smooth-mannered and obviously wealthy man? The grounds of their own suspicion had been stated, and were being reasonably met. The police had suspicions also, which might be no better founded.

Mr. Mildew went on: "And after that they persuaded you to become one of themselves? And without mentioning me? Don't you think you connect me with them on rather inadequate grounds?"

"Perhaps I did. You certainly put it differently from how I had looked at it before. But, to be fair to myself, there is rather more than that. There is the fact that; Miss Wingrove was able to communicate with you through them."

"Which I have no doubt that they were very glad to have that excuse to do! I told Inspector Cauldron last night that the man Wellard you mentioned, whom I met some years ago in a casual manner—and whom I couldn't even describe accurately—has been trying to force his acquaintance on me ever since. Mr. Limbrook, if you ever have the misfortune to be burdened with such wealth as mine, you'll learn to spend half your time avoiding those who wish to know you for their own ends, and whom it's no pleasure to meet.

"I shouldn't have been surprised even if you or Inspector Cauldron had told me that the scoundrel was using my own name. I had a hint of this happening some years ago, though, of course, there was nothing that I could prove. And I am glad to hear that nothing of the sort is occurring now. But"—he started suddenly at the recollection—"it must be a quarter of an hour since I rang for some refreshment to be brought in. I suppose those rascally servants thought I was safely out of the house, and have found some way of amusing themselves. No, but I must really insist!"

His hand moved toward the bell, and drew back. "I'll go myself," he said, with a slight but rather grim smile, and give someone a shock!"

His two visitors, left alone, looked at one another in a common doubt. That he had not won their belief was evidenced by Eustace's low whisper: "Not now. We might be overheard. Wait till we're outside," and Billie's silent assent. He had not won their belief, but he had brought them both to a bewildered uncertainty. He had given them something more than a plausible explanation. It was one which, to an impartial judgement, might appear far more probable than that of which they had been so sure.

The telephone rang again. Twice. Billie, who was the nearer to it, said: "I'd better ask whoever it is to hold on till Mr. Mildew returns." She rose, and went to the instrument.

"Who—" she began, and stopped abruptly. She was silent for the next minute, and then laid the receiver down, and returned to her seat. "It's nothing," she said; "whoever was there has cut off." The next moment Mr. Mildew returned to the room, bearing a tray of biscuits and wine.

"The fellow," he said angrily, "must have slipped out of the house as soon as he saw me go to the car. He may not find it easy to get his next job. There's port here, and sherry, Miss Wingrove, if you'll say which you prefer."

"Sherry, if you please. And you'll take the same, Eustace, won't you? We really ought to be going. Mr. Mildew, I've let Eustace talk till now, but I should like to say for both of us that we're very sorry if we misjudged you in any way, and very grateful for what you've done."

"That's all right, Miss Wingrove," Mr. Mildew replied. "It was a quite natural mistake to make. But I should like to ask you again, Mr. Limbrook—I shouldn't like there to be any possibility of misunderstanding on such a point—did I hear rightly that you had consented to work with this drug-trafficking gang?"

The moment's pause which was evident before Eustace replied might be interpreted differently. It might have been no more than the slight confusion of a man who is required to confess to his own shame, and it was possible for Mr. Mildew to take it in that way. But Eustace saw, as he had done when it was first asked, that he was faced by a subtle trap. To say that he had consented to join such a gang, on the bare possibility that Mr. Mildew was all he professed to be, was to declare himself an outcast from the society of all decent men. It was a confession which Mr. Mildew might repeat; and to assert that he had only said it because he had thought that gentleman to be of the same persuasion would not have a very convincing sound.

Yet, if Mr. Mildew were the scoundrel which he was still disposed to consider him, to deny that he had ever intended to join the gang would be to bring instant suspicion of treachery upon himself: it would finally close the door upon any hope that Mildew might admit to them his illegal activities, or expose his friends. The question might be the crucial test, after which, if it were answered in the right way, Mr. Mildew would show his true colours, and invite the cooperation of his guests. Or he might think it more prudent to maintain the pose of rectitude he had assumed, and the invitation might come through another channel.

"You might make some allowance, Mr. Mildew," he said, "for the very difficult position in which I was placed. When a man is financially on the rocks he is tempted to do things he would not consider under easier circumstances."

"And I suppose that trouble is over now? You ought to be able to get substantial compensation for the amazing blunder of your arrest, if you play your cards in the right way."

"There hasn't been much time to think of that yet. As a matter of fact, I'm still technically under arrest. I suppose I shall have to attend the remand hearing and be formally discharged. But the police are making it as easy as they can for me in the meantime. Of course, they made a mistake, but I'm not sure that I wasn't the more to blame."

Mr. Mildew's manner had become indifferent. He said: "Well, that's for you to consider. Mr. Limbrook, this has been a most interesting talk. As to any little thing I may have been able to do for you, we may agree to put it out of our minds. For the future, you cannot be greatly surprised if I ask you to consider that our acquaintance is closed."

"And after that," Billie said rather sharply, putting down a half-empty glass, which she had not tasted until she had observed that their host drank from the same bottle. "I think we'd better go."

Mr. Mildew turned to her apologetically. "You may be sure, Miss Wingrove, that what I said was not meant for you."

"But it goes for me, too, Mr. Mildew," she said, meeting his eyes steadily, and wondering, as the words passed her lips, how he would take them, and whether they might not be the most foolish she had ever spoken.

But he only answered, with a slight bow: "I can see that you are a young lady who is loyal to her own friends."

Silently, with no attempt at formal leave-taking on either side, he conducted them to the door.

CHAPTER XXX

Amazing Penalty of Success

"Don't hurry," Billie said, as they turned from Mr. Mildew's gate. "Don't show that you're in any hurry, but come round the next corner, and then step out."

"Why are we to do that? You think someone's following us?"

"I *know* someone will be. I suppose it's that car crawling along on the other side of the road. But don't look back to see. There's a taxi rank just round the corner. We can sit still for a bit in one of the cars there."

Without clearly understanding her purpose, Eustace had the wisdom to fall in with a plan which was evidently already developed in his companion's mind. They turned the corner in a leisurely manner sprinted for the farthest of the three taxis which stood in a row facing the same way as themselves, and were seated in it, and out of sight, when the following car turned into the road.

"Don't start just yet," Billie said to a driver who had been dozing upon his seat; "we haven't made up our minds where we want to go."

Any hope she may have had that they would shake off pursuit by this simple ruse was quickly ended as the driver of the following car, after a moments hesitation, during which he gazed with natural astonishment down what must have seemed to him a miraculously empty road, came slowly on, with a sharp glance right and left, which did not miss any possible place of hiding in the basements of the close-set houses, nor fail to look into the interiors of the standing taxis.

Seeing that discovery was inevitable, Billie said to a driver who had become wakeful and alert to what was occurring: "Scotland Yard, as quick as you can go. Never mind the traffic signals, or anything else, so long as no one gets killed. Superintendent Backwash will see you don't get into any trouble for that. Eustace, make sure of the number of that car before it falls back."

"I've done that already. Standard twelve, dark blue and lined black, MX263. Pockmarked driver, and sallow little skunk sitting behind. But do you think it's quite wise?"

"Anyway," she answered, her mind concerned first to defend the abortive ruse she had tried, "it made them show themselves. There may be something in that. Wise to make straight for Scotland Yard? Yes, I think it is. Isn't it a natural place for you to be going? He doesn't know on what conditions you were let out, or how soon we've got to go back to report. Besides, I hope we shall get rid of the car behind before we get there. But listen, Eustace. When I picked up that telephone, it was the biggest stroke of luck we've had yet. There was someone trying to get Mr. Mildew, whose voice I should have known among fifty speaking at once. It was the man I met at the Reader Grill. The one who wanted Mildew arrested. But I could hear Mr. Mildew also. The lines must have been crossed. He was saying: 'And don't let them out of your sight till Linford takes over from you.' At least, I think Linford was the name; but anyway, it was plain what he meant and why he'd gone out of the room. It hadn't ever sounded sense that there were no servants he could call in a house like that. I suppose when he rang three times it was a signal for them to keep away. But, just as he was saying that, he must have heard the other voice asking if he were there, and he said: 'I've got someone else on the phone now, Catsgill. There's some mix-up with these lines. You might ring again in ten minutes.' And then I put the receiver down and made sure I should be back in my seat when he returned, which he did with that tray so soon after that it was evident that he hadn't prepared it himself, but that it had been done by a servant, as you might suppose that it would.

"The only question is whether he heard me begin to speak. But I only said about one word, and I don't think he caught it, or he wouldn't have gone on talking the way he did."

"Catsgill's the name of the lawyer he was going to see? You've certainly done something to talk about if you've found out that he was the man."

"No. I think I've been very stupid. I ought to have thought that the man was like a lawyer before. I can see it now. If I'd suggested that to the police, they'd have known where to look. But can't we do better than this? The man isn't passing the traffic signals! It seems more like loitering about to give them time to turn red."

The man, to whom this remark, if not all the preceding conversation, must have been audible, turned round with a grin: "I'm doing the best I can miss. I've got two black marks on my licence now. The next means the dole for me."

"If you don't mind me taking a hand in the game," Eustace said, "now that I know what it is, I think I can do something better than shaking off our friends in MX263. Driver, you've no occasion to hurry. Give me time to write a short note, and then draw up by a traffic constable so that I can pass it to him, if possible so that it won't be seen by our friends behind, though I don't know that it will matter much if they do."

"Yes, sir. I'll manage that." Ignoring traffic lights was a different matter, but in any lawful act he was disposed, as most drivers are, to make the cause of his fares his own in these episodes of chase-and-dodge with which all taxi-drivers become familiar. Eustace tore a page from a notebook and scribbled:

> Inform Superintendent Backwash or Inspector Cauldron, at once, that Miss Wingrove and Mr. Limbrook are on the way to Scotland Yard on most urgent business, and that they are followed by a dark blue Standard twelve, MX263, with a pock-marked driver and a passenger, both of whom should be detained.

It would have been a barren formality to feel through his own pockets, which he knew to contain about seven shillings. He asked: "Got a pound note?"

"Yes. One."

"Then let me have it."

He folded it into the note, wrote "Most urgent" on the outside, and, a minute later, had passed it into the large palm of a constable not on traffic duty, but moving leisurely along the, pavement in the same direction as themselves"

"It was a bit of luck spotting him," he said. "A traffic cop mightn't have felt he could leave his job even for a note like that. I'm beginning to think it's our lucky day."

"It's a bit early to call it that."

"Well, we won't boast. Sorry to take that last pound, and I don't suppose it was necessary, but there's nothing like making sure."

"It doesn't matter. I've got a hundred at home, and you've got two thousand to come; but do you suppose it will be in time?"

"It will be five minutes, more or less, before we get there. The policeman will be 'phoning the message now from the nearest box. Yes, I should say it will."

The blue Standard was not following very closely when the taxi turned through the wide gates of the entrance to Scotland Yard. It had been an easy guess where it was going as it had approached the headquarters of the C.I.D. The driver did not feel it necessary to approach more nearly to a place with which he had had a previous unpleasant acquaintance. But he had been doing nothing of an unlawful nature today, and he had carried out his orders successfully in spite of that dirty dodge by which a less competent man might have been thrown off the trail. He expected praise and reward.

What he experienced was a uniformed constable on the running-board and a plain-clothes officer opening the door on the other side.

"Drive right in, Jimmy," the latter said, with untimely jocularity. "You've come all the way from Palace Gardens to see us. Don't be shy of the last few yards."

"I haven't come to see anyone. Can't a man drive along the public street without being interfered with by you?"

"Jimmy, if you didn't come to see us, what made you drive this particular way, and who told you to do so? There's some bad trouble coming for some people higher up; but if you answer that question properly, you may find that it will blow over for you."

The man made no answer. He turned sullenly in at the gate where the taxi had led the way.

CHAPTER XXXI

Experiences of Miss Charlotte Bingham

Superintendent Backwash was in the good humour which comes to most of us when events move in the way we would have them go. He was at his desk, with a surrounding litter of cablegrams and radio-grams witnessing to the activities which he had started in Paris and on the farther Atlantic seaboard, when Inspector Cauldron intruded upon him.

The surrounding litter had told him that the Houghton murder case was no longer likely to end in the doubly abortive manner which he had more than half expected to see added to the list of cases which are often spoken of within the privacies of the C.I.D., but of which it is not accustomed to boast abroad.

For Charlotte Bingham was about to return—might already be on her way back—to France. And from there her transit to England—voluntary or involuntary—was not likely to be long delayed. It had seemed unlikely, even by the earlier of the cablegrams which were now before him. The Bureau de Sûreté had professed willingness to help, but had been very dubious of what it could do.

It had already realized that Charlotte Bingham was a woman of some social importance who would not be brought back to England against her will without the attention of two continents being directed upon the event. He had been puzzled at first as to how she should have learned of her own jeopardy, or thought it prudent to use the radio of the *Île de Paris* as obviously she must have done. For it appeared that cablegrams, both from her own lawyers and a Government Department of the United States, had already arrived in Paris, emphasizing her American citizenship, and making it clear that any irregularity of procedure against her would be strenuously opposed.

But a long radiogram from the captain of the *Île de Paris*, worded with the freedom of one who knew that its cost would be borne by the taxpayers of the metropolitan area, had made it clear.

Miss Bingham was a woman of resolute character, as she had shown when she had gone to disarm her sister, and even more so when, having failed in the expected surprise, she had replied to that infuriated woman's random shots with others of straighter aim. Feeling the torturing impact of one of her sister's tiny bullets against the flesh of her lower arm, she had ignored a wound that bled little, and which had been well concealed by a hastily twisted scarf before Janet had come upon a scene which drew her eyes to another sight. Subsequently Miss Bingham had abstracted the bullet with her own fingers, during a night of agony the details of which remained private to her own mind; and after that she had expected no trouble which she would not have fortitude to endure without audible complaint.

But the wound had not healed, as it might have done under less septic treatment. It had festered. Her arm had become swollen and stiff. The time had come when its condition could not be concealed and when she had been glad to show it to the doctor of the *Île de Paris*. She did not wish to be hanged, but neither did she wish to die in a worse way.

She told him a tale of how the injury had occurred, by which no one with a rudimentary knowledge of wounds could have been deceived. In effect, she told him no more nor less than she had taken a bullet wound under circumstances which she did not wish to disclose.

He said that the condition of her arm was beyond his skill. It might have to come off, though he doubted how much benefit that might be. It was a matter for a specialist too decide. And every moment was of importance. It was proposed to her that a surgeon should come out to her on the *Bretagne* and that she should be transferred to that ship. It would save a day. Perhaps two. It would have the same result if the specialist should be transferred to the *Île de Paris*, but the captains of ocean liners must have some right of decision as to the way in which such emergency matters are arranged. It appeared that the surgeon chosen—of French extraction—would make it occasion of taking a holiday in his parents' land. The Bureau de Sûreté felt, with some confidence, that when it next asked a favour of the C.I.D. it would not be refused.

Miss Bingham also, in whatever extremity of physical distress she might be, had not been idle. There was a cablegram from one of her own lawyers to say that he was sailing on the *Europa* and would be in London within a week.

The subsequent fate of Charlotte Bingham is no more than a matter of minor consequence, which can be rapidly recorded and put aside. Most readers will be familiar with it already from the newspaper controversy which it aroused at the time, both in this country and throughout the United States.

Under the excellent care of the French specialist, she did not lose her life, nor even her arm; and under the excellent advice of her American lawyer she did not resist extradition when she had recovered sufficiently to make the journey; and under a clement construction of English law a plea of manslaughter was accepted, mitigating circumstances were allowed, and a sentence of nine months' imprisonment was considered sufficient to meet the justice of the case.

It may have been true that, either in her own country, or in France, she would not have been convicted at all (as Mrs. Houghton certainly would not, had she proved to be the one with the straighter aim), but English law has always regarded crimes of unbridled passion with less lenient eyes, and the fact that she had made no attempt to retreat through a door not more than three feet away, and that she had fired a second time into the body of a woman who must have been already collapsing, had been too much for a most capable defence to explain entirely away.

The enforced sobriety of her period of retirement did her much good. A longer sentence would have done more.

Mr. James Cadell Houghton, having been proved innocent of his wife's decease, inherited the whole of her very considerable wealth, after which he married, or, to be more exact, was married by a Russian refugee of dubious nobility, and uncertain age, who spent his money very much as such a woman would be likely to do. But she had no sister, which condoned many faults in his experienced mind.

Now Superintendent Backwash, vaguely foreseeing many of these forthcoming events, and feeling a pleasant measure of content at having brought them to the threshold of healthy birth, was in a mood to share his satisfaction with a subordinate almost equally responsible for them, but Inspector Cauldron was in no mood to listen.

He threw down the transcript of Mr. Limbrook's message, as it had just come through the telephone. "P.C. Jeeves," he said, "has just sent us this. It's a note which was handed to him from a taxi, while he was on his beat just this side of the park."

Superintendent Backwash frowned over it doubtfully. Mr. Limbrook's handwriting having been eliminated in the processes of transmission, he wrongly attributed it to a female mind. "I wish," he said, "that that girl hadn't developed such a passion for coming here. I spend half my time heading her off, and most of the rest telling her she shouldn't have come. Besides, we can't arrest anybody for following her through the streets. Not in another car. There's no insult in that. They seem to think we begin by arresting people, and then thinking out whether we can make up any charge against them."

"Well, that's rather like what we do now and then, sir. I've told Bream not to let that Standard car go, if he has to ram it with one of ours."

"Yes, I didn't suppose you'd be standing there if you hadn't attended to that! But it's foolish for her to keep slipping in and out here, all the same. She's proving that by the way they're following her now."

"It was we who fetched her here yesterday, and if we don't let these men who've been following her go back to report, they won't know that she's come to us."

"No. But when they don't return, it will be evident that something's wrong."

"Perhaps it may be too late to matter. The note reads as though there's something urgent on foot now. Mildew mayn't have received them quite as we hoped he would."

"Well, we shall know soon. I suppose you've given orders for them to be brought straight up here when they arrive?"

"Yes. I've done that. And it sounds as though they're here now."

As he spoke, Eustace and Billie were shown into the room.

"I ought," Inspector Cauldron said, when their tale was told, "to have thought of it being one of his lawyers."

"I don't know why you should," Superintendent Backwash allowed, with a silent reflection that he had been equally obtuse. "It looks obvious now. But so the truth usually does when you have got hold of it. It's a different matter before. But I think, Miss Wingrove, you've done the right thing in coming here. If Mildew couldn't be brought to trust you, we can't act too quickly on the knowledge which you obtained. But, first of all, we must know what has happened to your pursuers."

"There were some policemen round their car when we came up, and they were fetching out the two men, who didn't looked pleased."

"Then we can forget them. We'll have a little chat later but that can wait. I think, Cauldron, you might do worse than see this Mr. Catsgill at once, and I'll phone him first, to make sure that he won't be out. It's a position in which every second counts. If you're satisfied that the lawyer can put us on to the kind of evidence which we require, we'll arrest Mildew at his club this afternoon."

As he said this, the superintendent glanced at his watch. It was ten minutes to twelve. There should be time to catch Mr. Catsgill before he would leave for lunch, and then to arrange for Mildew's arrest at the place where Miss Wingrove had so fortunately heard that he intended to be. Like she, Superintendent Backwash was disposed to think that he had come to his lucky day. But after two minutes' conversation with Mr. Catsgill he was less sure.

He had no difficulty ill getting put through to the firm, nor to its surviving partner. Yes, it was Mr. Catsgill speaking. Billie, having been introduced to a companion instrument, from which she could listen-in, nodded emphatically. It was the voice she knew. But she did not fail to observe that it was formal, slightly impatient. Not what might be described as a coming-on voice.

Superintendent Backwash, conscious of this aloofness, felt some hesitation in his approach.

"I understand," he said, "that you are Mr. Mildew's solicitor."

"Well?"

"We are particularly interested in a message which you gave to a young lady whom you interviewed recently on his behalf."

"Are you sure that you have not got the wrong number?"

"Not if that is Mr. Catsgill."

"Then there is some mistake."

"I think not—I was about to propose that—"

"You say you are speaking from Scotland Yard?"

"Yes. Superintendent Backwash."

"I beg leave to doubt it."

The click of disconnection followed.

The Superintendent looked at Miss Wingrove with scepticism in his eyes. "You still think that was the voice?"

"I don't think. I'm sure."

"Then we'll give him another ring."

But Mr. Catsgill had come on the phone himself. He had thought it well to report to the Yard that he had been rung up by someone who made use of that address and professed to speak in Superintendent Backwash's name. Evidently some queer business. He might have acted foolishly in cutting off before learning more of what the game was. Being assured that the call was genuine, he could only repeat that there was some mistake. It sounded like an attempt to hoax the police. Anyhow, he had interviewed no young ladies recently. Most of his clients were business men. And he had certainly sent no message to the C.I.D. Had he wished to do so, he would not have selected such a medium. He would have written. Surely their own judgement would tell them that!

Less abruptly than before, but with evident impatience, he rang off again. As he did so, Billie rose. Her eyes were angry, and her mouth set in a stubborn line. She said: "He shan't get away with that. I'm going to see him now."

CHAPTER XXXII

Interview with Mr. Catsgill

Superintendent Backwash looked doubtful. "It may be a very dangerous thing."

"I don't care if it is. It's the only thing left to do."

"If she goes at all, it can't be too quickly," Inspector Cauldron said. "I shall go with her, of course."

She looked reluctant. "He mayn't be so likely to talk."

"And if you are alone he may say things and deny them again.

"Very well. Anything's better than wasting time."

Eustace rose too. "You're not going without me."

Superintendent Backwash interposed. "I think two's enough, Mr. Limbrook. There'll be two good men in the car. And he won't be more likely to talk if we all crowd in on him at once. Besides, I want you to identify the two beauties we've got waiting downstairs. You may like to hear what they've got to say."

Leaving the police car with its two sturdy occupants in the square below, Inspector Cauldron went up to Mr. Catsgill's second-floor offices, and was admitted without delay to that gentleman's presence.

To Billie's natural surprise, after the denial she had heard him make, he greeted her with instant recognition and the pleasant gravity of their previous meeting.

He shook hands with her companion, asked them to be seated, and commenced directly upon the subject which was on all their minds.

"Inspector," he said, "I was unfair to this young lady this morning—it was an aspect of the matter which did not immediately enter my mind—but I have given it further consideration since I was approached so abruptly upon the telephone, and I suppose you will have done about as much harm as you can, whatever attitude I may now take.

"At a great risk to myself—I literally put my life in Miss Wingrove's hands—I gave you a chance which you did not take. There is no more to be said, except that, by coming here, you are doing no good to yourselves, and—if your visit should be observed—putting me in a grave and most useless peril."

"I'm afraid, Mr. Catsgill, we can't leave it like that. You must know that your client is breaking the law, or you would not have advised his arrest. That being so, it is your evident duty to place your knowledge at our disposal, and I need hardly point out to one of your profession that, if you decline to do so, you run a serious risk of being subsequently charged with complicity in his crimes.

"And it is almost equally needless to add that, in rendering assistance to us, you will receive the utmost protection which it is in our power to give."

Mr. Catsgill smiled slightly, with a suggestion of bitter satire in the lines of his mouth. "Inspector," he answered, "that is easy to say. But I suppose it to be scarcely possible, under any circumstances, for one of your profession to incur such jeopardy as you have placed me in by your coming here. You are a policeman. Even the most desperate criminal would hesitate to attack your life, knowing that, if he should take it, he would be hunted down remorselessly by every one of your fraternity through the length of the land, with the energetic cooperation of a ubiquitous press. In a week—a month—a year—he would be caught, and mercy would be an unavailing word.

"When you come here now, to this quiet respectable office, the risk you run would be negligible to the most fantastic imagination, even had I been a criminal such as you had double reason for knowing that I was not. Yet, I dare guess, you have not come without an escort which is advertising your call upon me in the street below."

As he spoke he rose and walked to the window.

"Yes," he said, "it is as I supposed. You must pardon me saying that when you came in that conspicuous manner you were regarding a remote and imaginary danger to yourself as much more important than a most grave one to me."

"I am sorry, Mr. Catsgill, if it looks that way to you. But you must recall the denial you had made, and that I had to consider Miss Wingrove's safety as well as my own.

"Besides, I have said that, if you will help us, you shall have all the protection you require. You can come back with me now, if you like, and the escort of which you complain will be as much for your benefit as my own."

"And what use would there be in that? Am I to remain under your protection for the rest of my life? I have a wife who expects me home at the usual hour. I have professional duties to discharge. You speak of placing my knowledge at your disposal. I know little. I could prove less.

"Your chance was to begin with Mildew's arrest, while he was unsuspicious of the imminence of such an event, and before he could disconnect the currents which centre in his own hands.

"Had you done that and kept the secret for a few hours, the telephone calls to his house, his letters, the people who would have sought to establish contact with him—every nerve which would have quivered upward to the severed head—might have joined to give you the information which you require. But to alarm him first! You cannot have realized his caution or his resource. It is to ask for your own failure and to ensure the death of all who shall give you help. And whose death—you must pardon me again—you would exert yourselves less to avenge than that of the meanest constable in the land

"Inspector Cauldron listened to this indictment of the methods of his department without resentment, nor did he feel disposed—nor perhaps able—to contest it. He said amicably: "Yes. I see how you feel. I'm sorry if we seem not to have appreciated the matter from your point of view. But do you wish me to understand that you are unwilling—or perhaps unable would be a fairer word—to give us any further help?"

Mr. Catsgill replied with a slow deliberation, choosing his words with care: "Not precisely. You may understand that I am unable to supply you with sufficient evidence to secure Mildew's conviction on any serious charge; though, if he were taken into sudden custody, and providing that his suspicions had not been previously aroused, there are ways in which I think such evidence could be obtained.

"You may understand that, if you should ever arrest him on a charge of dealing in illicit drugs, I will give you all the assistance in my power.

"And, beyond that, I will give you the names of two wealthy and prominent men who, I have good reason to believe, are intimately associated with him in these transactions, of which you can make such use as you think well, remembering what the consequences will certainly be for myself, if you should reveal the source from which they have been obtained."

He wrote down the two names on a slip of paper and passed them across his desk. "No," he said. "Don't take it. You can write them down, if you wish."

"I can remember them without that. They are hard to believe."

"It is much the better way."

Mr. Catsgill rose. "And now," he said, "if you will go quickly, it is the kindest thing you can do. I must live—if I live at all in the hope that your visit has not been observed by any one of the gang which Mildew controls. When you consider that his own income is not less than £100,000 a year from these sources, and that it is to his own interest, and that of everyone who serves him, to remove, at whatever cost, anyone whose loyalty is suspect, you may judge the danger to which you expose me now."

"I have said that any protection we can—" Inspector Cauldron began uneasily.

"No. Half-measures would be worst of all. It is a risk I must take, unless you are prepared for a risk of another kind.

They shook hands, and parted. But they were not clear of the outer office when Mr. Catsgill appeared at his door again. "Miss Wingrove, I should like just a word with you." She went back into his room, Inspector Cauldron waiting outside.

She was there for no more than three minutes. The door opened again. Mr. Catsgill was saying: "You have been a brave girl; but you did not understand how much risk you ran."

He shook hands again, and she came out.

As they descended the stairs together—for Inspector Cauldron's possibly too-belated caution had led him avoid calling the lift—he asked her: "Did he say anything more? Anything which might give us a clue?"

"He said nothing that I can repeat."

There was a finality in her tone which did not encourage a further question.

CHAPTER XXXIII

Events of the Night Hours

"You think," the Assistant Commissioner said doubtfully, "that nothing can be done?"

"I don't see how it can now," Superintendent Backwash replied. "We've got two good names. Which means two more we can watch. That may mean a good deal, sooner or later. And we know that Catsgill will be ready to help when the time comes. But we are not ready yet. And the best we can do is to let Mildew think he has satisfied us, and we are busy looking in the wrong directions again."

The Assistant Commissioner did not dissent. As to taking any proceedings against the two whose names had been written down, without the most absolute proof, the mere thought was a nightmare to any prudent Assistant Commissioner's mind. And yet—there had been a scandal about one of them ten years before, which only high influence, and weakness of evidence, had combined to keep out of the public courts. He had appeared to live it down—to reform. And, anyhow, there had been no proof. But incredible might be too strong a word.

He was better disposed to accept this policy of caution, of further delay, than would have been probable had the Houghton case been proceeding in a less satisfactory manner. Had that developed into the public display of successive blunders which had at one time seemed probable, it would have been a matter of urgency to make some spectacular move against the drug-trafficking gang, such as would have enabled his department to say that they had let the murder case go for the prospect of bigger game. But that was no longer necessary, and there was much to be said for the policy of extreme caution, where great names would be involved, and the best legal brains in the land would be hired for their defence. Let them wait till they could be stricken a fatal blow, such as no cunning could turn aside. But there must be one or two matters to adjust. Some dust had been stirred, which must be assisted to settle quietly again.

"What about Wellard?" he asked. Superintendent Backwash smiled. "He's agreed to plead guilty," he said, "to a charge of drug-peddling, on condition that we get him out of the country as soon as he's served his sentence. He doesn't think London will be a healthy place for him in future. Fortunately for him, he was born in Hobart. We've told him we'll get him on to a ship for Australia, providing he works his passage out. A few weeks in the stoke-hole ought to be a real life-preserver for him."

"And the two men who followed Mr. Limbrook's taxi?"

"There'll be no trouble about them. The man in the car was an unregistered alien, whom we've been looking for for the last two months, and the driver has a maintenance order against him about nine months in arrears. Besides that, he was carrying an unlicensed pistol.

"The car's registered in the name of a man we've got nothing against—or, at least, hadn't till now—and we are notifying him that it's at his disposal here. But there'll be nothing said about drugs. It's just a case of two men we wanted coming under our notice, and we picked them up. Nobody'll be able to say whether they followed Limbrook or not. Or where he went, if they did."

"Then it boils down to what we're to do with Mr. Limbrook and his young lady. We can't keep them here for ever, and I'm by no means sure that they'll be safe anywhere else."

"They're quite happy at present. I've told Limbrook that a messenger may arrive any moment with a cheque for £2,000, and he won't be in any hurry to go till he's pocketed that. But I've been talking with Tolbooth, and he made quite a good suggestion.

"He thought if we see them on to an aeroplane, and send them off to somewhere a few hundred miles away, and then put it in the London papers—we might get a bit of natural publicity for it as relating to the man who was wrongly charged with the murder of Mrs. Houghton—Mildew would be likely to drop any suspicion he may have had. He will find that nothing is being done against himself, and he'll know that if we were relying on them as witnesses we should keep them nearer at hand."

"Well, I hope it will be all right. I can't suggest any better plan. I suppose you've got their consent to this programme?"

"Yes. I agreed with Limbrook that they should go to a place in Scotland that they know already. I didn't actually suggest that they should get married there, though that's obviously what they'll be planning to do. They ought to be able to think that out for themselves, without any help from us. They've got plenty of money now.

"I mentioned it to Miss Wingrove afterwards, and I did say something that just hinted that they ought to be getting married. She looked quite startled at first, and then laughed, and said she supposed anyone might think of getting married if they'd got to go to a place like that, because there'd be nothing better to do. She seemed to be most interested in getting her clothes from the hotel."

"We mustn't let her go back there. Not till the position's clearer than it is now."

"No. I'm not quite such a fool as that."

"Then there's only one other point. Have you been able to ascertain how far that Ashbarton woman's involved with Mildew?"

"I don't think she's in with his gang at all, beyond the fact that she's been taking drugs for some internal complaint, and was relying on Wellard for her supplies. She seems to have acted in good faith, and I should say that Miss Wingrove—or Mrs. Limbrook—will get the work if she's still wanting to take it on."

This conversation took place only a few hours after the interview with Mr. Catsgill. At its conclusion the Assistant Commissioner, who could not often have made a greater mistake, put the Mildew case from his mind, as one which no longer threatened his peace, and Superintendent Backwash returned to his own room, in the vain hope that he would be on the way home in the next hour to gain some much-needed sleep.

It was 12:45 A.M. when Inspector Cauldron communicated to the two who were most concerned that it would be necessary to be at Croydon Aerodrome at 7:50 A.M. for a 'plane which would take off within five minutes of that time; and must then consent, not without a long and stubborn argument, to Billie's insistence that she should return to her hotel in the early morning, to collect possessions which she was neither willing to leave behind nor to entrust to the packing of other hands, finally fixing the hour at which she should visit it with a suitable escort.

After that, he went to Superintendent Backwash's room, thinking that, even if that zealous officer should be still there, he would have no more to do than communicate the result of these final activities, and say good-night to an equally weary man. But he found himself speaking to one who showed no sign of exhaustion, nor gave much heed to his own words.

"That's all right," the superintendent answered, with more abruptness in his manner than he would often show, "or rather, I suppose I should say it's all wrong. Just look at this."

As he spoke he passed over his desk a police report of an accident which had occurred less than three hours before on the Bayswater road. There had been a collision between three cars. There would have been nothing in that sufficiently remarkable to cause it to be referred to the C.I.D., but for the fact that one of them had been driven by the surviving partner of Timbrel, Timbrel, and Catsgill, who, after working late at his office, had been returning home alone, as his custom was.

"They've taken Catsgill to the West London Hospital. I've just had the house-surgeon on the phone. He may live. He called it a fifty-fifty chance. There were two men in each of the other two cars. One's scarcely hurt. We ought to get something interesting from him. Two were dead when they were picked up, and one died within the hour.

"Of course, that wasn't how they meant it to be. It's a trick you know as well as I. One car wasn't meant to touch him at all. It was only used to crowd him into position for the other one to upset him with a blow which wouldn't cause it anything worse than a bad swerve, which the driver would be able to correct.

"It's supposed to be safe enough, if the drivers are sufficiently skilful, and keep their heads. But Catsgill must have seen what the game was, and though it was too late for him to get clear, it wasn't too late for him to give them something they didn't expect. If I've got the hang of what happened he must have swung his car right round, so that they both struck it at the same moment. It must have been next door to a miracle that he wasn't killed outright himself, but you know how oddly these accidents happen "

"I've just promised Miss Wingrove that we'll take her to the Envoy Hotel in the early morning to pick up her things. What do you think of that now?"

"They'll be watching for her to go back. I thought we had agreed she wasn't to do that. I told Sir Henry we shouldn't be fools enough to allow it."

"They won't expect her to get there at six A.M. Especially not if they think we've got her here, as I hope they don't."

"Perhaps not. But Greaves is still there. It won't do her any good if he reports that she came there in a police car."

"I might send a taxi, with a driver we can trust. And let Limbrook go along. If they drive straight from there to Croydon they ought to be safe. Should you tell them about Catsgill?"

"No. What good would it do? Only frighten them to no purpose. It's getting them away quickly and quietly on which their health depends."

"Very well. But I don't think I'll go home till I know they're safe in the air. After that I shall feel I've got one worry the less.

They're due in Oban about five hours after they take off, and that ought to be far enough."

CHAPTER XXXIV

Those Who Go Quickly May Soon Return

To those who have good health and the fresh vigour of youth, excitement will call up reserves of energy by which sleep may be lightly deferred, though it will claim its rights at a later hour.

The possession of a cheque for £2,000, and the information that arrangements for his discharge had been completed without the formality of his appearance in court for a remand hearing being required, combined in their different degrees to raise Eustace Limbrook's spirits to a sense of exhilarating freedom and satisfaction which was the more keenly felt because the sun had broken through what had appeared, even only a few days before, to be a most sombre sky.

On her part, Billie, although she had not experienced the bleakness of incarceration with empty pockets and an uncertain future, had equal reasons for being pleased by this abrupt close of a dangerous episode, which left them well rewarded for a shorter peril than she had expected to face; and she had an additional incitement to wakefulness in the fact that she had resolved that all Scotland Yard should not coerce her to enter the Croydon aerodrome before she had retrieved her possessions from the Envoy Hotel. And on this point she had less belief in the sincerity of Inspector Cauldron's promise than it fairly deserved.

Eustace had no similar difficulty to disturb his mind, his belongings at Charmian Crescent having been secured for him at an earlier date, but Billie's determination that she would take no flight in reliance upon the dubious shopping resources of a Scottish hamlet, was no firmer than her refusal to delegate the selection and packing of her requirements to a stranger's hands. And as to Inspector Cauldron, she remembered too vividly how he had handled her clothes, and where he had laid her shoes when—no, certainly not again!

Besides that, there were one hundred useful pounds (likely to be particularly so before that £2,000 cheque could be banked and cashed) hidden in a place which she preferred to keep in her own mind.

So, though they withdrew for three hours or four to the rooms which the resources of Scotland Yard had been equal to placing at their disposal, there had been little sleep for either when they were summoned at 5:40 A.M. to descend to a waiting taxi.

Inspector Cauldron was there, but did not offer to enter the vehicle. He said in a low voice to the ex-policeman who occupied the driving-seat: "Got your gun? Then don't hesitate to use it if there should be any sign of trouble. You'd better shoot first than second, with the kind of beauties you'll meet if you get molested at all."

The man nodded assent. He understood the position, and had been well chosen for the part which he might have to play. The chance that they would be interfered with might not be much, but it was certain that, if it should occur at all, it would be of an abruptness and to a purpose which would render argument of little value for its repulse.

But, as must often be, that which had been provided against did not occur. They arrived at the hotel door just as it was opened by a sleepy porter, still in his shirt-sleeves, to whom Billie did not omit to confide that she was about to set out on a journey to Scotland, though she was vague as to her destination there and silent as to the mode of transit selected.

If Mr. Greaves—from whose room, at that early hour, she heard no sound of movement until she was on the point of leaving, when she deliberately and loudly telephoned to the porter to fetch her two suitcases—if he, whose hastiest movements could not now avail him to follow her, even wearing the minimum of garments that convention and law require, should make subsequent enquiry as to whether her temporary absence had portended a permanent withdrawal from the hotel, would hear nothing to rouse suspicion in the minds of those to whom he would make report; nothing which would not be confirmed by the press notices which would appear on the following day.

The porter appeared promptly. With the caution which the experiences of such an establishment teach, even when dealing with its most reliable guests, he had already telephoned to Miss Hounder's bedroom, and been told: "Miss Wingrove owes for about a week and a half. I'll be down in five minutes, Thomas. You'd better keep her till then." But he found himself forestalled by the offer of five one-pound notes, and the remark: "I can't stop to get my bill from the

194

office, Thomas. But I must owe two and a half guineas for last week and about half that for this. You'd better settle it for me with these and divide the change with Ellen and Dorothy."

"Thank you, miss," he said, "and good luck." He might have some curiosity while he put the suitcases into the vehicle and observed the quiet and rather professional-looking gentleman beside whom the departing guest was now seated, as to what experiences had been hers during her recent absence, or what circumstances brought them together to collect her luggage at that early hour, but do people who have been detained by the police usually drive about London in taxis before six A.M.? It would not be a combination of circumstances which would readily occur to the most lively imagination—unless, of course, they had been released on bail after being arrested for disorderly conduct the night before: and Miss Wingrove was not of that festive type.

Billie, conscious of her object gained, yawned as she leaned back in the cushioned corner. Eustace was turning the pages of the early morning edition of the *Daily Express*, which he had purchased from the nearby news-stand while she had been in the hotel.

"Do you," she asked, "always occupy yourself in that way when you elope with none-too-willing brides in the early hours of the day?"

"I do when I'm as near asleep as I am now. If I don't read I shall go off in the cab. But I hadn't thought of you in that capacity. How sharp these policemen are!"

"Yes, aren't they? They need a few women on the staff; they'd learn a lot of things that they miss now. But you'd better give me half, or I shall be in the same state. We don't want to both be dead asleep when we get to Croydon, and probably be drugged by Inspector Cauldron, and find ourselves in Shanghai or Bogota when we wake up. I believe they'd like nothing better than to dump us down at the South Pole, now that they've given up the hope that we can be any more use to them."

"I don't suppose you're far wrong," Eustace agreed, as he passed her that portion of the paper which contained the sales advertisements and short paragraphs concerning accidents, suicides, and records of usually unsuccessful criminalities, such as might be considered of more probable interest to her than the political or commercial pages.

She glanced idly down a half-column description of a smash-and-grab, which had ended with a wrecked car and the arrest of a man with a broken head; and then her eyes paused upon the next paragraph—paused, and did not lift.

She became so still that Eustace looked at her more than once, thinking to see her sleep, but her eyes were open, with the expression of one who looks at something which is not there. They were in Streatham High Street before she spoke, but when she did they were words which he was not likely to disregard. "Eustace, we're not going to Scotland. We're staying here."

He looked bewilderment, apprehension, obstinacy; and then tried to smile the absurd suggestion away. "Nonsense. Don't try to frighten me like that. We couldn't change our plans now even if we wanted to, and I don't think you do. I won't read another newspaper for a month if you mean that."

His arm went round her firmly as he spoke. It was a gesture she did not repulse, but neither did her lips relax from the firm line which he had learnt to associate with her more difficult moods. "Don't be silly! As though I minded that! But read this."

She pointed to a brief but sufficient account of the "accident" of the previous evening. He read it carefully, and as he did so, he realized without understanding her mood that he was confronted by something more serious than a petulant whim.

"I'm sorry," he said, "that Catsgill's got hurt; and if you mean that it was deliberately done, I wouldn't dispute that. But it doesn't seem to be a good reason for staying here. Rather the other way."

"Yes. Most people would say that. But I know something you don't. I promised not to tell the police. Not while Mr. Catsgill's alive, as he may still be. That cuts both ways now, because they may try to get him again, and I may he the only one who could make things take a different course.

"But, anyhow, I didn't promise not to tell you, and I think I must. You remember when I went to Mr. Catsgill's office? Well, he called me back at the last minute and he gave me a name. And an address. He said he didn't know who the man was. He'd never been to the address. He knew nothing about either, but just the fact chat the man had been regarded as of such importance that a large sum of money—a *very* large sum—had been found about two years ago to prevent suspicion being directed upon him. Mr. Catsgill understood that the trouble arose from the man's own indiscretion when he was drunk—"

"There must have been something wrong about that. They don't allow any heavy drinking in such gangs. I believe that's one of the fundamental rules. They wouldn't find any money to save a man of such habits. They'd be more likely to do for him themselves."

"Well, that just shows the special position that man had. They didn't think of punishing him or clearing him out. They found means to protect him at any cost. And in the course of whatever they did Mr. Catsgill learnt his name and address. He told it to me and I promised not to tell the police, nor even to write it down, so long as he was alive, and without permission from him. But if I heard at any time of his death I was to let the police know."

"I suppose he thought that if the police got on the man's track after they'd been to see him, Mildew would connect the two things."

"Yes. But if Mildew did—what he has done—without that, he meant to have his revenge, even after he was dead."

"I don't know that revenge is quite the word. But as he isn't dead yet, as far as the report shows, I don't see that any question arises."

"Oh, but it does! There's no question of telling the police. I'm bound not to do that. But I think I ought—I'll say *we* ought, if you like—I know you won't let me go on alone—we ought to find out who the man is, and whether any use can be made of the information that will keep Mr. Catsgill."

"I don't see what you can do without getting the police to help. Not much, anyway."

"It might come to seeing him in hospital, and getting his permission to speak."

"You said it was two years ago. The man may have left the address beyond tracing now."

"That's the first thing we've got to find out."

Eustace had been thinking hard while this conversation proceeded, with more consideration if not for his own safety, at least for that of the girl beside him, than for that of a lawyer he didn't know, who might be already dead, but he was disposed to agree that some use should be made of information which had been given her in anticipation of circumstances which had so nearly arisen.

He used an argument which was both subtle and sound when he said: "I'm not sure that you're wrong, and I don't say that we oughtn't to see what we can do at the first possible minute. But when you say that we ought to give up going to Scotland I think you make a mistake. Suppose we come back tomorrow? Wouldn't that be better? After the newspapers have made a splutter about us, and said we're five or six hundred miles away? Shan't we have a far bigger chance of doing something really worth while than we should if it were known that we had stayed in London, and they might have their spies open-eyed for us, wherever their diggings are?"

She frowned doubtfully over this. "You're not saying this just because you want to persuade me to go? It's what you really believe?"

"Of course I do. It's common sense. If we had been planning to follow them up all the time, we couldn't have thought of a better way. Especially if Inspector Cauldron marries us in the morning papers."

Billie laughed at that. "Do you think he will? What fun these policemen are!" Her voice changed with the realization that the taxi had stopped and that Inspector Cauldron was at the door. "Yes, Inspector. There's nothing but these three suitcases, if you've got Mr. Limbrook's luggage in already."

"Then come along as quickly as you can. The 'plane's ten minutes late now."

They hurried across the ground, Inspector Cauldron on Billie's left side and Eustace on her right, holding her arm in what was certainly a firm grip, but it was a spirit of mischief which caused her to exclaim upon it: "There's no need to hold me us though you think I'm trying to get away! You might at least wait till tomorrow before you give me the first bruise."

She glanced at Inspector Cauldron, and was satisfied that he had interpreted it as she meant he should. He went back to the headquarters of the C.I.D. feeling that it was; a grey world.

Later in the day he consulted Superintendent Backwash upon the wording of the paragraph which was to be issued to the press agencies.

"I suppose," he said, "we mustn't put in as a fact that they're getting married?"

"If you know that—and it's the natural thing to expect—you couldn't do better. It'll show Mildew he's no more to fear from them."

"I don't exactly know it; but she as good as told me just as she was going on to the 'plane."

"Then if that's what she means it to be, there won't be much doubt about it. She's the sort of young woman who knows how to get her own way.

Chief Inspector Tolbooth was in the room. He had listened silently until now, but as he saw that Inspector Cauldron's pencil was busy upon the projected paragraph, he was moved to speech: "I'm not sure, but I believe the penalty's about seven years' hard.

Inspector Cauldron looked up. "Penalty for what?"

"Marrying a sister."

"Marrying a—but that's absurd. They're not even the same name!"

"Half-sister, I should have said."

Inspector Cauldron's mind went back over many little incidents and words of the past weeks, to which a new interpretation must be applied. He saw truth clearly, unmistakably, now. "And to think," he said bitterly, "that I couldn't detect that!"

In the 'plane, Eustace was asking: "You're sure you remember that address correctly? It sounds rather risky, never having written it down."

"Yes. It was quite easy: 4 Adams Street, off Whitechapel Road. The name's Beal—spelt without a final 'E'."

"It doesn't sound a very good one."

"Well, we shall soon know."

And so they did; coming thereby to so strange and terrifying an experience that we might make a thousand guesses and all be wrong. But that story must be left for a later day.

www.ingramcontent.com/pod-product-compliance
Lightning Source LLC
Chambersburg PA
CBHW032007240626
47153CB00003B/1159